Covered Bridge

GHOST STORIES

Covered Bridge

GHOST STORIES

BY KARYN ZWEIFEL

Published by

CRANE HILL
PUBLISHERS

2923 Crescent Avenue • Birmingham, Alabama 35209

Published by Crane Hill Publishers
First edition, first printing, September 1995

Front cover photo by Christine P. Patterson
Book design by Bob Weathers

Cover photo: The Harrisburg Bridge in Sevier County, Tennessee. Restored by the Great Smokies Chapter and the Spencer Clark Chapter of the Daughters of the American Revolution.

Library of Congress Cataloging-in-Publication Data
Zweifel, Karyn, 1962-
     Covered bridge ghost stories / by Karyn Zweifel — 1st ed.
       p.   cm.
     ISBN 1-881548-23-6
     1. Ghost stories, American.   2. Covered bridges — Fiction.
PS3576.W368C68   1995
813'.54—dc20   95–25027
                                                    CIP

Crane Hill Publishers
2923 Crescent Avenue
Birmingham, Alabama 35209

This book is dedicated with love to my fellow travelers, Kathryn and Doug.

Other books by Karyn Zweifel:

Southern Vampires
the forthcoming *Dog Ghost Stories*

Table of Contents

INTRODUCTION

"Is it true?"

When I tell these stories, that is the most frequent question I hear. And one of the most difficult to answer. Why do some people feel a chill when they cross a certain bridge or hear a noise that can't be explained by physics or common sense? I would hesitate to deny the experiences of the many people I've interviewed, though there will continually be skeptics who can explain the inexplicable.

For myself, I am content to believe there is much, much more to this universe than I can understand. And being ignorant of so much, I believe it is prudent to be respectful of all that lies beyond my limited awareness.

Most of these stories started with the reported appearance of a ghost or an unexplained occurrence, and I wrote about it as I think it might have happened. For stories based on historical events, I started with the documentation, which was sketchy at times, and embroidered on the factual details for the sake of presenting a good story.

These stories are written primarily for fun, for telling around a campfire at night, for raising a few goosebumps here and there. Ghosts are rarely reported at the site of happy events, so I have necessarily written about a number of tragedies. In those stories where living people might be affected by the publicity, I have used fictitious names.

There seems to be an interesting correlation between water and the presence of ghosts. Spirits are frequently seen near the ocean, like the famous Gray Man of South Carolina and the many reports of shipwreck victims who return to warn others of hazardous conditions at sea. So I would not be surprised if there were reports of supernatural activity at almost every bridge. There are many intriguing tales on ordinary bridges that I did not have room to include here, and I am sure there are many other covered bridge ghost stories, too. I regret that I didn't have enough time to uncover them all. If there is some "real" explanation for the supernatural activity, maybe the properties of water play a role.

Another fascinating thesis about the presence of ghostly sounds and sights deals with our understanding of time. We usually think of time as a straight line. What happened in 1898, for example, we consider to be past and irretrievable. But recent research in the field of theoretical physics suggests that time may not be linear. Perhaps some people are more attuned to their surroundings and catch more fragments of "past" events, because in reality, past, present, and future events are actually occurring simultaneously. Maybe every space around us is crowded with unseen but very real people, past and future, going about their business, just as we are. The structure of some of my stories reflects this theory, although I did not consciously write them with that intention.

When I began researching this book, I was surprised to find so few ghost stories collected in the wealth of available covered bridge lore. My best source for stories was to travel to the location and ask local people about their experiences. Although people often are reluctant to speak about ghosts and hauntings at first, some will eventually share their stories.

I was fortunate to find a number of covered bridge enthusiasts, librarians, publishers, historians, and ordinary people from Oregon to Vermont who were willing to stop and chat. Most of my best stories came from people who live near the covered bridges, and I thank them for their time. Lisa and Pleasy in Missouri, in particular, were most helpful, as were Bea and Thelma at the Kymulga Grist Mill.

I owe a great debt to all the people I contacted who are associated with the Society for the Preservation of Covered Bridges. I have the greatest admiration for the work of this dedicated group. Their enthusiasm is contagious.

There is nothing equal to the feeling of standing in the center of a structure that is a hundred years old or more and thinking about the hundreds of lives that have passed through—and the thousands of stories, big and small, sheltered within. When you consider the tools these early builders had to work with and the monumental size of their project, it inspires a sense of awe about their resourceful spirit. I hope public authorities across the country will use their resources wisely in order to preserve these graceful structures that have played a major role in our history.

Without the encouragement of my family, this book would have never been completed. Ellen, Catherine, and Kim at Crane Hill are a continuing source of support, and I am grateful for their faith in me. I am truly blessed to have this opportunity to do work that I enjoy so much.

A note on the directions to each bridge: Mileage is approximate. Road conditions are always subject to fluctuations in the weather, so please use caution. Although I've done my best, the directions might not be the best way to find a particular bridge. If you see signs directing you to the bridge, follow those in preference to my directions—they may offer a more straightforward route. Remember that it always pays to stop and ask the local people if you're unsure. Enjoy your trip!

Covered Bridge Ghost Stories

CRY BABY HOLLER

"Stop it, Bobby!" She laughed as she slapped his hand away. The boy took the laugh as a signal to continue. The girl laughed again and slipped loose, sliding across the seat of the Chevy and pushing down on the door latch.

"Where are you going, Cheryl?"

"Can't catch me!" She threw the taunt over her shoulder as she half-ran, half-walked down the asphalt road. The boy struggled out of the car—the springs in the upholstery had given out years ago—and stood watching her, his arms resting on the rounded curves of his '49 Chevy.

The road was swallowed up by a large rectangle of soft darkness: the mouth of Swann Bridge. Cheryl's footsteps slowed as she approached the black gaping entrance, and she looked behind her for Bobby's comforting presence.

"I wouldn't go in there if I were you, Cheryl!"

She took it as a dare, and her slender form melted into the shadows in a matter of moments. Uneasy, Bobby began to walk down the gentle slope toward the bridge.

The waters of the Warrior River sang softly, unseen below the thick hand-hewn timbers that formed the roadbed of the bridge. Between the crisscrossed slats glowing slightly in the light of the crescent moon, Bobby could see the stark white stone of Scarum Bluffs.

1

He shuddered, remembering the legend of the Indian murdered there whose blood could never be washed away from the rock.

Cheryl was just ahead, standing stock-still in the center of the bridge. Over the sighing and cooing of the water, a new sound rose. He quickly stepped up alongside her, and Cheryl reached out and clasped his hand tightly as they listened.

It started out broken, hesitant at first: The sound of a baby waking in an unfamiliar place. Gradually the sound gained strength and duration, building to the cry of an infant lost and alone, rage battling with fear in every shrieking call.

Tears glistened on Cheryl's cheeks. Bobby, too, was affected, feeling strangely chastened as he led his girlfriend out of the bridge, not speaking a word. His romantic hopes for the evening were abandoned, and they climbed back into the car to head for home.

****

Thomas Brown trudged slowly down the center of the road, his boots stirring up a little cloud of dust as he walked. The sack over his shoulder was heavy. The blacksmith in Oneonta had been able to repair the plow blade, sparing Thomas the unexpected expense of a new one, and so he had spent some of his carefully hoarded cash on a small bag of white sugar and five yards of pretty gingham. The seven-mile walk from town was pleasant in the late October sunshine.

A jingle of harnesses coming up from the bridge made Thomas move to the side of the road. Before long, a small wagon appeared, drawn by a mule and carrying Thomas's neighbor from across the road, Cornelius Cole.

"Howdy, Mr. Brown," Cornelius pulled his mule to a stop. "Been to town?"

"Yeah, Cornelius, my plow blade snapped off. But Earl got it fixed, so I reckon I'll get another season or two out of it."

"We'll be puttin' in a bit more cotton this year," Cornelius commented. "Never thought I'd see the day when cotton got to 13 cents a pound."

"Makes me scared to put in more, though, remembering that it only fetched just over 5 cents a pound 10 years ago," Thomas said with a grin.

Cornelius returned the smile. "God willin', we'll all prosper this comin' year. Gee-up!" he commanded the mule. "You need anything else from town?" he asked as he moved off.

"No, thank you, Cornelius. Give my best to your family."

"You do the same, Mr. Brown."

Rachel was feeding the chickens when Thomas reached the top of the hill. He slipped an arm around her waist and they surveyed the gently sloping fields his wife had inherited from her uncle. To the west they could see the white scar of Scarum Bluffs. The massive stone formation was nearly hidden by a line of trees bright with fall foliage, a line that curved gracefully to mark the bed of the Warrior River.

"Nice place, Mrs. Brown," Thomas teased, nuzzling her neck. They had been married a scant six months.

"You made it so, Mr. Brown," Rachel retorted. "I believe that house you built will stand a hundred years or more." The white clapboard house, three rooms one behind the other, stood just below the crest of the hill. Just to the right was a barn, considerably older and currently unoccupied except for Rachel's chickens and a couple of cats.

"Supper's ready," she continued. "I made some cornbread, and went over to Roscoe's for a little butter, too." She felt her husband stiffen. "I traded him a dozen eggs for it, Thomas. His hens have stopped laying for some reason."

"Prob'ly scared by that pack of dogs he keeps," Thomas grumbled. He worked the pump outside the kitchen door, moving the handle furiously up and down until water splashed out into the bucket. He scrubbed his hands and sputtered as he threw water on his face to sluice off the road dust. Rachel watched him with affection.

"You'll be takin' the pump in for repair, next, if you don't stop being so hard on it. Roscoe is a good boy. He misses his father."

"He misses his father's hard work, more like it. I've never seen anyone lazier."

"You should know. You worked with him for years."

Inside the kitchen, warm from the heat of the stove, Rachel and Thomas sat down to their supper of cornbread, green beans, pickled beets and lima beans seasoned with fatback. Just before they finished, they heard a horse gallop wildly up to the doorstep and stop at a shouted command.

Rachel slid back her chair and went to the door.

"Evenin', Roscoe."

Thomas came to stand behind his wife, his hand on her shoulder. "What brings you out, Roscoe?"

"How's the hired hand tonight?" The young man slid off his horse and slapped Thomas on the shoulder as he entered the kitchen.

Rachel felt Thomas stiffen again and sighed. Her uncle had hired Thomas six years ago, when she was just 13 and her cousin Roscoe had been 12. Thomas had proved to be a natural farmer, with a sixth sense when it came to farm animals and growing things. Rachel had fallen in love, and when her uncle died in an accident 18 months ago, he had left half his farm to her and Thomas and half to his only son, Roscoe.

Roscoe lifted up the lid to the pan on the stove and sniffed deeply.

"Have you had supper?" Rachel asked politely. "Let me fix you a plate."

"Don't mind if I do," Roscoe sat down and grinned at Thomas. "If I'd known you were goin' to town today, Thomas, I'd have loaned you the mule and wagon."

"Didn't want to inconvenience you, Roscoe," Thomas said shortly.

"No inconvenience, Cuz." He attacked the food on his plate with such vigor that Rachel shook her head.

"You need to find a wife to cook for you, Roscoe," she said with a laugh. "You eat like you haven't had a bite in days."

"No one can match your cookin', Rachel."

Thomas scowled and threw his napkin on the table. "Let me get the water for washin' up, Rachel." He took the bucket and went outside, barely restraining himself from slamming the door behind him.

Rachel busied herself at the sink, scraping the dishes. "What brings you out this evening, Roscoe?" she called over her shoulder.

"I came to ask Thomas for some help fixin' the roof. It's gotten so I have a bucket in every room, now."

"Your father loved that house. He'd be glad to see you take care of it."

"He shoulda left me the means to care for it, then."

"He nearly lost everything in '99. We should all be grateful to have a roof over our heads."

"I'm planting more cotton next fall. That damn nigger across the road made enough this year to buy a mule, and if he can do it, I can, too."

"You already have a mule, Roscoe," Rachel pointed out impatiently. "And a fine horse, and a big house, and a cow—you're very lucky."

"It's not right that I have to work so hard and he just brings in the cash year after year," he continued stubbornly.

"Cornelius has six children, four nearly grown, and they all work hard from dawn to dusk."

Thomas brought the bucket of water in and sloshed some into the kettle to heat up for dishwater. "If you'd get married and have some children, in a few years you could have more success than him. We've got better land."

"It ain't right."

Rachel turned to Thomas. "Roscoe needs some help with the roof at the house, Thomas. Can you give him a hand tomorrow?"

"Glad to." His tone belied his words, and Rachel hurried to dispel the tension.

"What news from town, husband?"

"I brought a paper. I'll read you some." He drew the newspaper out of the sack and settled himself at the table again. "Any coffee?"

"Here." She set a cup in front of him. "I'm afraid we're out of sugar."

"No, we're not." He rummaged through the bag again and brought out the sack of sugar.

"Oh, goody!" She threw her arms around him and smacked his cheek. "I'll make a cake tomorrow."

Roscoe stood up, barely covering his mouth as he belched. " 'Scuse me," he mumbled. "I'll be headin' out now. Thanks for supper, Rachel. See you tomorrow, Thomas."

After he left, Rachel stood behind her husband and rubbed his neck and shoulders while he commented here and there on the news from Oneonta and the world.

"Four miners died in an explosion in Birmingham," he said. "I'm glad I left the mines."

"I'm glad God sent you down this road, Thomas Brown." She bent over and kissed the crown of his head. "God's sending us something else, too."

It took a moment for her meaning to sink in, then he stood up and gathered her into his arms. "Are you sure?" he whispered.

She smiled and nodded. "He'll be a summer baby. He'll get here about the same time the blackberries do."

With a whoop, Thomas picked her up and swung her around. Then he suddenly set her down. "Can I do that anymore?" he asked anxiously.

"I reckon," she said with a smile. "Until I get so big you can't pick me up."

****

The lights bobbed up and down, in and out of the trees, making the darkness seem more oppressive. Dogs raced through the underbrush, stopping occasionally to sniff and raise their heads to howl. Behind them, in camouflage jumpsuits made pointless by orange vests, three hunters followed, shotguns cradled in their arms and lanterns dangling. "They sound like they're on to something," one man grumbled as he disentangled himself from another blackberry vine.

"It's a big 'un, I know it," said the man in the lead. "Buddy sounds more excited than usual."

"We grow 'em big in Blount County." The third hunter was breathing heavily as they reached the crest of the hill above the south bank of the Warrior River. They paused to listen again for the dogs.

"How much did you say that dog cost you?"

"Well, I traded a couple other dogs and then paid him 12 hundred on top of that. His daddy was a champion coon hunter in '92, and I 'spect Buddy'll be next year. Hush."

The dogs' cries escalated to a frenzy, echoing and reechoing across the narrow valley. Then, abruptly, the barking stopped.

"What's wrong?" asked the second hunter.

"I dunno, but I'm gonna go see," came the reply as his friend crashed down the hill to the road that wound its way to Swann Bridge.

All five dogs clustered outside the opening to the covered bridge, whining, their tails between their legs.

"You don't suppose they got a bear trapped in there, do ya?"

The experienced hunter laughed. "We don't have any bears around here."

Buddy, the prize coonhound, ran anxiously between his master and an unseen border three feet from the bridge entrance.

"He acts like they got the coon cornered in there."

The third hunter moved to kick the dog past the threshold of the bridge.

"Dammit, you idiot, don't kick my dog!"

"Sorry." He retreated sheepishly.

Just then, an eerie wail floated up from the riverbed below.

"Jesus! What was that?"

The cry came again, long and drawn out, and the dogs whimpered and cowered close to the men.

"Do coons cry?"

"That's no coon," came the whispered reply. The voice sobbed and wailed again, the plaintive moan of a baby abandoned. The men stood in a tight little group, circled by the coon dogs. Again the cry repeated itself, sobbing and whimpering until it tailed off to an exhausted finish.

"What was that? Is somebody hurt? Should we go see?"

"There's nothing down there. You'd just break your neck in the dark, crawling around all the rocks. Let's go."

Fortunately, their pickup truck was on this side of the river. No one wanted to enter the dark mouth of the bridge and cross to the other side.

"Have you heard that before? What was it?"

One man shrugged. The other lit a cigarette and exhaled softly before answering. "It's been going on as long as I remember. It's why this is called Cry Baby Holler."

They climbed into the truck, the dogs leaping into the back, grateful for the human companionship and unconcerned about the interrupted hunt.

"Let's go get a drink."

****

Thomas folded the newspaper with a snap. Rachel, sitting placidly across from him with a pile of yarn in her lap, looked up.

"What would you think of us growin' pecans?" he asked. "I keep hearin' more and more about it, and I think it would be a good source of extra income."

"It seems like you already have plenty to do, but I know you'll do what's best, Thomas." Pregnancy had given Rachel an aura of calm well-being, which sometimes enveloped Thomas as well. He laughed and came over to hug her before moving to lay two more logs on the fire.

"We'll be goin' to bed soon, Thomas," Rachel protested mildly. "Should we save the wood?"

"We'll have plenty of firewood. I've decided to sell off the timber on those five acres down by the river. Now we're gonna have a baby, we'll need a horse to get back and forth to town."

"We can always borrow Roscoe's mule. That's what Uncle intended."

"My wife ride on a mule? Never!"

Rachel giggled as she wound the yarn in a ball. "I'd break the poor thing's back now I've gotten so big."

"Why, you must have gained all of 10 pounds, you heifer."

"Oh, stop it, you." She threw her half-wound ball of yarn at Thomas just as a gust of wind blew smoke back down the chimney into the front room.

Down by the river, the tall trees tossed and danced, shaken by the chill February wind. Four men, oblivious to the cold and clad strangely in white, hurried their horses across the bridge and up the rise.

"Old man Staton's farm is up on the ridge to the left," the leader shouted over the noise of the river and the wind. "His son has been talking a lot around town about how the black man has cheated him out of his fair share."

"He's one of us, then."

Roscoe blinked to see four figures draped in white on his doorstep. Their heads were covered by odd masks and they appeared menacing, but when the leader spoke, Roscoe recognized with relief the voice of the storekeeper from Cleveland.

"Hail, brother! You have been selected for the honor of initiation into an organization of the highest caliber."

"Yeah, William? Come on in here and tell me about it." Roscoe held open the door and gestured for the men to come in. "You put your horses in the barn?"

"Do you believe in the natural superiority of the white man?"

Roscoe nodded, his eyes narrowing.

"Do you believe in maintaining that natural superiority at all costs?"

He nodded again, a smile beginning to curve the outside corners of his lips.

"Do you pledge to support and uphold your white brothers in the face of any adversity?"

His face now broken by a wide smile, Roscoe nodded a third time.

"Will you submit to the rules and regulations, agree to abide by the decisions of your leaders, and hold in confidence the identities of your fellow members?"

"Hell, yes! I can't wait to get started! Was it you, Will, that chased that teacher all the way back to Boston where he belonged?"

The man's answering smile was revealed as he removed his mask. The three men with him followed suit.

"I hear Cole's been giving you trouble."

"That damned Cornelius' been doing something to my fields so my cotton won't grow. My corn had the blight last year, my hens won't lay any more, I just can't hardly make ends meet. What's this world coming to when an honest white man's farm starts failing and a no-'count black man's getting rich?"

"We can help, Roscoe. All you gotta do is help us out. That's what we do, we help each other out."

Down the road, Ida Cole had just put the lamp out, over the protests of her oldest daughter.

"Just let me finish this chapter, Mama, please!"

Ida smiled. "You'll wear out your eyes, girl, and then where will you be? Out in the cotton fields all your life?"

"Not me! I'm gonna go to school and be a teacher and wear fine clothes. You'll see!"

"I believe you, Baby. Now let's go to sleep. Your daddy and your brothers should be back from Tuskegee tomorrow, and they'll be full of new ideas to try out."

Hoofbeats rang out on the hard-packed dirt road leading up to the little house, and Ida's mind flew from one thought to another. Horses riding fast at night rarely brought good news. A rifle butt pounded the door, jarring Ida's three youngest awake and causing all four children to huddle near their mother, shivering.

"Hey!" A falsetto voice ripped through the thin wood of the door. "We wanna talk to you!"

Ida held a hand over her son Zeke's mouth. He was so frightened he could barely keep still. Ida was figuring furiously how to protect her family. Another blow to the door, and the wood shuddered, cracking under the force.

Ida made up her mind. Holding 6-year-old Zeke in her arms like a baby, she ran to the back door of the cabin. She looked out. To her relief, the night visitors had not thought to post anyone around back. She gestured for the other children to follow, and they ran out into the night just as five men dressed in white burst through the front door.

Ida and her children hid in the barn. "They'll come out here next, Mama!" Mary whispered. "What do they want?"

Ida looked at the sixteen-year-old girl and gestured again for the children to follow her into a stand of river cane next to the barn. Soon enough, the men were in the barn and Ida could hear their conversation.

"Where did they go?"

"There wasn't enough time to hitch up the mule. They must be out visitin'."

"I know where they went! I read in the paper they were givin' out free seeds over in Tuskegee. They must have left this mornin', 'cause I saw that woman on the road yesterday."

"Let's leave 'em a present."

"You got that kerosene?"

Covering her mouth in horror, Ida realized the light of the fire they intended to set might reveal their hiding place. Quickly, she sent each child out of the cane down toward the riverbank, praying the shadows would hide them well.

Ida stayed, hoping to put out the fire as soon as the men left. But they stayed and left the barn standing, so they could shelter themselves and their horses as the wind whipped the flames into a fiery inferno, sending sparks climbing high into the winter sky. Ida wept as she watched her home burn, and then she turned to find her children and a safe place for the rest of the night.

****

Sarah Groves rolled her car window all the way down, letting the cool night breeze wash over her and clear the cobwebs from her head. She'd been driving since dark, after spending the weekend with her sister in Birmingham. If she wasn't in her place at the mill by 7:30 a.m. on Monday, though, she'd lose her job.

"There's a war on, sister," the foreman liked to say. "Production can't stop for anything. Our boys need their uniforms, and that's why you're here!"

The mill made low-grade cotton fabric, and since last December, they had been running two shifts. The work wasn't hard, just boring, and the tremendous noise of the mechanized looms crashing hour after hour had made Sarah a little hard of hearing.

She sighed in relief as she saw the lights of Oneonta up ahead. Only nine more miles until home. The old house surrounded by pecan trees was practically falling down around her ears, but it was hers, free and clear. She'd had romantic fancies about living on a farm when she was a kid in Birmingham, but 12 years married to a small farmer washed that romance right out of her. When Dave died last year, she'd gladly sold all but one acre and the house.

She thought she heard the kids stirring behind her, and she twisted her head to look. No, Mary Ellen, who was eleven, and Petey, five, were sound asleep. Sarah smiled at the little boy's wide-open mouth and soft snores. Petey sounded amazingly like a miniature Dave when he slept.

Swann Bridge was up ahead, and Sarah slowed the car down to a crawl. She hated driving across the bridge, the way her tires whined and thumped across the heavy timbers. It didn't seem logical that the bridge would support itself, much less the weight of the car as she crossed, and she always had vague pictures in her mind of the bridge cracking in two, tossing her into the water below.

At night the bridge was even spookier. It was dark, and you never knew when another car might suddenly come thundering onto the bridge from the other side. Right after she and Dave had gotten married, a snake had fallen out of the rafters onto the top of the car with a thump and she had shrieked so loudly her throat hurt for days. Dave thought it was funny, but he'd grown up going back and forth across the bridge.

Tonight she drew her arm inside the car but kept the window rolled down—the breeze felt so good. She heard a moan and thought it was Petey in his sleep. She glanced back but saw he hadn't stirred. The sound was repeated, this time louder and more prolonged. Panicked, Sarah stopped the car in the middle of the bridge and reached back to shake the kids awake. "Are you okay?"

"What, Mom?"

Another cry filled the bridge, chilling Sarah to the bone. It reminded her of a baby crying—it sounded so lost, so forlorn. The river below made a hushing sound, but the cries would not be stopped. They grew in strength and sorrow, and Sarah couldn't make herself move from the spot. Her eyes filled with tears, and her children sat bewildered in the backseat, waiting for the sad wails from an unseen baby to die away again.

****

"That sneaky hen managed to hatch five baby chicks, Thomas!" Rachel held one out to her husband, who was washing up at the pump. "Isn't this a wonderful spring?"

"Can we have fried chicken every other day?" He laughed as she hurried awkwardly to return the chick to the barn. Her belly was full and round now, and he loved to rest his hands across the smooth, firm skin as she slept. The baby's leg or arm would sometimes thrash out, creating an odd bulge that shivered across her midriff. The whole farm was filled with new life.

It had been a perfect spring, with just enough rain and plenty of prematurely hot weather. The cotton was thriving, and the corn was already two feet high. Thomas was in the fields every day till dusk and awake before dawn, but he loved the rhythm of this life. Now he had a fine horse, and Rachel rode out to the fields every day to bring him dinner and a bucket of cool water.

As they sat down to supper, Rachel told him bits and pieces about her day. "After lunch, I heard Bessie mooing up at Uncle's place. She sounded really distressed, so I went on up there."

Thomas looked at her, his mouth too full to comment, but she knew what he would say.

"That poor cow hadn't been milked in a day or more, Thomas! I couldn't leave her in misery, could I?"

Thomas swallowed. "Where was Roscoe?"

"He came out to the barn—scared me half to death—said he'd overslept."

"I just don't understand that boy. He complains about poor crops, but his cotton's full of weeds and he sleeps all day."

"He said he'd signed a lease on the Cole land, too, and he'll put cotton in. He wants to plant a pecan orchard like ours up by the house, and I said you'd give him some advice."

"You've taken more care of those trees than I have. Without your attention, they'd have probably shriveled up and died by now."

"I think it was a good idea."

"They won't bear enough to make any money till after junior there is in school." Thomas pointed with his fork at her belly.

"That's good—it'll keep him in shoes!" Rachel pushed herself up from her chair with a little grunt to clear the table and start the dishes.

"A colored lady came to the house when I was starting supper tonight. She was looking for Ida Cole—her cousin or something."

"It's a shame they left—though I understand why they did after the house burned. He was a fine farmer. I could've used his mule last month, too—two mules can plow twice as fast as one."

The next morning Rachel was making pies from the last of her dried apples when Roscoe appeared on her doorstep. "Come on in, Roscoe. You want a cup of coffee?"

"No, thanks, Rachel. Too hot." He lounged back at the table, tilting the chair back on two legs.

"What brings you over here on a weekday?"

"Is Thomas here?"

"No, he's at work," Rachel said pointedly.

Roscoe let the chair legs down on the floor, leaning over the table and idly tracing designs in the flour Rachel had scattered to roll out the pie crusts on. "My cotton's not doin' too well," he said, not meeting her eyes.

"You really have to keep it hoed." Rachel tossed the dough down on the table and began to forcefully roll it with a rolling pin smooth and worn with use.

"I need help on my farm." Roscoe began to tap his foot under the table.

"You should start callin' on the Wilson girls. There's five of them—surely one would suit you."

He laughed unpleasantly. "My dogs are prettier and prob'ly cleaner." He started to get up from his chair. "Damn—what's that?" He shook his foot and a kitten scurried out from under the table, mewling loudly.

Rachel laughed in relief. "It's just a kitten—Tabby had a litter a month ago, and they keep gettin' in the house. Look—she must have gotten into the flour—her paw prints are all over your boot."

"I'll be goin' now." His chair legs dragged across the floor, making an angry scraping sound.

Rachel stood back from the table, surprised by her cousin's suppressed fury. A strand of dark hair had straggled loose from her bun and draped across her forehead. With the back of one flour-dusted hand, she tried ineffectually to push it out of her eye. Roscoe reached out, and she flinched. He gently tucked the hair behind her ear.

"Shall I—shall I tell Thomas to ride over when he's through?" Rachel stammered.

Roscoe only turned and looked at her as he mounted his horse. With a shake of his head, he rode off and turned right, away from his farm, toward the bridge and town.

This close to summer, daylight lingered on until eight o'clock, so Rachel always planned a light, late supper. Tonight they'd have apple pie, some cold leftover chicken, and fresh string beans from her kitchen garden.

Thomas was tired, and they didn't speak much during the meal. "I'm ready to go to bed," he confessed right after supper. "I've still got two acres near the river to hoe tomorrow, and the corn needs tending to."

"I could help," Rachel offered. As Thomas patted her shoulder and smiled tiredly, they heard horses gallop up to the yard. "Who could that be?" Rachel picked up the lamp and walked to the door.

"I'll get it." Thomas took the lamp from her hand and moved in front of her to the door just as someone began to pound on it.

"Open up," came the falsetto cry.

Thomas opened the door with a jerk. "What d'you want?" he asked. Over his shoulder, Rachel glimpsed the spectacle of the nighttime visitors and gasped. They were dressed in white from their heads to the tips of their boots. Any other time she might have laughed at the sight, for the men looked as if they had pillowcases on their heads, with eye slits slashed crudely through the fabric. But at night, and in a group of five, the robed masked men were strangely menacing.

"Do you, Thomas Brown, believe in the natural superiority of the white man?" The falsetto voice came from the man at the far left—the tallest figure.

"Well, I 'spect I've known some smart white folks. I've known some pretty dumb ones, too, though," Thomas drawled. Rachel could tell by his slower-than-normal speech that he was weighing every word before he let it drop.

"Do you believe in the natural rights of white men?" The speaker in his urgency let the falsetto drop, and Rachel struggled to put a face to the familiar voice.

"I've had a hard day, and I don't have time for this foolishness," Thomas said.

"That, sir, is an unwise thing to say." Another man spoke, making no attempt to disguise his voice.

"State your business with me," Thomas insisted.

Rachel's eyes traveled frantically from man to man as they stood in a semicircle at her doorstep, sweeping from head to foot trying to find any clue to the identity of this menace to her home.

"We are looking for loyal white men," the original speaker said, remembering the falsetto. "Finding none here, we ride." He turned, striding to his horse in the shadow of the barn. The other men followed him, and as they turned, something about the left boot of one of the silent men caught Rachel's eye. Marching across the toe were the distinctive five-toed tracks of a kitten. She gasped and stumbled back into the kitchen, falling into a chair.

"Don't worry, Rachel, they're gone." Thomas stroked her hair and tried to soothe her, but all she could do was clutch her belly and weep.

****

The doctor smiled again and shook the new father's hand for the third or fourth time, trying to free himself so he could begin the long drive home. He'd already run the gauntlet of proud relatives in the living room and spoken at length to his patient's anxious mother.

"Really, Doc, I can't tell you how much I appreciate it. I mean, this is just wonderful. It's a miracle! Didja see the little fella's toes? They're just so, so tiny! And all that hair, he looks just like me, don'tcha think?"

The older man extricated himself gently, patting the man on the shoulder and hurrying down the stairs to his buggy and elderly Nell waiting patiently. He'd sent someone out to feed and water her six hours ago, but still, she nickered softly to see her old friend approach.

"That's a good girl, a good old girl," he said, pulling a small apple out of his black bag and offering it to her. "I've brought another one into this world, girl, so now you do your job. Let's go home." He spread the blanket across his knees and picked up the reins, but she needed no encouragement. She moved away from the curb at a brisk walk.

It was nearly midnight, but the doctor still kept an eye out for traffic as they crossed the streets of the small town, heading for his farm above the Warrior River. Old Nell didn't much care for those noisy, sputtering automobiles, and neither did Doc, for that matter.

"You really ought to retire that old horse, Charles," his wife scolded him regularly. "You'd get to and from your patients faster. After all, this is nineteen-and-twenty-two—it's the twentieth century, and you should act like it!"

"Bless your heart, Clara, I'm only acting my age," he'd chuckle. "When Nell's old enough to retire, I will too. My patients need me in one piece, not scattered by the roadside somewhere. I'll take my horse and buggy any day over that smelly, noisy, mechanized monster!"

After they were safely out of town, Doc dozed a bit. Nell knew the way home and needed no urging. His head nodding up and down in time with the soft clip-clop of her hooves, the doctor and his horse wound their way downhill toward the approach to the Swann Bridge.

A baby's cry, shrill and anxious, made the doctor's head snap up. "Dammit, Peggy, I told you to take care of the child," he muttered. "I've got my hands full with the mother, here!"

He shook his head, disoriented. It was dark, and he was alone, except for old Nell, who stood still in her tracks. Oh, it was the bridge. He'd dreamed he heard a baby cry.

"I'm getting too old for these long deliveries, Nell," he chuckled, and clucked gently to get her started again.

Another wail rang through the bridge. Moonlight slipping through the side slats revealed a shiver running across Nell's back, a strange rippling motion of her silky skin.

The doctor sat quite still, the reins motionless in his hands. The sob broke up, then built again as a plaintive moan. The cry was familiar to this old family doctor—the cry of a baby alone and frightened.

"There, there," he murmured. Whether he was placating himself, the horse, or the unseen baby, he had no idea. Tears welled up in his eyes, and threatened to spill over. "Hush, now," he said softly, over and over, until the pitiful cries died away.

****

Rachel was down the road collecting blackberries in an enameled dishpan when the first pains struck. They left her breathless but dispelled for a full 15 minutes, long enough for her to get back to the house. She had just sat down in the kitchen chair, panting slightly, when a fresh wave broke over her. She sucked in great drafts of air, a little scared, but mostly excited.

When these pains too passed, she pulled the shotgun out of the cabinet and carefully loaded it, just as Thomas had taught her. Walking slowly outside, she aimed the gun straight up into the air and fired.

The roar sent the chickens in the yard running and squawking, and the recoil made her stagger. But the gun's report rolled across the fields and down to the river valley, and she knew Thomas would soon be on his way to her.

He'd been riding the horse to the fields the past week since her time was close, so he could return quickly if she needed him. She didn't allow herself to think of the sinister visitors they'd had a few months ago. She had almost been able to dismiss their presence as a bad dream, faintly remembered, but not quite.

"Are you okay?" Thomas flung himself off the horse before it even came to a full stop and stumbled a bit in his haste to reach her side.

"I'm fine," she laughed. "But that old rooster thinks he's been shot." She pointed to a venerable old Rhode Island Red, who reeled and tottered around the yard, still shaken by the shotgun blast.

"Why'd you call me, then?"

A pain snatched low in Rachel's back, then widened and grew, marching steadily across her belly to writhe there evilly for a few moments. Thomas watched as the pain wrote itself on his wife's face, and he clasped her by the upper arm to keep her from swaying and falling.

"Come on, sweetheart, let's go to bed," he said, gently steering her to the kitchen door. When the pain loosed its grip she panted slightly and smiled.

"It'll be hours yet, that's what Lonie says, and she's birthed dozens," she protested. "Let's sit at the table and have a drink of water."

The next pain seized her 15 minutes later, so harsh and unforgiving that she vomited up the water Thomas had drawn for her. She cried this time, ashamed of the mess, but Thomas soothed her.

"That's all right, you just come with me. Let's lie down. You'll feel better." He led her to the bedroom, sandwiched between the sitting room and kitchen, which was cool and dark with the curtains closed tightly against the hot summer sun.

She lay there for a while, dozing in and out. The pains were infrequent, coming every 15 to 30 minutes, and it was not yet time to fetch the midwife. Thomas tried to read an old newspaper and then went out and fed the chickens and then wandered aimlessly around the house. Right before dusk, Rachel struggled out of bed.

"I want to walk around a bit," she said, over Thomas's protests. "I'm too restless to stay in bed. Lonie said walking was good, so long as I felt okay."

When the moon rose over the river, Rachel's pains were coming regularly, every 10 minutes, and clutching her tightly for a full 60 seconds.

"I want to lie back down," she said, and they walked back to the bedroom.

He helped her loosen her clothes and got a cool cloth to lay across her forehead.

"I'm going to ride across the bridge to get Lonie now, okay?" Thomas stood in the doorway, lit from behind by the oil lamp flickering brightly on the kitchen table.

Rachel lifted up her arms, mutely begging for a kiss before he left. He came to her, gently smoothing the hair away from her eyes and mouth. She was pale. "I'll try to be brave, Thomas," she whispered. "I love you."

"I love you, too, Rachel," he said fiercely. "Don't worry about a thing. I'll be right back."

Rachel listened to the thunder of the horse's hooves pounding down the road and tried to relax, knowing that another pain would soon overtake her.

Thomas had just reached the bridge when a ghostly figure detached itself from the shadows.

"Who rides?" the man demanded, and Thomas recognized the white robes and crude mask with a rising sense of panic.

"My wife, she's having a baby, I've got to get the midwife," he said. "Let me by!"

"It's Thomas Brown," said another figure, materializing from the trees beside the bridge road.

"No friend of the white man," said the first one.

"A traitor who refused to join our brotherhood," hissed a third form in white.

"You don't understand, she's frightened, she's just a girl," cried Thomas. "Please, you've got to let me get the midwife!"

In the house up on the ridge, Rachel allowed herself first to moan through clenched teeth as the pains swept through her body and then to cry out with a full-throated bellow. A sudden warmth seeped through her clothes. With horror, she realized she had entered the final stage of her labor.

"I understand she's too good for you," growled a white-robed figure whose shape was faintly familiar.

"How do we treat traitors here?" called the leader to the five men assembled. One man now held Thomas' horse, and as unfriendly hands reached to pull him from the saddle, he began to realize how serious his plight was.

Rachel's moans would begin low, almost guttural in the back of her throat. Then, as the pain wrapped itself around her, tightening cruelly, the cry would build to a harsh crescendo of wordless agony. In the scant seconds between pains, her breath came out raggedly.

"Soon, soon," she panted. "Ah, Thomas, soon now."

"Death is for traitors," chanted the men. "Death to traitors!" Thomas struggled savagely now, knowing that these men were beyond all reason. His struggles were in vain. The familiar figure in white approached with a knife in his hand, and whispered cruelly as he drew the blade across Thomas's throat.

"She's mine now, Thomas—you can be a hired hand in hell."

Rachel made a last, herculean attempt, shrieking with the effort, and the baby heaved out and onto the wet, sticky bedclothes beneath her. The baby gasped, and cried, at first tentatively but then with the lusty yowl of a healthy newborn.

When Rachel awoke, she was laying on clean, dry sheets and the baby slept peacefully beside her. Lonie rose from the rocking chair when she saw Rachel's eyes open. "Is he all right?"

Lonie's eyes widened in shock.

"Is the baby all right?"

The midwife's expression relaxed. "Of course he is, dearie, he's just perfect."

"What took you so long?"

"What do you mean, Rachel? I came as soon as I heard."

"After Thomas left, it took so long," Rachel murmured, her eyes fluttering closed.

"You sent Thomas to me?"

"Lonie." Rachel recognized her cousin's voice at the sitting room door, but she was too tired to puzzle out the meaning.

"Don't tell her yet," Roscoe whispered to the midwife. "I don't know where Thomas ran off to, but his horse turned up back at the barn. There's no sense in upsetting her."

Lonie eyed Roscoe with some degree of suspicion. He'd come to her door late last night with a tale of hearing his cousin screaming, but she didn't trust this boy. She shrugged and turned back to the bedroom.

"Lonie, can you stay with her for a day or two? I can pay you."

The midwife shrugged again and nodded as she sat back down in the rocker.

A few hours later, Rachel was moving slowly around the house. When Lonie told her Thomas was missing, she didn't believe it.

"Thomas went to get you," she insisted. "He didn't run off. He wouldn't do that."

Lonie was inclined to agree, but she kept her own counsel.

The day after Lonie left, Roscoe arrived at Rachel's doorstep leading the mule with a long cylindrical shape, wrapped in a sheet, draped over its back. Her heart rose up into her throat.

"Rachel, sit down for a minute," Roscoe said, pushing her down into a chair. "I'm afraid I've got some bad news."

She began to shake her head and then moan softly as Roscoe spoke.

"I think Thomas got scared when your baby was coming, Rachel. He must've run away, and the horse threw him."

The baby began to whimper in the next room as Rachel's cries steadily grew. She threw off Roscoe's restraining hand and ran outside to tear the sheet away from the mule.

Thomas's vacant face stared up at her, with a terrible wound, bloodless but gaping, across the throat. It was an ugly parody of his wide smile that had so often greeted her.

"I'm afraid he drowned, Rachel," Roscoe said, standing next to her. "It must have been a terrible accident."

"It was no accident!" The cry burst from her, a furious, shrieking accusation. "I know about you! I know what you are!" Sobbing wildly, she darted back into the house, slamming the door in his stunned face.

"Rachel, you're upset, I understand that!" Roscoe pounded at the door. As the kitchen door splintered and Roscoe tumbled in, Rachel snatched up the baby and flung herself out the front door.

When she reached the barn she didn't even pause to throw a saddle on Thomas' horse. She knew she had to ride to safety and get away from the man who murdered her husband.

Ruthlessly she crashed her heels into the horse's side, gripping the baby with one hand and the horse's mane with the other. They flew down the road, the horse neighing in protest at the return to the bloody scene of its master's death.

At the opening of the bridge, the very spot where Thomas's blood had poured out, the horse balked, stopping dead in its tracks. Forward momentum carried Rachel and the baby she held so tightly up and over the horse's head. As they tumbled toward the unforgiving rocks below, the baby cried out—a long, drawn-out forlorn wail.

To visit Swann Bridge, go to Oneonta on US 231, in north central Alabama. Take US 231 north out of town toward Rosa. (Near Rosa, you'll see a sign for a covered bridge, but it's Easley Bridge, not Swann Bridge. It's a nice bridge, but I didn't find any ghosts there.) Drive through Rosa, and continue to Cleveland. Just outside Cleveland, US 231 splits off to the right; continue straight on Alabama 160. In less than a mile, turn right onto Alabama 79 North, and then turn left onto Swann Bridge Road. Swann Bridge is about one mile down the road.

THE GHOST OF YANKEE CREEK

Enormous forks of lightning splintered the ebony sky. Thunder roared across the fields, shaking the ground with savage power.

The little house, white clapboard with blue shutters, withstood the onslaught of rain and wind, but the windows chattered in their frames at every roll of thunder and gust of wind. Isolated at the end of a winding, unpaved road, its bright lights shone bravely, trying without success to hold back the gloom of the stormy summer night.

"I don't know, Alex," Hal Evans was telling his eleven-year-old son. "Even if the storm stops, the ground's gonna be really wet. It can wait till next weekend, can't it?"

Alex slumped down in despair. "If I don't research six wild animals by July 30th, I won't get my merit badge." The pitch of his voice climbed higher. "Dad, I've got to go out!"

"Why not let him go out tomorrow night?" Beth Evans had been eavesdropping on the conversation. "You'll both get what you want."

"What about Sunday School?"

Beth shrugged. "So he misses one day. He'll be all right."

Alex jumped up and ran to the phone, throwing his mom a quick grin on the way.

"Where you goin', Sport?" his dad called.

"Gotta call Les," the boy replied, his hand on the receiver.

"Wait till this storm's over," his father suggested. "I don't think it's a good idea to use the phone during an electrical storm like this."

Alex made a face, but set the phone down anyway.

The next afternoon, Alex was carefully checking his gear: sleeping bag, plastic tarp, flashlight, Fritos, Snickers, sandwiches, canteen, camera, notebook, pencil, and a little plastic baggie with plaster to make casts of any paw prints he might find.

"Got everything?" his father asked, dropping down on his haunches next to the boy's pack.

"Yep, sure do," Alex replied.

"Not gonna build any campfires, are you?"

"No, sir." Practically surrounded on all sides by national forests, Alex had had the danger of forest fires drilled into him from an early age. Smokey the Bear was a more familiar figure than Mickey Mouse.

"Let's go pick up Les, then."

Les was loaded up in no time flat, and the sun was still well above the horizon when Hal Evans dropped the boys off in a field a few miles from the Evanses' house.

"What are you boys looking for tonight?"

"Creatures like skunks, raccoons, bats, mountain lions . . . "

"Lookin' for any ghosts?"

"Aw, Dad!"

With a beep of the horn and a wave, he drove off. He stopped the car a few hundred yards down the road and backed slowly up to the spot where the boys stood. "If you need to get home, we're just three miles straight across those fields." He pointed south. "I think old man Coldwater's got his bull penned up these days, but be careful if you cut across any open fields, okay?"

"Yeah, Dad. Thanks." The two boys shouldered their packs and headed off the road toward a bank of trees, not waiting for the car to drive off a second time.

The noise of the car had faded before Les asked a question. "I didn't know we were looking for mountain lions," he ventured.

"Naaah. I just said that. There aren't any mountain lions left around here."

Soon they were among the trees, looking for signs of small wildlife.

"I don't smell any skunks," Alex said.

"They don't make that stink until you threaten 'em," Les pointed out. "I hope they don't mistake your camera for a threat."

"We'd better find a place to make camp," Alex said. "Near the water would be good since raccoons hang out by the water."

"Skeeters are worse by the water, too," Les pointed out.

"Any sacrifice for a merit badge," reminded Alex.

"Yeah, right," Les said gloomily. "Lead me to the water."

The two boys found a level spot above the bank of the creek and spread out their sleeping bags. Les had a Coleman lantern, but they decided against using it, since it might scare the animals away.

"Let's eat," Alex said. "I've got baloney sandwiches and Fritos. What've you got?"

"Banana and peanut butter and Cheetos. We'll have to chew softly. How good can raccoons hear?"

"I'm more worried about the skunks and mountain lions, myself," Alex said cheerily.

"Quit it about the mountain lions, okay?"

The sun had set. Both boys took out their notebooks and pencils, ready to make notes on any creatures they saw, and then they ate with a businesslike efficiency the raccoons they were seeking would have admired. The crickets and cicadas had started their evening song, and Alex was the first to spot the bats swooping and diving through the trees.

"Look," he said. "Nocturnal creatures seeking food." The bats were consuming insects as rapidly as they could catch them. Alex scribbled a few notes, and then picked up his bag of Fritos. "Look," he called quietly. "Nocturnal creature seeking food." He stuffed a handful of chips in his mouth and crunched noisily.

"Don't," whispered Les. "I can't hear if any creatures are coming."

The woods started coming alive with little sounds amplified by the deep blackness that surrounded them. Once their eyes adjusted to the loss of light, they could make out the indistinct shapes of each other and the trees. Suddenly, a heavy rumble tore though the peaceful woods.

"Cripes! What is that?" Alex stood up, scattering his notebook and pencil.

"It sounded like an earthquake!"

Both boys looked anxiously at the treetops—but they were still and undisturbed. When a car's headlights suddenly blinded the boys, they both recognized the source of the noise at once.

"It's the bridge," they chorused in relief. They had followed the treeline on the creek far enough down to be within a few hundred feet of Yankee Creek Covered Bridge. The summer vegetation was so thick they hadn't seen the road or the white structure of the bridge through the trees. A car's tires passing over the thick wooden floorboards made the throaty thrumming sound that had frightened them.

"You wanna drink, Alex?" Les held out his canteen.

He drank deeply, then spit it out in disgust. "Yecch! What is that?"

"It's Kool-Aid, I think." Les took a swig and just as quickly expelled the liquid. "She forgot the sugar again."

Alex rolled his eyes. Les's mother was very, well, unorganized was probably the nicest way to put it. Les was a little touchy though, so Alex was glad the darkness hid his gesture.

"I've gotta find my pencil."

"That mountain lion probably ate it."

"Wha?" Alex was almost caught, but pulled back just in time. He whacked Les across the shoulder. "Gimme a pencil, barf-breath."

They sat in silence for a good 20 minutes, listening intently to the little noises of the forest and the sound of each other's breathing, before they heard a regular pattern of tiny footfalls trotting in their direction. Les froze, gesturing to Alex to stay still.

A rotund figure, as tall as a cat but much bigger around, waddled between the trees and down the bank to the creek. As it passed him, Alex noticed the hairless tail, like a big rat's, and the tiny little eyes that gleamed and reflected what little light there was under the trees.

The boys tiptoed to the edge of the bank and peered down. The animal seemed unconcerned about their approach, even after they began to descend to the creek toward it. Alex pulled a flashlight out of his back pocket and shined the light through his fingers to diffuse the brightness.

"You'll scare it away," protested Les in a whisper, but the creature just turned to stare at these two nocturnal intruders. Its fur was graduated white to gray, and its eyes stared beadily.

"It's a possum," exclaimed Alex.

"It's not afraid of us," Les said, advancing toward it. Just as he closed within a yard of it, it scurried off down the bank, its white-and-gray back bobbing up and down.

"That's two creatures," Alex said as they climbed back up the bank. "If we see any raccoons tonight, we'll be halfway to our badge."

A long moan interrupted him.

"Whatsa matter, Les, those bananas gettin' to you?" Alex jumped when Les grabbed him around the waist.

"I didn't do that," Les gasped.

"C'mon, it's not funny," Alex protested. Just as he was peeling his friend's fingers loose from his waist, the ghastly moan sounded again, louder—more like a shriek this time.

The boys looked at each other, their mouths open comically, as the noise died away. "I don't like the sound of that," Alex said, trying desperately not to sound afraid.

Les shook his head wordlessly.

The moan repeated itself, but it seemed a little more distant this time.

"Mountain lion?" croaked Les, and the two boys dissolved in nervous laughter. They moved their sleeping bags closer together and huddled for a long moment, waiting for the melancholy groan to come again. When it didn't, Alex brought out a pair of Snickers bars and they feasted again, in silence this time, the only sound the quiet crackle of the paper wrapper slipping off the candy.

"You wanna go home?"

Alex thought about arriving at his house just hours after they had left. He thought about his father's reaction. He considered the merit badge he wanted so badly. "Naah," he said, and stripped the wrapper off a third Snickers, throwing half to Les.

The only noises they heard for the rest of the evening were ordinary wind-in-the-tree sounds and the soft humming of insects. At last, reluctantly abandoning hope of seeing any raccoons at work, the two boys crawled into their sleeping bags. When Les checked his watch, he was amazed at the time. "Hey, Alex," he whispered. "It's only ten o'clock."

"Yeah," his friend said sleepily.

"I thought it was like midnight or something."

"Go to sleep, Les."

"G'night."

When the boys woke the next morning, a fine mist had risen from Yankee Creek. It was a little chilly, and they were glad for the cover of their sleeping bags.

"Les."

"Uh-huh?"

"What was that we heard last night?"

"I dunno."

"It wasn't, like, a bird or anything?"

"I never heard a bird cry like that."

"You think it might've been, well, a ghost?"

"It is possible, I guess. This bridge has been around a long time."

Alex threw off his sleeping bag, stood, and stretched.

"Oh, no," he cried.

"What's wrong?" Les sprang up. "Oh, crap."

The two boys surveyed the wreckage of their packs. Their notebooks were scattered, and the two bags of chips, half-filled last night, were now empty and shredded. Dainty little paw prints circled the area and led down to the creek.

"Raccoon?" suggested Les.

"That was breakfast," moaned Alex.

"How could we sleep through that?"

"I guess we were tired. Or maybe it was a ghost raccoon."

"Aw, quit it."

Alex made a few clumsy casts of the paw prints, the plaster dotted with bits of leaves and debris from the creek water he used to mix it, before hunger drove them out of the woods to the road. A green Chevy station wagon, its battered condition hinting at long and rough use, was approaching as the boys reached the edge of the road.

"Hey, Mr. Coldwater!" Alex shouted and waved his hands. The dust-covered car slid to a halt.

"Boys need a ride?" The farmer was a native of Jackson County, and both boys had known him all their lives. He had always been old, it seemed, but as tough as nails, they agreed. He'd probably helped chase the Indians out of Oregon a hundred years ago.

Alex and Les threw their packs in the back through the rear window that had broken out long ago. Then they climbed into the car, glad for the ride back to civilization and breakfast.

"Whatcha doin' out so early?" Mr. Coldwater carefully steered the car down the narrow road, bumping across the little white bridge.

"We camped out last night, lookin' for animals to study for our merit badge," explained Alex. Les stirred the pile of accumulated junk on the backseat floorboards cautiously with his foot. He could see part of an old chain, the rusted blade of an old axe, a bit of a bridle, a few tin cans, and a few dozen crumpled cigarette packs. The debris reached nearly to the top of the seat.

"Find any?" Mr. Coldwater lit a cigarette and flung the match out the window. Alex followed its course with his eyes, unsure if the match was still lit.

"Yes, sir," Les piped up. "Found a possum and some bats, and a raccoon ate our food while we were asleep."

"They'll do that."

"Mr. Coldwater, do you believe in ghosts?" Alex wasn't sure what made him ask that, but Mr. Coldwater would be the one to know if anybody did, he reasoned.

The old man paused. "Well, now, I do, mebbe, sometimes." He turned off to Alex's house.

Les lost his fascination with the rubble at his feet. "Are there any around here?"

"Mebbe." They were almost up to the little white house, and Mr. Coldwater paused again. "I'll tell you sometime, but not today. I've gotta get on over to the feed store."

Disappointed, the two boys climbed out of the car and grabbed their packs. "Thanks for the ride, Mr. Coldwater," they shouted as he backed up, turned around, and drove away.

"Ah, hello, boys!" Beth Evans greeted them cheerily. "Just in time for bacon and eggs and then Sunday School!"

"Aw, Mom," protested Alex.

"You boys must've gotten up at the crack of dawn." She ignored his groans as she laid out two more plates. "Any luck?"

"Yeah, we found a possum and some bats."

"And a raccoon broke into our packs in the middle of the night!"

"That must've been scary." She spooned a pile of scrambled eggs onto each boy's plate just as Hal came into the kitchen.

He poured a cup of coffee and then sat down. "Hey, where's my breakfast?"

"These boys got here first, Hal. I'll put some more on. Don't get your feathers ruffled."

The following week, Alex begged again to plan an overnight trip to study wildlife. "Time's running out, Mom," he said. "If I don't hurry, I'll never finish! And we know right where that raccoon lives. I'll stay up all night long and catch him in the act."

"Your grandmother's coming this weekend," his mother said crossly. "And if I don't get this house cleaned up first, I don't know what she'll say."

"I'll help you clean house, Mom," the boy negotiated. "She won't get here till Saturday, so me 'n Les can go Friday night, please, please, please?"

"All right, all right," she conceded. "As long as your dad says it's okay."

It was overcast all day Friday. Hal called Beth from work three times to discuss a change in plans, and Alex was nearly beside himself with apprehension. Finally they agreed that the boys could go, and Alex slung his pack in the backseat of the car quickly before anybody changed their mind again. Picking up Les, Beth dropped the boys off at the entrance to the bridge.

"If it starts raining, you can get in here," she called to their retreating backs. "Have fun!"

Before they were halfway down the bank, they heard a car horn beeping. Alex groaned and turned around. "If she's changed her mind again . . . " Relief bloomed when he recognized Mr. Coldwater's dusty, low-slung station wagon.

"You boys out huntin' again?" the old man bellowed, thrusting his head out the window.

"Yes, sir!"

Mr. Coldwater carefully steered his car to a spot only partly blocking the road. "You boys gonna have a fire? I'll go get some weenies, and we can have a regular feast, if you want."

"Yeah! That sounds great!"

Alex wasn't sure about campfires, but Mr. Coldwater was an adult and ought to know what he was doing.

"I'll be back. You boys gather the wood."

"Won't the fire scare away the raccoons, Les?" They had piled up a small mountain of deadwood, and Alex started to worry again.

"Aw, don't worry about it. Maybe he'll tell us about the ghosts!"

The old man scrambled down from the road to the campsite the boys had used before. After carefully clearing away all the nearby underbrush, he started the fire. He'd brought a bucket with him, which he filled with creek water and set near the fire. "Can't go startin' any forest fires, now can we, boys?" He winked at Alex.

It was nearly dark, and all three were leaning back, stuffed full of hot dogs and chips. The boys' sandwiches intended for supper were scattered along a trail: bait to lead the raccoon back to their camp.

"Mr. Coldwater, you remember, you were gonna tell us about the ghosts?"

"I was?" Seeing the disappointment on their faces, he relented. "Oh, yeah, that's right. But I don't wanna scare you, since you'll be all alone out here in the woods tonight."

"We won't get scared." Alex leaned forward, eager to hear the tale.

"Well, you know back in the twenties there was an awful lot of bootleggin' goin' on around here." The old man stretched out his legs and shook a cigarette out of the pack. After lighting it and sending a wreath of smoke curling around his head, he continued.

"Folks were makin' a pretty penny on that bootleg liquor, too, and you know money makes people awful mean. Well, my cousin Jack was not quite 20 but he did pretty good, bringing cases down into town and sellin' 'em to interested parties. His daddy was the sheriff, you know, but that's the later part of the story.

"Some folks up in Portland heard Jack was doin' a pretty good business, and they heard he was just a little pip-squeak. Now I was real young— 'bout six, I reckon, but I remember my cousin Jack bein' a pretty strong man. He wasn't mean at all—in fact, he would pull candy outta his pocket fer me.

"Those Portland gangsters—that's what they were, plain an' simple—came roarin' into town lookin' for Jack. They couldn't find him anywhere. He was out collecting liquor from his sources, see, and he'd be gone a day or two. But nobody tol' them strangers nothin' at first.

"The men from Portland got tired of waiting and were actually on their way out of town when they saw a car pullin' onto Main Street, ridin' low like a car does when it's loaded down. Sure enough, it was Jack, and they pulled in behind him. People said they stuck their shotguns out the window in broad daylight and started tryin' to put holes in ol' Jack then an' there.

"But Jack was crafty and managed to give 'em the slip. He turned into a side street and cruised out of town. It was his bad fortune that one of the shots had punctured his radiator, and the ol' car overheated and quit right up there on that bridge.

"The gangsters were lookin' all over for him, and somebody—if I knew who it was I'd've cut his throat years ago—told 'em to look out by Yankee Creek. Meanwhile, the sheriff had heard there was some shootin' in the middle of town, and he was worried about his boy.

"The men from Portland pulled up behind Jack's car, and he didn't even have a chance. They pumped him so full a' holes he looked like Swiss cheese. They were jus' loadin' up the bottles—them that weren't broke by all the shootin'—when the sheriff pulled up to the bridge. He took one look at his son, Jack, layin' there dead, and he went crazy. He killed every last one a' those gangsters—shot two and beat the third one to death. There was so much blood they said the creek would never run clear again."

The boys were quiet, awed by the scope of the tragedy. After a minute, Alex spoke. "What about the ghost, Mr. Coldwater?"

"For a long time, cars goin' over the bridge would jus' stop dead, right in the center. And one night, I was crossin' over to home a little late," he winked again, "and my car just quit. I pulled up the hood, fussin' and fumin', and then I heard footsteps on the bridge. I stood up so quick I cracked my head good on the hood of the car, but there wasn't anybody there. And sometimes, people say they hear screamin' round here, but I never did."

The boys looked around nervously at the dark woods surrounding them and over at the bridge, its bulk barely gleaming in the reflected glow of the campfire.

"Well, I've got to go," Mr. Coldwater said finally, standing up and brushing off his pants. "You want me to help you put out this campfire? I don't think coons'll come around with all this light."

Reluctantly Alex and Les helped the older man douse the fire. After he climbed back up to the road, they heard his car start up and pull away. The forest seemed impossibly dark and full of inexplicable noises.

"Reckon that's the raccoon?" Alex whispered after one particularly loud crash, not too far away.

"Probably so," admitted Les. "It must be pretty late."

Alex turned on his flashlight and shielded the glow with his fingers while he looked at his watch.

"It's only ten-thirty," he murmured. "You wanna get some sleep while I stay up?"

"Naah, I'll stay up with you. That coon oughta be along soon."

The moon was hidden behind a thick screen of clouds. Suddenly, the chorus of insects stilled, and even the night birds ceased their song. Something was crashing through the underbrush, headed straight for the boys' camp.

They could hardly sit still, waiting for the creature to approach. Alex's hand clutched the flashlight tighter and tighter, until he was sure the thin metal casing would surely crumple. When it sounded like the creature was nearly in their laps, Alex switched on the flashlight with a barely suppressed cry.

The flashlight's beam exposed the mild, myopic stare of a fat possum, following the trail of sandwich scraps the boys had laid down hours ago. With a sigh of disappointment, Alex switched off the flashlight.

"You s'pose that's the same one we saw last week?"

"If it is, it's gotten fatter," Les said bleakly. "Do possums eat raccoons?"

"Naah. That raccoon comes out really late, I bet. We'll get him. We'll just have to stay awake, that's all."

Something cold and wet touched Alex's cheek, and he jerked upright. He'd dozed off. Les, too, was asleep sitting up. A light rain was falling, sifting through the tree leaves landing quietly on the sleeping boys. In the distance, thunder crackled faintly.

By the wavering light of his flashlight, Alex gathered up his sleeping bag and stuffed it haphazardly into his pack.

"Les," he shook his friend by the shoulder. "Wake up."

"Huh? Is it here? Did I go to sleep?"

"It's raining. C'mon, let's go to the bridge before it starts pouring."

They clambered up to the road, sliding a little in the mud created by the light rain. Preoccupied by the weather and their awkward packs, they didn't hear the noise until they were right at the mouth of the bridge.

An unearthly howl floated out from the white structure, and Alex dropped his pack. Another scream, and the boys hesitated, not knowing in which direction lay safety. The ghastly cry began again, echoing from the rafters of the bridge. Paralyzed by fear, the boys could only stand in the rain. Within an instant, a white shape floated out of the bridge and away, just as the rain began to descend in sheets.

The boys had no choice but to dash into the shelter of the bridge. Shaking, chilled by more than the rain, they stared at each other and then rummaged through their packs to find their flashlights.

The faint yellow beams offered meager comfort. They shone their lights up and down the structure, looking for signs of anything that might explain the eerie noise and the amorphous form that had escaped the bridge as the rain began.

"What's that smell?"

Les looked at his shoes. "I think I wet my pants," he admitted. "I've never been so scared in my life."

Thunder cracked again, closer now, and both boys jumped.

"I could care less about that merit badge right now." Alex's teeth were chattering. "I wanna go home."

"What time is it?"

"Almost three o'clock. Unless my watch stopped." Alex shook his arm and held the timepiece up to his ear.

The blood drained from Les's face, and he clutched his friend's arm. "Omigod," he whimpered, pointing out the mouth of the bridge. "They're coming, Alex!"

The twin beams of a car's headlights were bearing down on the bridge at full speed, slicing through the raindrops that fell like bullets.

The boys huddled in the corner of the bridge, waiting for the carful of gangsters to arrive. A cold wind blew over them, and they closed their eyes and shuddered, certain of their doom.

"Hey, you guys, you wanna ride home?"

It was Hal Evans, in the family's blue Monte Carlo. The boys were so relieved they didn't know whether to laugh or cry. They were subdued during the short trip home and slept only a few more hours in their sleeping bags on the floor of Alex's room, with all the lights turned on.

On Wednesday, Alex called Les.

"Hi. It's me."

"Hi."

"I been thinkin'."

"Me too."

"We gotta find out what that was."

Les sighed. "I know."

"You game?"

"If you are."

Hal and Beth noticed there was a certain measure of reluctance in their son's preparations for yet another overnight campout, but they attributed it to an eleven-year-old's short attention span.

"He's probably tired of the project," Beth told her husband.

"He's put a lot of effort into it. I'm glad he's sticking with it."

On Friday afternoon, the boys persuaded their folks to let them take their bikes out to Yankee Creek. "That way, at least we have a chance of getting away," Les whispered to Alex.

"I don't know about this," Alex replied, but then Beth began to stuff a couple of apples in his pack.

"Have fun," she said brightly. "At least there's no rain in the forecast."

The boys pedaled off slowly. Halfway there, they passed Mr. Coldwater on his way to the store. He honked and they waved, wishing he would join them again for a cookout.

"Maybe it's not a ghost," Alex said hopefully as they spread out their sleeping bags in the twilight gloom under the trees.

"Maybe it's a creature from outer space," retorted Les. "It moans, it flies, it comes out only at night. What else could it be?"

Darkness fell. Again the woods became animated with the rustlings and creakings of its nocturnal inhabitants and every sound made the boys jump. They expected the stout possum to reappear, its friendly shape a comfort to their apprehensive minds. But they waited in vain.

It was nearly midnight, and they were still waiting for a sign of the ghost or even the elusive raccoon. Then, floating over the fields from a great distance, they heard a familiar spooky cry. Alex moved closer to his friend.

"We should go up to the bridge." Les spoke in a harsh whisper.

Alex nodded but didn't move.

"C'mon." Les prodded him with his flashlight.

The cry came again, closer this time. Les shuddered. It seemed to circle the bridge, repeating over and over, louder and louder. Alex forced his legs to move, climbing automatically through the sparse undergrowth that covered the approach to the road. Once they reached the road, their steps slowed to an imperceptible pace.

The uncanny screech came again, almost right on top of them. With a whoosh and another shriek, a shapeless blur streaked over their heads and into the bridge, causing the boys to fall flat on the ground in an instinctive attempt at self-preservation.

"We've got to go see," moaned Les.

"No, I can't go in there," protested Alex, but he allowed his friend to clasp his hand. They crawled into the mouth of the bridge.

The cry came again, shrill and terrifying. With trembling fingers, lying on the rough wooden timbers of the bridge floor, Alex nudged the switch on his flashlight.

"It's broken," he breathed in panic.

Les's flashlight came on, flickered, and went out.

"Shake it," he commanded Alex. Suddenly, both beams shone out, clear and pure. The light swept across the walls, finally pinning down a pair of eyes that glowed with an eerie fire. With another bloodcurdling screech, the great horned owl stretched its wings. It rushed over the boys so low they could discern individual feathers and muscles pumping hard underneath them.

They stood, awed by its power, and watched it dwindle into a speck of gray against the deep black sky.

Unfortunately, Yankee Creek Covered Bridge was dismantled in 1974. But Jackson County, in the southwestern corner of Oregon, still has a number of well-preserved covered bridges. An excellent guide is Oregon Covered Bridges *by Bert and Margie Webber.*

THE SCOURGE OF TALLADEGA CREEK

The young Creek stumbled as he stepped up on the rough wood planking of the primitive bridge. The other members of his band, at his insistence, had already gone ahead. They were on their way to fight the white man in a mighty battle that would, once and for all, establish the superior force of the Creek.

The white men needed to be fought. It had been only three years since Running Wolf had first caught sight of one of those strange, arrogant creatures. A band of them had ridden by, never seeing Running Wolf crouching in the underbrush. Since that time, they had been steadily encroaching on his village, often riding right up and enticing the women and little ones to come close and see their pretty baubles.

But that was not all they brought, Running Wolf thought darkly. They brought the fever, too, which had stormed through his village in the course of a week, making strong men weak as babies and making mothers go mad with grief for their children who lay consumed by the heat from within. Those who survived were marked for life, their pitted and pocked faces and bodies mute testimony to the terrible gifts the white man had brought.

Running Wolf's own family—his squaw, five-year-old son, and infant daughter—all fell victim to the sickness. Grief gave Running Wolf the power to be a terrifying warrior. It had propelled him headlong into the preparations for war and brought him miles from home in spite of the battle that raged within his body.

But now the fever wracked his frame. His steps faltered as he forced himself across the bridge, and he shook his head to clear his vision. He nearly fell at the far end of the bridge but managed to stumble on down the path a few more feet. Ahead he saw the curious log dwelling the white men built, and he heard the joyful shrieks of children playing in the just-plowed field. His children, too, would have run and shouted through the rows of beans and corn and squash planted outside the stockade of his village. If they had survived the fever.

He could walk no farther. He collapsed in the center of the path, falling with a barely perceptible thud to the grassy path. From a distance, his slight frame resembled a pile of rags. The two little girls who approached him circled cautiously, and then ran screaming back to the cabin. "Papa! Papa! There's an Indian on the path!"

The man was bent over, examining the plow blade. He jerked upright. "How many?"

"Just one, and he looks dead!"

Roughly, the man shoved his daughters inside and snatched up his rifle before running across to the path. He slowed as he neared the prone figure. It did not stir, but he could see by the steady rise and fall of its chest that it was still alive. Using the tip of his boot, he rolled the body over.

The flushed cheeks and glazed eyes gave the settler all the information he needed to know. As he watched, the deep brown eyes flickered shut, and the breathing slowed even more.

Impulsively, he took off his shirt and stepped down to the creek to wet it in the fast-running, cool March waters. He laid it across the fevered man's brow. "There, you poor creature. Not long now, I reckon."

He hunkered down and watched the man's labored breathing. Suddenly, the Indian's eyes flew open, and the startled settler reached for his gun. The Indian's eyes cleared, and a stream of words flowed from his mouth. The settler didn't understand a single word. The Indian's eyes closed again, and life slipped away.

He took the dead Indian's hand in his own and marveled at the similarities. It was shaped exactly like his own, except it was a little smaller, slightly more brown, and, of course, marked with the pockmarks, unmistakable sign of the affliction that had taken his life.

"Well, I hope you didn't touch him," his wife said later. "You know those savages carry all kinds of horrible diseases."

****

Years later, music and light streamed out the open doors of the gristmill that stood on the banks of Talladega Creek. A crowd of 30 people, waiting for the last of their winter's supply of corn to get ground, or waiting for lumber from the sawmill, or gathered at the forge to have their horses and mules shod, had all come out for a Saturday night dance. They had come from a distance of 40 miles, some of them, just to see their neighbors and conduct a little business on what was still essentially a frontier.

"I declare, Simon, you've just about spun me off my feet," laughed Sally Stewart.

"I'd like to think I swept you off your feet," he replied gallantly. Then he led her just outside the circle of light thrown out by the merrymaking at the mill. "Sally, you have no kin for me to ask, so I'll ask you directly. Will you be my wife?"

"Oh, Simon." Sally clasped his hand in hers and raised her eyes to meet his. "I will, gladly." A widow of six months, Sally had been struggling to make ends meet on the few acres her husband had cleared before he died.

"The preacher's here already. Would tomorrow be too soon for a weddin'?"

Sally laughed again and shook her head. "March 25th sounds like a wonderful day for a wedding, Simon. All I ask is that you take a bath in the creek before we get married."

"I'd do anything for you, Sally," he exulted. "A hundred baths, if that would make you happy."

The next morning dawned clear, and Sally went down to the creek early. Simon was already there, in the shadow of the newly covered bridge, splashing and laughing and vigorously rubbing strong, homemade lye soap over his arms and face and head.

Sally watched for a moment. Suddenly Simon's happy bellows changed to a cry of fear. She could only watch, stunned, as the big man was dragged beneath the surface of the water by an unseen force.

Later she held his cold, lifeless hand as the carpenter at the sawmill measured his body for a coffin. "Must be a whirlpool or somethin' that comes up in the spring," he commented, taking the stick and laying it even with Simon's feet. "Seems like every year in the spring, somebody jes' drowns for no good reason." He notched the upper end of the stick even with the crown of Simon's head. "I'll git that box built by tomorrow noon. Lucky for you the preacher's here. Not everybody gits buried by the preacher." He turned and left before Sally could tell him it was supposed to have been her wedding day.

****

In 1853 the little community of Waldo boasted a cotton gin, a blacksmith shop, a sawmill, and a gristmill. Saturday nights were still a time for dancing and courting, but Saturday afternoons were the time for children to take advantage of the company of others. Small bands would roam around, their elders preoccupied with the price of cotton or the cost of corn.

"Don't play in the creek," was the constant admonition, but the lure of the water was irresistible. The older children knew how to carefully shed their clothes before slipping into the creek so wet clothes never betrayed them. The younger children just splashed on into the water anyhow, trusting in the leniency of adults who were on a holiday of sorts, gathered with other families to tend to business.

"I'm gonna tell," singsonged little Jason McBride to his big brother Bradley, who was splashing naked in the creek. The bridge, source of so many paying customers for the busy miller, blacksmith, and sawyer, cast its shadow across the water.

"You wouldn't dare," hollered Bradley. "If you do, you'll be sorry! I'll tell Mama you've been sneakin' into the sorghum jug when she's not lookin'."

Jason sat down and struggled with his shoes. Although it was almost the end of March, his parents had insisted that he wear his shoes this morning since they were in town. Finally they slipped off his feet, and he ran down to the edge of the water.

As he watched, Bradley began to strike the surface of the water with the palms of his hands, making great gouts of water spray up. "Help me, Jason," he roared, and then his head disappeared beneath the water. It took a moment for the small boy to recover enough to run, screaming, up to the mill.

"It doesn't happen very often," the miller assured Jason's parents. "Just sometimes in the spring the waters rise up. It's perfectly safe most of the time."

The couple were too dazed by the loss of their oldest son to even attempt a reply.

****

The mill stood silent for much of the four years of the War Between the States, but hooves regularly thundered back and forth across the covered bridge. One March, not quite a year after the war began, three soldiers passed through Waldo.

"I'm gonna get a bath, right here," announced one, dropping his backpack on the bank of the creek. "This water looks too good to pass up."

"You think Caroline will git a little closer if you sweeten up some?" His friend poked him slyly but also began to unbutton his frayed shirt.

"That ain't what we're goin' home fer, Frank," laughed the third. "We're s'posed to spend all our time at home plantin' crops an' head straight back to our regiment."

Before long all three men were submerged in the water, talking idly among themselves.

"You plantin' just corn, Frank, or some cotton, too?"

"Oh, I reckon I'll plant me a little cotton. The war's not gonna last forever, you know."

"Ol' Jeff Davis said it's our duty to the Confederacy to plant corn."

"I'll plant it to make sure I got plenty to eat come winter," agreed the third soldier.

"I don't care what Jeff Davis says," argued Frank. "Cotton is where I'll make the most money, an' that's what I'm plantin'. Jeff wants to come pull 'em up, he kin do that." He splashed over to a rock where his shirt was laid out and balled it up in his fist, wringing the dirt and sweat of a long hard winter out of the homespun fabric.

His friends shrugged and began ducking their heads under water, trying in vain to dislodge the lice that had taken up residence. The youngest soldier looked around after a few minutes.

"Frank, where'd Jimmy go?"

Frank shrugged, busy hanging out his shirt to dry a little in the warm March sun.

"He was right here, in the water with me," insisted the other. "I didn't see 'im git outta the water." He took a deep breath and dove below the surface, straining to catch sight of his friend in the depths of the swimming hole. He splashed out of the water onto the bank and began to walk up and down the side of the creek, calling as he walked, "Jimmy?"

Frank finished hanging out his shirt and walked back down to the creek, certain that Jimmy was playing a trick. When he caught sight of an arm floating among the cattails on the far side of the stream, he called out in relief. "Jimmy, you dog, you scared poor Thomas half to death!" He splashed through the water and pulled up short. The hand was lying in the water palm down. He parted the cattails gingerly, afraid of what he might see.

Jimmy floated face down, bobbing gently in the current.

****

The war had been over for less than a year, and strangers traveling through Waldo were not uncommon. The residents had adapted to the defeat; after all, no one around the little village had owned any slaves, so life continued much as before.

A little boy, no more than six, had slipped away from his chores at home and sat fishing underneath the cool shade of the bridge. The Confederate army, fleeing, had often burned bridges during the past five years. The Federal army, too, had sent their share of bridges crashing into creeks and rivers. But Waldo was far enough out of the way that the bridge survived. In the dim waters below were fish of enormous size. The little boy was prepared to wait a while in order to present a fat fish to his mother for their supper.

A whistling figure made him look up. "Howdy, mister," he said, friendly enough.

The stranger only nodded and proceeded to unbutton his shirt after setting his bag down on the bank.

"Hot, ain't it?"

The stranger nodded again and sat down to remove his dusty shoes.

"I wouldn't get in that water if I was you," the boy continued.

"And why is that?" The stranger paused, one shoe off.

"Folks drown in that creek in the spring."

The stranger studied the placid water and then turned to stare at the boy. "Looks fine to me. How long's it been since anybody drowned?"

"'Bout a year."

"Do you swim here, young man?"

"Yep, sure do. All summer long, till October, usually."

"Just not in the spring." The man sounded skeptical.

"No, sir. Somethin' comes up every spring. My gran'ma says it's in March, but Mama says she thinks it's April, so they won't let me swim at all till May."

"I think you don't want me splashing around, scaring off your fish."

"Oh, no sir, I don't mind that at all," the boy said earnestly. "I'd just hate to see you drown."

"I've swum against the strongest currents in the Atlantic Ocean," the man boasted. "I think I can manage to paddle around in some little no-name creek."

"It don't matter how good you swim," the boy protested. "And it does too have a name. It's Talladega Creek."

The only reply was a splash as the stranger dove into the deepest part of the swimming hole. The boy sighed and pulled in his line, watching the water with great curiosity.

In seconds, the stranger's head reappeared on the surface. "Nice 'n' cool," he crowed. "Beautiful swimming hole, here."

The boy shrugged and kept watching. The stranger's head disappeared again, and although the boy waited patiently, it never reappeared. He painstakingly counted on his fingers.

"March," he said with some satisfaction. "March 25th. Gran'ma was right." He gathered up his fishing gear and started back along the path toward home.

****

Sweat ran down into his eyes, making them sting and blurring his vision. He stopped his work long enough to wipe his face, then picked up the hammer again.

From his perch on the roof of the bridge, he could see the dilapidated mill building and the grassy swath of lawn that led up to it. It was easy for him to imagine the political rallies, revivals, dances, and socials that were a central part of life in Waldo from 1843 until 1930, when Alabama 77 bypassed Old Socapatoy Road and the covered bridge.

The bridge and the mill had fallen into disrepair over the next 50 years, until he had come along with a grand scheme to make the grassy area enclosed by the curving Talladega Creek come alive again. The mill would become a restaurant, and the bridge would draw tourists from all over the Southeast, he envisioned.

But for now, all he had was a falling-down old bridge with no approaches to it and a crumbling mill filled with rusted-out machinery. It would be a while before his dreams were realized. He nailed a few more shingles onto the roof and scrambled down. His first priority was to stop the deterioration, and the interior of the bridge needed a little work to keep the rain out.

It was nice and cool inside the bridge. He had to use a ladder to climb the 15 feet to the inside since the unenclosed bridge approaching it had collapsed. He hammered up a few boards, expecting to scare out a few birds and maybe some lizards while he worked. The bridge would be a tailor-made hideout for mice and squirrels, he thought, since they could easily scamper up the rough stone pilings and enter the bridge from the holes in the floorboards.

He looked around. There was no sign of any animal life. No messy tangles of leaves and debris marked the home of a squirrel or mouse; no droppings betrayed the presence of birds, large or small. That was strange because barn owls in particular liked the shady, quiet confines of these old open structures. He struck a match and held it high, straining to see the rafters. No bats hung from the massive old beams.

In fact, he hadn't even noticed any spiderwebs, even though he was the first person inside the bridge in a year or more. The structure was completely devoid of life. He suppressed a shiver and hurried down the ladder to head back up to the mill. He had a good three months of hard work before he could even consider opening his doors to paying customers.

The people around Waldo eagerly awaited the opening of the Old Mill Restaurant. Someone had tried to make it into a family amusement park some years back, but it had never really gotten going good. But a restaurant with good, hearty food would surely draw folks from miles around.

On the day of the grand opening, the proprietor greeted all his guests at the door. He knew many of them since he'd grown up in the area. In his head, he was calculating how many $6.95 dinners he needed to sell in order to make the mortgage payment on the old place. It had been a struggle over the last four months, and he had done most of the work himself, but maybe it would start paying off.

"Mrs. Pierce," he exclaimed, taking one old lady's hand between his own. "I'm so glad to see you!"

"You've done well, Lloyd, and I'm proud of you." This slightly bent lady had once been the terror of his life. She had taught second grade the old-fashioned way, with a hickory stick. Her family had been among the original settlers in the village of Waldo.

"I have a riddle for you to solve, Mrs. Pierce. You go eat, and I'll come sit with you while you have dessert." The proprietor spent the next 30 minutes running between the kitchen and the door and the dining room, making sure that everything was proceeding according to plan.

At last he sat down next to Mrs. Pierce with a sigh. "This is hard work, Mrs. Pierce!"

"Hard work is good for you, Lloyd." She patted his hand. "Now what did you want to ask me?"

"I know you grew up around here," he began. "I've noticed something odd about the old bridge. There are no birds nesting there, no squirrels, no lizards, not even any spiders."

She opened her mouth to speak, but before the first words came out, he interrupted her. "I checked to see if the beams were treated with creosote because I knew birds don't like that, but they're not."

She shook her head. "You still haven't learned not to interrupt, Lloyd."

He hung his head, amazed at how quickly she could reduce him to feeling like a seven-year-old.

"I never would have told you this story when you were young," she continued. "In fact, I must be getting pretty senile to tell it to anyone at all, because I doubt anyone would believe me."

Lloyd leaned forward, eager to hear.

"I was the youngest of five girls," she began. "The next oldest was Lucy, and she was about as contrary a girl as you would ever care to meet.

"We were allowed to swim in the creek just about any time— except March and April. There was some old superstition that people getting into the creek in the spring would drown mysteriously. My mother said she didn't believe it, but she wouldn't let us swim in the spring anyway.

"Well, one March—it was late in March, I remember, because my birthday is March 15th and I was wearing a new hair ribbon my daddy gave me for my birthday—Lucy got it into her head to go swimming."

Mrs. Pierce paused to glare at Lloyd. "You're paying attention, aren't you?"

"Yes, ma'am."

"I was seven and Lucy was nine. She could swim like a little fish, and she was always teasing me because I hated to get my face wet. Still do.

"Lucy stripped down to her knickers and jumped right into that creek. I was mad because she'd called me a scaredycat, and I turned my back on her. She was swimming and splashing and calling out that the water was so cool, I should jump right in.

44

"I didn't know what to do. Lucy and I were very close, and I knew she'd tease me unmercifully if I didn't get in. At the same time, Mama had a mean hand with a switch, and she absolutely did not want us in that creek in the spring.

"I had just made up my mind to get in anyway and reached up to take out my new hair ribbon when Lucy gave a shout.

"I thought at first she was playing because we all played like that, to scare each other—you know how kids are. But then I ran right down to the edge of the water and I could see she was really struggling. Just like someone was pulling her, forcing her under the water."

Mrs. Pierce paused and took a swallow from her water glass. The chatter of voices and the chink of forks on plates had receded as she spoke, so that she and Lloyd seemed to be all alone in the old mill, with its plaster walls freshly whitewashed and the machinery cleaned of rust.

"I know you'll think I'm just a crazy old lady, but I saw a hand pulling her down. It reached right up through the water and held onto her forearm so tight I could see the knuckles turning white. But it wasn't just any old hand. It was small and brown and covered over with pockmarks like I've never seen before.

"Lucy died, and I couldn't save her," Mrs. Pierce said simply. "I don't know if that has anything to do with that old bridge out there, but it wouldn't surprise me. Not one little bit."

That night, Lloyd took a walk out by the creek after the restaurant closed. He tried to imagine what it would be like to see somebody drown right in front of your eyes, but his imagination failed. He listened to the water instead. The murmuring sound which had seemed so peaceful just yesterday now carried a menacing undertone. Almost like a voice, muttering in a tone just beyond hearing.

Perhaps it is a voice still murmuring, speaking in a language no one understands. No human witness to the death of Running Wolf in March 1814 understood his words, but maybe some of God's creatures were perceptive enough to comprehend his meaning all the same.

Listen. Maybe it's the rocks and the water repeating the message of a long-dead Creek saying endlessly that he shall have his revenge.

The old mill and covered bridge over Talladega Creek is near Talladega, Alabama, in the north central part of the state. Take Alabama 77 south out of Talladega and continue until the road splits; turn to the left—this road isn't marked, but it's still Alabama 77. Go about 4.7 miles; you'll find the mill and bridge on the left side of the road.

THE KISSING BRIDGE

The photographer entered the shade of the old covered bridge with relief. She had been clambering up and down the river bank for hours, now on the south side, now on the north, once even scaling a tree, trying to find the best possible angle for her shot. Hauling 20 pounds of equipment all over creation in the August heat made her wonder why people thought a photographer's job was glamorous.

Once her eyes became accustomed to the dimness, she noticed the profusion of initials and messages carved into the venerable old beams. The graffiti looked old and carefully inscribed. The bold, angry strokes of paint so common in the city she lived in were conspicuously absent. It was peaceful here, with the light filtering greenly through the branches at either end. Smiling faintly, she ran her fingers across a heart carved near the center of the bridge.

A whispering sound behind her made her turn sharply. No one was there. It was probably some tree branches scraping across the roof of the bridge, she thought. Odd how it sounded like voices. Like a whispered endearment. This fanciful notion made her smile again, and she leaned closer to the wood to study the carvings on it.

****

"That's it!" The foreman shouted loudly as the final beam was guided into place. "Set the bolts now, Matthew!"

The young man straddled the huge beam, white and still oozing sap from its fresh-cut surface. Before he took his hammer and knocked the bolt into place, he eased his pocket-knife from his pocket. There, hundreds of feet above the murmuring waters of the Doe River, he painstakingly carved the initials MT, intertwining them with the letters JS. This job would give him the money he needed to ask for her hand. And their love would last as long as this bridge remained standing across the river, he vowed.

"You gonna stay up there all day, man?"

The foreman's demand startled the young builder, and his hand slipped. The knife nicked his finger before sailing through the air to land with a tiny splash in the shallows.

"After lunch we'll put the roof on it, okay, Matthew?" The foreman's eyes flashed, the vivid blue evident even from Matthew's perch in the air. He wasn't an ill-tempered man; just a busy man. And that was fortunate for Matthew, because the foreman was also destined to become his father-in-law.

****

Someone lightly tapped a car horn at the mouth of the bridge, and the photographer looked up from her study of the carved initials. She waved, and the car slowed to a halt as it approached her.

"Hey, young lady." The car was a boxy old Rambler, at least 50 years younger than the driver. His hair was a bright white, and his eyes shone blue even in the dusky interior of the old structure.

"You like this bridge?"

"Yes, sir. I hope these photographs will be in a book I'm working on."

"Pictures can't do this bridge justice. You need to hear its history. There's something mighty unusual about this bridge."

"It certainly does make me feel peaceful to be here," Sarah admitted.

"You go see Mattie Billings. She'll tell you a thing or two about this bridge. She lives on this road and can see everybody comin' and goin'."

"Mattie Billings," the photographer repeated. "Where can I find her?"

"'Bout this time every day, she's down at the post office. She gets around for an ol' lady, she does. You like old things?"

"Yes, sir."

A pocketknife materialized in the palm of his hand. "Found this knife buried in silt by the river when I was a little tyke." It was rusty and obviously more than a century old. "It's done its share of carving on this old bridge, I can tell you that."

Sarah examined the knife closely and then handed it back. She stepped back as the elderly man continued across the bridge, giving him a little wave.

"Hey," she shouted. "What's your name?" He just smiled and piloted the car gently off the ramp and onto the asphalt road.

Sarah shrugged and dusted off her hands. She needed to buy some stamps anyway, so she might as well stop off at the post office.

****

She met him at the door, flying into his arms as if she hadn't seen him in a year. Actually, it had been a little more than two months since he'd joined the army, and she hadn't seen him in uniform. After the first hug, she stepped back and pulled him by his arm out onto the porch.

"My, don't you look fine in that uniform," she said, admiring the smartly buttoned tunic and tight leggings. "Let's take a little walk, shall we?"

He held her arm tenderly as they strolled down the hill.

"You look thinner," she commented, just as the silence between them grew awkward.

He shrugged. The silence lengthened again.

"How's your mother?" She already knew the answer since they were practically neighbors.

"All right, I guess."

They were nearly to the bridge. As they entered the shadowy space, her words came out in a rush.

"I wish you weren't going."

"President Wilson says we have to make the world a safe place."

"France is so far away."

It was easier to speak in the bridge, their faces hidden in the dimness.

"I love you."

She turned to him. "You know I've always loved you."

"Will you be my wife?"

Her only response was to stretch up on her toes and kiss him swiftly on the cheek.

"We'll get married next spring. I'm sure I'll be home by then."

"I'll be ready."

They clasped hands and held on as if their life depended on it. Absorbed in each other, they didn't hear the creak and jingle of a horse and rider approaching.

"Good afternoon, folks."

The couple guiltily jumped apart.

"Kissin' Bridge earnin' its name today?" The rider laughed and spurred his horse up the hill.

"I've got to go now."

"When does your train leave?" She fought the urge to cling to his arm.

"Seven tomorrow morning."

She clasped his hand again until at last he tenderly worked it free. With a soft kiss on her cheek, he left.

Halfway up the hill he turned to look back. From that distance he couldn't see the tears glistening. She stood framed by the dark opening of the bridge and the graceful tendrils of the weeping willow on the riverbank.

****

Sarah drove slowly along the main street until she came upon the post office. Just stepping outside was a petite, white-haired woman.

"Excuse me, ma'am?" The photographer threw her Jeep into park and jumped out. "Can you tell me where to find Mattie Billings?"

"You've found her. Who are you?"

"Sarah, Hamilton. I've been photographing the bridge, and I was told you might know some history about it."

The old lady laughed. "Mercy, yes. I could tell you stories all day."

"Can I buy you a cup of coffee?"

The diner was just across the street, and Sarah carefully held Mattie Billing's elbow as she stepped off the curb. Her bones felt as fragile as a bird's, and her skin had the crepelike texture of great age.

When they had settled into a booth, Sarah pulled out a notebook and pen.

"They say if you declare your love on that bridge, it will last forever," Mattie explained. She fumbled in her billfold for a picture. "See here?" It was the picture of a very young man in an old-fashioned uniform, the edges of the photo tattered from years of handling.

"We pledged ourselves to each other on that bridge in 1917. We were married for 68 years."

Something about the young soldier looked familiar to Sarah, but she couldn't quite place it. She examined it closely before handing it back.

"Are there any other love stories connected to the bridge?"

"My land, yes. Just about everybody in Elizabethton has spent some time spoonin' in that old bridge. Why, on a Saturday night, you just about couldn't get a car through there for all the couples!"

Incredibly, the woman winked. Sarah blinked, not sure she'd really seen it. Then Mattie leaned closer over the table.

"Of course, you'd find all those same couples lined up pretty as you please on the pews of all the different churches come Sunday morning!" She laughed at her own joke, and Sarah smiled.

"But they all lived happily ever after?"

"As happily as folks can, I reckon."

"Mattie!" An older lady, tall and imposing, sailed into the cafe and across to their booth. "You didn't tell me you had guests coming!"

"She's just in town for the day. She's come to take pictures of our bridge."

The woman nodded, a smile forming on her lips. She reached to her shoulder and touched a brooch pinned there, as if to assure herself that it was still there.

"That's a beautiful pin. It's Italian, isn't it?" An oval frame held a delicate mosaic, tiny chips of opaque stone forming flowers in a vase.

"Yes, I got it a long time ago."

"Is Hank waiting outside for you, dear?" Mattie pointed out the window to a man who was waving a cane in great sweeping motions, trying to get the attention of the woman inside.

"Oh my, yes. I'd better go. See you Wednesday night, Mattie?"

"Of course. Bye!"

Through the glass, Sarah watched with some amusement as the woman placated her husband. Reconciled, the couple strolled off arm in arm.

****

"I can't stay long." The girl was tall and thin, her hair pulled back into a tight knot at the base of her neck.

"Are you cold?" The young man rubbed his hands together and shifted from foot to foot. "Let's at least get out of the wind."

Shivering a little in her thin cotton dress and holding a sweater around her shoulders, she followed him to the shelter of the bridge.

"I've got a job."

She squealed and started to throw her arms around him but he stopped her.

"I've got to go to Nashville."

"No," she whispered. "You promised me we'd get married!"

"We will," he said fiercely. "I swear it. We'll just have to wait a year, maybe a little longer. Things will get better, and I swear I'll come back to get you."

Now her eyes and nose were red from more than the cold December wind. "You'll never come back. I know it."

"Of course I will." He tilted her chin up to look her in the eyes. "I've never broken a promise to you yet, have I?"

She shook her head, sniffling a little.

"I promise 1934 will be our year," he pulled her close with one arm, reaching into his coat pocket with the other. "Here, you can wear this and think of me."

She studied the little oval pin. "It's beautiful," she whispered. "I've never seen anything like it."

He turned it over so she could see the writing on the back. "It's from Italy. Flowers that will never stop blooming."

"Hank, I love you."

"You'll wait for me?"

She answered him with a tight embrace that lasted until a car horn made them break apart. They stood holding hands, watching as the car clattered across the bridge and down the road.

****

"If you'd care to come home with me, dear, I have some old photos of the bridge." Mattie had finished her coffee and was sliding out of the booth. Sarah checked her watch. She wanted to get some late-afternoon shots of the Elizabethton bridge, anyway, so she might as well talk to this entertaining old lady.

"You got married in 1918?" Mattie walked deliberately with small steps, planting each foot with great care.

"Yes, in December. Just after the war. You should see the way we decorated that bridge to welcome home our troops."

"There were a lot of men from here who fought?"

"Oh, yes, Elizabethton sent men to all the wars. Grieved over many of them, too. That's my car." She pointed across the street.

"You must've married very young." Sarah hurried to open the door of a big old Cadillac parked outside the post office. Mattie slipped inside, and Sarah got in on the other side.

"You're fishing to learn how old I am." The key made a grinding noise, and then the engine purred into life. Mattie threw the car into reverse with a jerk and began to back out.

"I'm 93 years old." She drove like she walked, with a deliberate pace, calm and implacable.

"I'm sorry, I didn't mean to be rude."

The car glided to a halt at a stop sign. Mattie put on her blinker to signal a left-hand turn. A red car roared past them, after pausing only briefly at the stop sign. Mattie sighed.

"Billy French. He always was a reckless boy. Thirty years married and five children would settle some people down, but not him."

She continued down the street, the Cadillac positioned firmly in the center of the road.

"They say my husband's grandfather helped build that bridge. Of course, half the people in town say their kin helped build it. It was built in 1885, or did I tell you that already?"

They pulled into a driveway that led up a gentle slope. At the top, Sarah looked around curiously at the old house and the barn beside it.

"I know he built this house," Mattie continued with pride. "Of course, all I keep in the barn now is junk and old cars."

Sarah helped Mattie up onto the porch and into the house. The woman directed Sarah to a cabinet in the dining room and asked her to pull out an ancient, round hatbox.

"Somewhere in here I have pictures of Robert and me on the bridge," she said, rummaging around. "It was when we bought our first car."

****

"Yeeeeooooooowwwwww!" The young man did a flip off the side of the riverbank, landing into the water below with a sharp smack.

"You're crazy!" protested the young woman standing next to his car.

"That's right, baby," he replied, breathless from running back up to the car right outside the bridge. "I'm crazy about you." He smoothed his hair back carefully and squeezed a few drops of water out of the ducktail at the back.

"You'd say anything," his date said, laughing.

"I mean it," he said, resting the palms of his hands on either side of her, flat against the two-toned red car. "I love you."

Just then a car filled with teenagers roared up into the center of the bridge. Moonlight poured in through the arched windows. Laughing and screaming, the kids piled out of the car and ran around to switch seats, ringing cowbells and shaking noisemakers. The driver took off with a squeal before the doors swung shut, and he tooted the horn as they careened off the ramp past the couple and their parked car.

"Oh, I bet they're on their way to see 'The Thing That Wouldn't Die,'" the young woman said eagerly. "I want to see that. Can we go?"

Without a word, he helped her into the passenger side and shut the door with a solid clunk.

The moon was full when he pulled up to her parent's house. They hadn't been sitting there more than two minutes before the porch light flashed off and then on again.

"I'd better get inside," she sighed. "Mama worries."

He buried his face in her neck and growled. "She oughtta be worried."

His girlfriend giggled and hopped nimbly out of the car. "See you tomorrow?" Without waiting for a reply, she was gone.

He sat for a few minutes, pondering his options. Then, his mind made up, he drove home.

Back at the bridge, it took some time to figure out how to juggle the paint can and the brush while hanging onto the rope, but the moon provided ample light. The letters were nearly 3 feet tall and marched unevenly across nearly half the length of the bridge. He stood back to admire his handiwork. The first "M" was a little shaky and the exclamation point dripped, but he was pleased. It looked like a serious proposal: "MARRY ME, RUTH WHITFIELD!"

****

"We kept that car till 1955," Mattie said, shaking her head as she looked at the photo. "Of course, we only drove it once a week or so. Robert always walked down to work, and I'd walk back and forth to the store and to the post office. It's such a small town, a car was really kind of frivolous." When she turned to Sarah and smiled wistfully, the photographer could see a shadow of the beauty that had been Mattie's before time wore it away.

"When we were young, couples used to take their buggies into one end of the bridge and the young men would see how much they could slow their horses down before the young ladies complained. In the dark they could slip their arms around their girlfriend and maybe even steal a kiss."

"I guess that stopped when cars became common."

"No," Mattie replaced the photo and began to stir through the box in search of another. "I think the young men still drive real slow through the bridge. Robert did, even after we'd been married for years."

"Did you always live in Elizabethton?"

"Of course." She presented another photo with a flourish. "Where else would anyone want to live? This is a picture of the bridge in 1953 when we welcomed the soldiers home from Korea. See how we strung flowers and crepe paper across the opening?"

****

55

It was dark. Not even a sliver of a moon brave enough to face this Tennessee night, the woman thought as she leaned over the rail to stare into the gleaming black water. She'd come back to town to help bury her grandfather, and it was like stepping back in time.

"Why on earth would you chop off all your hair like that?" her mother had hissed when she arrived at the funeral home after a 2,000 mile cross-country trek. "It's so unbecoming."

"I'm glad to see you too, Mama," she had said, gingerly pulling the older woman into an embrace. "It was a hard drive but I'm glad I came."

After the funeral, they all gathered in her grandfather's house, standing around tables with dozens of pies, cakes, casseroles, salads, and breads. Her grandfather had been well-loved, and the quantity of food pouring in from her friends and neighbors was mute testimony to that fact.

The woman's classmates and former friends had all been there, too, some with children running around, all of them a little thicker around the middle, a little grayer, a little more tired. None of them questioned her about her life in distant California. They talked about her grandfather or the latest scandal in Tennessee politics (news of which hadn't reached the West Coast) or their own lives bounded by the Doe River and the Appalachians.

Grace found it all very unsettling. After a while, she let their voices wash over her, the mosaic of food spread out before her went out of focus, and she only nodded vaguely in response to the kind queries directed her way. She wandered to the porch and then to the streets beyond. These streets, where she had learned to ride a bicycle, played tag, first steered a car, and walked with her first sweetheart.

Michael must be gone now. She hadn't heard anyone mention him, so he must have moved off the edge of the world—out of Elizabethton.

The darkness was healing. Like a bandage over her eyes and ears and mouth, it screened out the flow of sensory input, brought it down to a manageable level. The only two senses fully functional were her sense of smell and touch. She could smell the rich, fertile odor of the damp leaves piled by the sides of the street. Not too far away, she could smell the river's water and the fecund scent of mud at the river's edge. Her toes, poking through the sandals that were a bit unpractical for Tennessee in October, could feel the dew on the grass. Her fingers glided along the handrail and gripped the splintery old wood of the bridge.

"Hi."

The figure materializing out of the shadows of the bridge made her shriek softly. "My God, you scared me," she complained. Then recognition dawned.

"Michael?"

"That's me."

She strained to see his face and then laughed.

"I was just thinking you must've escaped. I've been here two days, and no one's said a word about you."

"I'm still here."

Her hand slipped easily into his, just as if the years had never gone by. Without a word, they walked slowly through the mouth of the bridge.

"Let me show you something," Michael said at last. He patted his pockets for a few minutes. "I don't have any matches. Do you?"

She shook her head before she realized it was too dark for him to see the gesture. "No."

"Here." He took her hand and drew it up to the beam in the center. Blindly, her fingers moved around and over a familiar shape.

"A heart?"

"Now look inside."

Her fingers now smoothed over a pattern of lines and circles.

"I always heard that if you declared your love on this bridge, it would last forever."

The pattern began to take shape under her fingers.

"I was too shy to tell you. But I never forgot you, Grace."

"G.O. and M.K. Michael, how sweet."

The darkness of the bridge made their kisses sweeter. Their embrace lasted until a beam of light pierced the shadows, announcing a car that thundered across the river and over to town. Silent again, the couple wandered off the bridge, hand in hand.

****

"Are you all right, Mattie?"

The old lady had been silent for several minutes, staring at the picture in her hands as if she could change it by a force of will.

"Robert, Jr., never came back," she said softly after a moment. "I never can look at this picture without remembering him."

Sarah touched her gently on the arm. "I'm sorry."

"Robert asked me to go back to the bridge with him in 1986." She placed the photo back in the box and sat up straighter. "He had just come home from the hospital after his second heart attack."

Sarah nodded, unsure how to respond.

Mattie laughed. "We must have made a sight. It was in December, and he was in a wheelchair, so I wrapped him up in three blankets and just wheeled him right on down there.

"It wasn't as cold on the bridge, you see, because the walls acted like a windbreak. We walked up and down the bridge three or four times, talking about all the things that happened to us on that old bridge, and then we went inside and had hot cocoa."

She lapsed into silence again.

Sarah couldn't tolerate the quiet for long. "I'm sorry if I've brought back old memories."

Mattie looked up and shook her head, a smile growing slowly on her face. "Mercy, no. Don't be. Memories are all I've got, and I cherish them." She grasped the arm of the sofa and pulled herself to her feet. "There's one more thing I'd like you to see, and it's out in the barn. I have some copies of a book about the bridge published at its centennial in 1985. If I can find it, you can have a copy."

They walked out to the porch and across the yard to the barn. To Sarah, it seemed as if Mattie's steps had slowed even further.

"I'll never forget the last thing Robert ever said to me," Mattie said over her shoulder as she picked her way carefully across the lawn. "He said, 'Meet me on the bridge, Mattie.'" She stopped and turned to face her guest.

"The nurse said he was wandering and out of his head, but I believe he knew exactly what he was saying." She turned to continue her passage to the barn.

The old structure was filled with shadows and unexpected gleams of pure sunlight, streaming in through random holes in the siding. Dust motes danced in the sun, and spiderwebs glistened in the shadows. The old barn seemed to be alive with magic. Mattie headed straight for a corner littered with old wooden crates and cardboard boxes.

"I'll just look through here," she declared. "They're in one of these boxes."

Sarah looked around. Still hanging on the walls were old, rotten pieces of leather held together by metal—bridles and harnesses, she guessed. A wheel leaned against the far wall, next to an indistinct pile that might have once been a wagon or a buggy. Far back in the barn, hidden by the darkness and partially covered by a piece of old green canvas, Sarah spied the wide round headlights of an old Rambler. Just as she started to move toward it, Mattie let out a triumphant cry.

"Here it is," she said. "I knew I'd find it!"

Sarah walked over to the other woman and thumbed through the book. They walked back to the house, Sarah ready to head back to capture the bridge in the afternoon sunlight.

"I never showed you Robert's picture, did I?" She led Sarah into the dining room to a framed photo resting on the sideboard.

"He's, he's very handsome," Sarah stammered. "Such blue eyes."

"I'll take you back into town now," Mattie announced. "Let me get my keys."

Sarah didn't speak on the short ride back to her Jeep at the post office. She thanked the woman profusely, promising to send her a copy of the book when it was finished.

"Oh, by the way," she mentioned in what she hoped was a casual tone. "Did you two ever have a Rambler?"

Mattie laughed. "Robert drove a Rambler from 1964 until the day he went into the hospital in 1986. He loved that old wreck."

Sarah gave a little wave as Mattie pulled away. She pulled the jeep off the road near the bridge and scrambled down to the river's edge to catch the last of the afternoon sun for the photograph.

The next day, working in her darkroom, Sarah hummed as she moved around, printing the last two rolls of film she needed for her book. She had put the incident in Elizabethton out of her mind, telling herself she must have imagined it, that there were lots of blue-eyed men around, and old cars were common in the country. She had almost convinced herself.

Sarah pulled the last print out of the chemical bath and pinned it up to dry. She cocked her head to take a look, and what she saw made her unpin it and hold it up close in the dim light.

The long, white, angular bridge over Doe River was surrounded by a soft, definite glow. It looked like the sun had created an aura, a halo of light and warmth. But that wasn't possible, Sarah realized. Doe River ran north to south through Elizabethton. There was no rational explanation for the radiance that enveloped the bridge that had sheltered a century of love.

The bridge in Elizabethton, Tennessee, is on Third Street between Main Street and Riverside Drive. Elizabethton is east of Johnson City in Carter County, in the southeastern corner of the state.

THE LINE

He flinched as a small projectile flew over his head, making an almost inaudible hiss as it continued its course past his left ear and landed on the ground by his foot. His first thought was dismay—he had always pictured his death occurring when he was surrounded by his comrades, nobly defending the company colors or leading a gallant charge that would ultimately prove to be the turning point for the Confederacy.

Instead, here he was, half-naked, rinsing out his drawers in a creek, not even where he was supposed to be. His friends were building defenses up on the hill. They had all agreed to take turns bathing and washing down at the stream since it had been nearly a month since their last opportunity.

The second fatal shell never came, and the private opened his eyes to look at the bullet that had missed him by a whisker. He rolled it over with his toe. It was a big, green pecan, still in its protective outer covering. He looked up to see that the tree towering over him was indeed a pecan tree. The creek was thickly bordered by trees of all types: redbuds with their distinctive heart-shaped leaves, mimosas with lacy fronds barely stirring in the thick heat of late June, crooked little dogwoods and tall arrow-straight pines.

He picked his way carefully through the water, headed for a rock that sat in the sun. Spreading his pants out to dry, he splashed again to the bank. He watched the water flowing for a few minutes, idly wondering if the stream might eventually join up to the creek that ran by his mother's house in Athens, Georgia. A fierce longing, quickly squashed, rose up in him: to be that stick, floating harmlessly downstream, toward someplace that was always quiet and safe and where a falling pecan didn't sound like death coming down.

He lay back, using his arms for a pillow, and thought about writing Delia about being scared by that pecan. She'd laugh, picturing him with his britches in his hands, crouching, trying to get ready to meet his maker. Maybe the sergeant would have some more paper and envelopes this afternoon. The supply train was supposed to have been through here by now, but Private William Beckman knew better than to count on that.

He could count on a few more minutes of peace, right here by this creek, and he intended to enjoy it. The sky was an old, faded, worn-out blue, like it was already tired of summer. But the branches and leaves that crisscrossed his field of vision were bright, defiant green. Wisteria twined and twisted around every available support, a riot of exuberant growth, and late-blooming honeysuckle tinged the air with faint sweetness.

William reached to scratch absently at a chigger bite on his chest. The birds called to one another beneath the sheltering arms of the trees, but their calls didn't seem too urgent. The laziness of late June seemed to affect every living thing along the winding path of the stream. A lizard sunned itself next to William's pants, blinking languidly. A couple of squirrels chased each other and then stopped suddenly to chatter. William listened to the soothing babble of the water over the rocks and let his eyes close. His imagination drifted back to a June day three years ago, when he was fifteen and sitting on another creek bank with Delia.

He felt a shadow fall over him, blocking the shade-dappled light, and sat up with a start.

The man standing over him was about his age, holding a rifle loosely in one hand and a canteen dangling by its strap in the other. His uniform cap was stuffed roughly into the back pocket of his pants, which were precariously secured above his hips by a belt cinched tight. The tunic coat that hung open, unbuttoned in the heat, was blue.

"Howdy," William said cautiously, gently patting the ground behind him for his rifle and cursing himself for not keeping it close at hand.

"Howdy," the soldier replied. "You seen anybody from the Twenty-seventh?"

"Who?"

"Ohio Infantry. The Twenty-seventh. I went out after a wild turkey and got turned around. I know they're right close."

"Naah, hadn't seen 'em." William scratched his head and then flicked a few lice from under his fingernail. "I reckon they're upstream a bit."

The tired soldier turned and trudged away. A few yards away, he turned back. "Say, what division're you from?"

William's mind scrambled to latch onto a number that might make sense. "Hunnerd an' twenny-first," he blurted.

The man nodded and waved. "See ya."

William looked at his pants, still drying on the rock in the middle of the stream. His shirt hung on a bush just out of sight. The soldier had mistaken him for one of his own, and that made a second brush with death in the space of an hour, he thought. Delia would really like this letter.

A figure came crashing through the undergrowth, from the high ground where William had left the men of his company earlier. It was John Coffee, who lobbed a pinecone at William's reclining form.

"You gonna take all day, Smelly?"

"You kin call yerself Smelly, now. I've had a bath, and I'm now fit to spend an evening in the finest company." William stood and stretched.

"You'll have to settle fer us old boys, I'm afraid."

"Saw a bluecoat jes' now."

"What? And didn't take 'im prisoner?"

"I was nearly naked. He went thataway if you wanna go after 'im." William pointed upstream.

"I'll jest have myself a bath instead."

"Y'all finish them fortifications?"

"We left you about a mile or so to dig."

"Hope we'll stay in 'em longer than the last ones."

John Coffee stripped down and waded out into the water. "It seems a shame to dig 'em 'n' then leave 'em," he agreed. He looked into the current. "If I jest had my fishin' pole, we'd have ourselves one heck of a dinner," he remarked.

William gathered his clothes and slipped them on. After refilling his canteen, he turned to trudge up the hill.

****

"Anybody want any more Cheetos?" The red-haired woman rattled the bag in vain. No one was in earshot. She stuffed the bag into the wicker picnic basket and stood up. She saw a glimpse of something gray through the trees near the creek and strolled in that direction, noting the signs of wildlife all around her. Squirrels ran and chattered through the trees, chipmunks scurried between the rocks on the banks, and birds flitted everywhere beneath the lofty canopy of pines, oaks, and old pecan trees.

"Jim?" she called. Every time she got near, they slipped off again. Really, it was a bit too hot to play hide-and-seek.

"What?" He was right behind her, holding a map. Josh was right behind him, clutching the bag of Cheetos she had just packed away in the picnic basket.

Sherry looked at her husband blankly.

"I thought I saw you over there." She pointed up a little rise.

"No, but let's go up that way. I think that's where the entrenchments were."

She shrugged and followed him, their son falling into line behind her.

"The bridge that was here was burned," Jim said over his shoulder. "That one there," he gestured to the right, "was built a little after the war. Both armies burned a lot of bridges." He grinned. "But if I were an infantryman in the summer of 1864, I wouldn't mind wading through a creek every now and then."

"Can I go wading in the creek, Mom?" At the prospect of getting in the water, Josh showed more enthusiasm than she'd seen from him in the three days they'd spent touring Civil War battle sites.

"It's a private creek, honey. Maybe we'll find a motel with a pool, and you can swim then." The boy dropped back, discouraged.

A booming sound made all three jerk to a stop, startled. Jim said with a laugh. "Tires on the old timbers of that bridge sound like cannon, don't they?"

"I think that's poison ivy, Jim, isn't it?" She pointed to a suspicious-looking plant. "Are these trenches very far away?"

He stopped walking. "They must've been around here somewhere." A horde of gnats rose up around him like a malevolent cloud. He swatted in vain. "The battle of Ruff's Mill was exactly 131 years and one day ago. The Ohio boys just put on their bayonets and swarmed over the top of the trenches. 'Course, the Rebels were fighting pretty hard. Lots of 'em had family near here."

Sherry shuddered. "I'm ready to go," she said firmly. "Take me back to the twentieth century."

As they drove toward the center of Smyrna, Sherry noticed red-and-white signs sprouting in a number of yards, like a crop of exotic mushrooms.

"Save Our Covered Bridge," she read curiously. "I wonder what that's all about?"

Josh never looked up from his comic book. Jim, although he drove the car, was still lost in the battle of Ruff's Mill. "Um," was all he said, and Sherry began to look for a motel with a pool as they entered the more populated area of the Atlanta suburb.

* * * * * * * *

It was dark before the sergeant told the men to quit digging. William gladly threw his shovel aside and sat down, dangling his feet over the edge of the trench.

"Pretty damn big," he commented. "Room for a lot more than our regiment."

"I reckon we'll have some company." John Coffee had come back from the stream refreshed, but now they were all dog-tired. "I don't think we were diggin' jest fer us."

"Let's go, boys."

William and his fellow soldiers looked up in surprise.

"Where we goin', Sarge?"

"Back to Kennesaw. Them's my orders."

"Damn." They looked at each other in amazement. "All that work an' we're gonna leave now?" No one rose to their feet.

"Come on." The sergeant was just as tired. "We got to get there by midnight."

One by one, the men straggled up to form an uneven line. Swearing and muttering, they began the eight-mile hike back to Kennesaw Mountain and the trenches they had dug there last week.

"I 'spect we'll see these ditches again," John told William. "I'd like to think so, anyway. It'd be nice to think somebody had a plan that made sense."

John and William and all the men of their regiment felt at home in the trenches below Kennesaw Mountain. They could work their way half-crouched through the maze of ditches and get almost anywhere up and down the line. The secret was not to stand up straight. Sometimes a new soldier would forget, and his head appearing above the trench would prove too tempting a target for the Union sharpshooters. Then his fate depended on luck, or the skill of the soldier a few hundred yards away.

Bullets whined and moaned across the tops of the trenches all day. Confederate soldiers returned the fire. The constant noise was something every soldier adjusted to. Sometimes one side or the other would yell taunts and insults, provoking an extra flurry of bullets or even a rock or two, hurled by an angry soldier.

William made his way through the trenches clutching a true prize. He'd traded his tobacco ration for two sheets of paper and an envelope. When he reached the section of fortifications he'd been calling home, he raised his hand above his head.

"Look what I got, John," he called, waving the paper triumphantly. A bullet whined overhead but he ignored it. "Today's my lucky day. As soon as she gets this letter from me, Delia will sit right down and write me back, you wait and see."

John pulled William's hand down roughly. "You idiot," he said. "Ain't you been here long enough to learn anything?"

Neatly piercing the two sheets of stationery was a bullet hole.

William stared at it in surprise. "I guess today really is my lucky day," he said. "Mebbe I've got nine lives, like a cat."

John shoved him lightly. "If that stationery don't make Delia write back, nothin' will." He sat back down on an overturned bucket to gnaw reflectively on a piece of hardtack. William smoothed out the paper and began to write.

"I heard we're goin' South again," John interrupted him.

"Mebbe that's what we dug them ditches for," William muttered, chewing on his pen and carefully considering his words. "My dearest Delia" sounded a little too serious, but she ought to know by now that his feelings for her were pretty strong.

"If we don't hold this next line, some people say the Union army's gonna overrun all of Georgia." John watched William carefully. His family had gone west to his uncle's farm in Alabama, but he knew William's mother and sweetheart were still ensconced in Athens.

"Uh-huh." Should he start off by saying how much he missed her, or jump directly into his adventures over the past few days?

"That creek we was at, it's called Nickajack Creek. It's jest 15 miles from Atlanta."

William looked up, startled. "We're that close to Atlanta?"

John nodded, switching a soggy chunk of hardtack from one side of his jaw to the other.

"Atlanta's not 65 miles from home."

John nodded once more as William bent over the page again. Now he had some real news to write. He didn't expect that Delia's father, who ran Athens' best hotel, would leave town. But maybe he would consider sending Delia and her mother and sisters out of harm's way. He wrote furiously for a few minutes and then slowed down as he began to recount his encounter at Nickajack Creek and explain the hole in the stationery.

He stopped altogether as he debated how to close the letter. Love? Deepest affection? That sounded about right. But it needed something else. The pauses between the bullets singing overhead began to grow longer and longer, and William realized the sun was setting. Maybe he should tell her that he was fighting for her. That was it.

"As I fight to hold that crucial line above Atlanta, I shall hold thoughts of you close to my heart. With deepest affection, I remain your devoted William."

He stretched, careful not to extend his limbs above the top of the entrenchment.

"What's for supper?" he asked John cheerfully. "Can we light a fire tonight or not?"

****

"Concord Village was established nearly 200 years ago." The woman spoke in the deep drawl of a native Georgian. "It's a practically perfect example of the villages typical during the Civil War."

"I can't believe we're so close to Atlanta." The journalist looked around at the thickly wooded landscape and the creek that murmured gently through the trees. "It's almost like being in another century."

Nancy nodded. "We want to preserve that feeling," she said. "The creek was named after a Cherokee Indian chief, Chief Nickajack. There are some Indian burial grounds nearby and some graves from some early white settlers, too."

"Cobb County started trying to put the highway through here in 1985, is that right?" The reporter scribbled in her notebook.

"Yes, and the Army Corps of Engineers has granted them a wetlands permit so they can start construction. But the highway will probably destroy the ruins of the old woolen mill, which is that way," she pointed east. "It will definitely ruin this location as a recreational area, and the bridge probably won't survive the blasting they'll have to do in order to build the freeway."

"I saw some people here earlier, before you got here. I tried to stop them, to interview them about their opinion on the construction, but I guess they didn't hear me call."

Nancy shrugged. Tourists were not uncommon here.

"I think I have all I need. Thanks for your help." They turned and began to walk back to the parking area at Ruff's Gristmill. She consulted her notes. "Your group's called Protect Endangered Areas of Cobb's History, right?"

"That's right. P-E-A-C-H. Will you send me a copy of the article when it comes out?"

"I'd be glad to." They shook hands, and the reporter drove off with a little wave.

****

It was the Fourth of July, and William couldn't help but feel a twinge of nostalgia for the celebrations he'd witnessed before the war. Now, he supposed, the Confederacy would celebrate something like it, but he wished sometimes that it had never come down to all this. Here he was again, bent over and hustling up and down the ditches, shooting and getting shot at.

They had abandoned the fortifications at the base of Kennesaw Mountain a day or two ago. The Federal troops had followed close behind. The last few days had been a confusion of marches and shouting and shooting. William wished that he and his friends had dug the trenches a little deeper, but they could improve upon them. It was only a little harder to dig now that there was constant fire overhead.

Suddenly the frequency of the firing increased dramatically. Somewhere, William heard an officer yelling.

"They're coming over the top, men! Hold your ground!"

William looked around to see John crouching next to him, his face pinched and grim. "Gotta hold this line, John," William grunted. "Can't let 'em get by."

They took turns cautiously peering over the embankment and firing, then falling back into the trench to reload. Each time William looked over the brink, a wall of smoke and fury seemed to be edging closer. He couldn't make out any individual soldiers, just indistinct blurs, first a 100 yards off, then 50, now 10.

"Fix bayonets!" An officer screeched, a clear note of panic.

William and John had abandoned their bayonets months ago. They had large hunting knives, though, and had them loosely tucked into their belts.

Both soldiers had fought before. They and about half of their regiment survived the battle at Missionary Ridge and a number of small skirmishes. For William, the memory was dreamy and disconnected, an incoherent roar of artillery, the sharp smell of gunpowder, masked by a cloud of smoke. He remembered men falling on either side, but the most painful memory was the agonized screams of the horses when they were hit. That seemed the greatest injustice of all. The poor dumb animals, led into this chaos against their wills, without even the comfort of knowing that their death served a higher purpose.

As William stuck his head above the trench, a figure resolved itself out of the smoke. To William, crouched in the trench, the soldier in blue seemed impossibly large and too close to shoot.

With a shout, John leapt up and whacked the Union soldier across the side of the head with his rifle butt. When he fell, John quickly finished him with a neat slice across the neck. William watched, fascinated and sickened, as the blood spurted out of the soldier's throat. The man had shaved that morning and nicked himself on the chin, right next to a deep dimple.

William's hand reached involuntarily to his own chin, hidden by a beard. He'd grown the beard to hide a boyish dimple just like the Union soldier's.

"William!" John kicked him, hard. "Shoot!"

He snapped out of his reverie and loaded his gun. With mechanical precision, they shot and stabbed at the men coming at them for what seemed like hours before they heard a bugle sound.

"That's retreat," John shouted. "Let's go!"

"I can't leave," William said. "I promised Delia I'd stay."

"You're crazy!" John pulled at William's belt, hauling him backwards. "We can hold the line back here. Come on!"

William resisted for just a moment, then felt John go limp.

"John?"

He shook his friend.

"John?"

The battle roared around him, the sound now louder and more immediate. Looking around, William saw they were all alone in the trench—except for the dead men. And some vaguely blue shapes that were swirling around in the smoke to his left.

William tossed John over his shoulder and climbed awkwardly out of the trench. He staggered a few hundred yards before he saw an officer directing the retreat.

"John," he gasped. "He's hurt."

"There's a house over there, about a half-mile away. Take him there. The doctors'll see to him." He clapped William on the shoulder. "Good man. Anybody left in the entrenchment?"

William shook his head and shuffled off in the direction he'd been told. John lay still across his back, but William didn't think about what that meant. He wanted to get John somewhere safe and get back to the line. Any other thoughts were meaningless.

Men were piled up on the porch of the big house like firewood. Someone yelled at William to lay John down outside, but William walked right into the frenzy that filled the house. He found a man with bloodstained hands and shook him by the shoulders.

"This is John," he shouted.

"I can hear you, son." The surgeon spoke kindly.

"Take care of him. I've got to get back to the line."

The man held out his arms and William gently passed his friend over. He squeezed John's hand and turned to leave.

****

Nancy was tired. She had spent the day in court, fighting with county officials and lawyers about the Concord Historical District. The battle seemed endless, without respite, one petty legal struggle following upon the heels of another.

She turned left onto Spring Road, past the big mall with its satellites of Taco Bell, KFC, and Hardees. Every store was draped with a big, brightly colored plastic banner declaring the virtues of the products inside. The traffic, the signs, the condensed litter of an affluent, late-twentieth century society seemed to scream at her that to resist the future was impossible. She snapped off the radio, cutting off a litany of snarled traffic in midstream. There—one manifestation of progress was eliminated.

A few blocks down Spring Road the buildings were spaced a little farther apart. A little more green surrounded the concrete, although it was still dominated by offices, businesses, and stores. Two miles away from the mall, the office buildings disappeared, replaced by single-story bungalows built at the century's midpoint. Solid, practical houses with aluminum awnings, sensible lawns, and American cars in the driveways. The trees along Spring Road at this point were tall, embracing the sky with wide-spread branches. They were planted 50 years ago or more by the same down-to-earth people who built and bought the bungalows. A wide strip of lawn bordered the road, was briefly interrupted by a sidewalk, and then continued to the doorsteps of the houses.

Nancy could breathe more easily now, and she rolled down her window to take advantage of the breeze that only began to stir about seven o'clock on a midsummer evening in Georgia. It was not a cool breeze by any means, but it managed to convey a promise of relief from the sultry air, a promise that might or might not be kept.

Spring Road became Concord Road at a sharp bend, and the four lanes narrowed into two. Trees crowded even more closely around the road now, and the houses, set farther back, looked like they had been there before the road was paved. At last the road began to slope gently down toward the creek, and Nancy pulled aside to let a stream of cars heading back toward town pass through the one-lane bridge.

She glanced to the left, and her heart skipped. Up on the hill were row after row of ragged trenches, the dirt thrown carelessly to one side. The trees she knew as veritable old giants were mere saplings, overshadowed by other trees she'd never seen. Long rifle barrels protruded from the trenches, each one marked by a puff of smoke as it fired.

Approaching the trenches were rough lines of men in Union blue. As she watched, horrified, they halted to pull long pieces from their pack that glinted evilly in the sunlight: bayonets. They fixed the weapons on the ends of their guns and advanced into the little puffs of smoke. Some fell. More came forward to take their places. They scrambled over the edge of the trenches, and Nancy shuddered, imagining the carnage taking place as the battle moved into hand-to-hand combat. She heard the cannon roar and felt her skin crawl with a chilling premonition of danger. She saw a figure on a horse ride across the battle line, exhorting his troops, heedless of the risk to himself. And as she watched him, clearly encouraging them to hold their position, she felt as if he were talking to her. She felt a sense of protection—of being watched.

The cannon roared again, and the sound of a car horn made her tear her eyes away from the compelling, unnerving battle scene. It wasn't a cannon at all. It was the last car from the opposite direction, its tires thundering across the bridge. As she swung out into the road, she glanced up to the left again. The trees were familiar, the fortifications long overgrown, the men in gray and blue long at peace. Or most of them, anyway.

****

William walked slowly down the road to the creekbed. The guns still thundered around him, but they sounded strangely distant. Men were streaming past him heading south, and some men on horseback stopped to talk to him, gesturing widely. He only shook his head and walked, step by step, north to the edge of Nickajack Creek.

There were a few stones piled up, remnants of the bridge that had stood there before someone—Confederate or Federal, William didn't know—had decided the bridge made it too easy for armies to move back and forth across the creek. William sat down on the stones and methodically began to load his gun.

"This is the line, Delia," he whispered. "This is the line I will hold."

In front of him, across the creek, stood a line of soldiers in blue. At a shouted command, they began to cross the creek, holding their guns and ammunition above their waist to avoid the splashing water.

William began to shoot left to right. He'd shoot one, and then carefully reload and shoot the next. He didn't know how many he'd shot before he felt something strike him hard in the chest. As he spun down, off the pile of rocks and toward the ground, he noticed the mimosa tree above him was in bloom. The vivid pink blossoms, looking like absurdly painted miniature feather dusters, spiraled down toward his face. Or maybe he was spiraling up toward them. The sky became bright, then white.

****

Calvin Phillips walked slowly down his driveway to fetch the newspaper. It was almost dark, and there might be a hint of a breeze off the creek to cool him off. He breathed deeply, noticing a faint scent from the late-blooming honeysuckle that wound itself around the trees by the road. The smell was nearly overpowered by the smell of exhaust from the cars passing to and from Smyrna. But the traffic was practically nonexistent now, at 8:30 on a July evening. The narrow Concord Road wound its way down to Nickajack Creek and the single-lane covered bridge that crossed it.

Calvin peered through the shadows at the mouth of the bridge. Someone was there, standing motionless at the entrance. Calvin moved a little closer to warn the man that sometimes cars came through the bridge at high speed and that he should move to one side before he was struck.

"Hey!" he shouted.

The figure did not move.

Calvin walked a little closer, then shook his head in disbelief. The forage cap with the black leather brim. The tunic buttoned smartly up the middle. The round canteen on a long leather strap. The long-barreled rifle. It was unmistakably an infantryman from the Confederate Army.

"Hey!"

Still the man did not budge.

"What do you want?" Calvin was now distinctly uneasy, but determined to make a stand here, practically at the foot of his own driveway.

The soldier's lips were moving. Calvin moved a little closer.

"This is the line, Delia." The whisper was so faint it barely carried above the song of water over stones in Nickajack Creek. "This is the line I will hold."

Concord Bridge, outside Smyrna, Georgia, is in danger of being lost due to construction of a new freeway. At the time this story was written, you could visit the bridge by taking U.S. 41 north through Smyrna. Just before the shopping mall, turn left onto Spring Road, and continue for several miles. Spring Road becomes Concord Road and will lead you straight to the bridge.

Whispering Waters

L isten to this, Papa." The young woman bent over the newspaper, straining to make out the smudged type by the lamplight. "The Iowa Equal Suffrage Society has adopted the motto of the State with the change of a single word, thus: 'Our liberties we prize, our rights we will secure.'"

The man seated in an armchair, dozing next to the fire, only grunted. "Ephesians 5, verses 21 through 24."

His daughter rattled the paper. "What about Ephesians 6, verse 5? Are we to take that to mean slavery is acceptable?"

"Don't try my patience, Jenny. God created Adam first, not Eve. It is not our place to question the wisdom of our creator."

"Yes, Papa." She was silent a few moments longer, then spoke again. "Mrs. Johnson and her daughters went to Des Moines to visit her sister again. I wonder if they are back yet?"

Her father only grunted, and she sprang up out of her chair like a mechanical toy and paced the parameters of the room. "Winterset, Winterset," she singsonged in a tone perilously close to mocking. "Do they call it that because winter sets in early and stays late?"

"You are restless this evening, my dear," her father commented, barely opening his eyes. "Regardless of why they named it, you had best become accustomed to it. I plan to stay here until my retirement and beyond, God willing."

"I miss Ohio," she started to say but bit back her tongue. What's past was past. Ohio and her life there were as lost to her as Iowa was lost to the Indians, she supposed.

"I will feel brighter in the morning, Papa," she said, trying to sound certain. "It is time for me to retire, I think." She kissed the crown of his head and lit a lamp to take upstairs. In Cleveland they had had all the modern conveniences, like gaslights in every room, but it seemed all they had in Winterset was corn. Corn to the east and corn to the west. Corn to the south and corn to the north. And in the winter, even that distraction was gone. The fields lay bleak and barren, waiting for the advent of spring and the farmer's attentions.

The congregation her father had come to lead was fairly large, about 30 families, but all the young ladies Jenny's age were married and mistress of their own place. Jenny, at age nineteen, was a distinct oddity.

In fact, she was a somewhat more agile and singular version of the Misses Lavender. They lived alone on the edge of town, the spinster daughters of the town's first banker. They subsisted, somewhat precariously one might assume, on some kind of pension. The first time Jenny had come to call they had hovered over her like bees over a fragrant rose.

"Oh, what a lovely bonnet," one exclaimed. "Is this truly the fashion now?"

"However do you get around in that skirt, my dear?"

Jenny rather expected one of them to pull out a magnifying glass and begin to scrutinize the stitchery on her gloves. She almost enjoyed the attention, until she had a sudden vision of herself 30 years from now latching onto a newcomer like a dog snatching at a bone.

"Have you joined our literary society yet, Miss Cooper?" Miss Lavender—the one who looked a little more like a plum than a prune, Jenny thought unkindly—was pouring tea. Jenny would have to stay a little longer.

"We have begun to read *Saint Elmo*," continued the elder Miss Lavender. "Do you enjoy reading?"

"Oh, yes," said Jenny, glad for a familiar topic. "I read that last year. Right now I'm reading *Leaves of Grass*, by Mr. Whitman."

The ladies were shocked into silence. After a moment, the younger ventured a word. "Does your father approve of such reading?"

Jenny wished the ground would open up and swallow her. To put herself in a bad light was one thing. But to make her father appear permissive or to make it appear that his daughter would not bow to his wishes was even worse.

"I'm afraid he has not noticed my little excursion into this book," she stammered. "I've not enjoyed it, and I really think rereading *Saint Elmo* would be a pleasure. When did you say the literary society meets?"

"On Tuesdays, dear." The elder Miss Lavender leaned over and patted her hand. "Do come join us. We usually meet at Mrs. Scott's house. She has such a big parlor in that nice new house of hers."

Jenny had hurried home that day and hidden her copy of Mr. Whitman's book that her best friend had given her when she left Cleveland. She didn't even think to ask Papa for his approval of her reading material—Mama had always allowed Jenny to read anything that interested her. But Mama had always been a little less strict than Papa, Jenny though guiltily.

Tonight she picked up her copy of *Saint Elmo* with a sigh. They would discuss the final chapters tomorrow at Mrs. Scott's house. Then on Wednesday she had the church supper to look forward to, with all the ladies vying to present the most elaborate dishes. Thursday she would write letters, and Friday she could prepare the Sunday school lesson for the little girls of whom she had been given charge. Saturday, well, perhaps Saturday she could find some mending to do.

Jenny nodded off into sleep, then awoke with a jerk. Not even the combination of the book and a catalog of her life's exciting events could keep her awake, she thought wryly.

The next morning she found herself late leaving for the club meeting. "How," she scolded herself silently, "can you possibly get so far behind when you have absolutely noth-ing to <u>do</u>?" She picked up her skirts a bit and took long, steady strides, not quite running, her book tucked under one arm and her muff under the other. Jenny spun around the corner to Mrs. Scott's house and collided full force with a figure just closing the gate. Her book flew to the left, her muff landed in the street, and her hat was thrown off her head by the power of the impact.

"Oh, I am so sorry," gasped the young man, whose hat had also been knocked off by the blow. "Are you all right?"

Red-faced, Jenny assured him that she was. "It was my fault, completely," she insisted. "If only I had been paying attention."

"Let me get that for you." He retrieved the book for her and read the title with interest before placing it into her hand.

"*Saint Elmo*. You must be a member of the famous literary club."

Jenny blushed further, feeling like her face must surely explode.

"Well, I am," she admitted. "I'd already read it, but when we moved here I had so little to do that I needed the company, and the Misses Lavender invited me first thing."

Then it occurred to her that she was rattling on to a complete stranger, on the streets of a very small town on whose goodwill her father's future depended. "I'm late," she concluded abruptly. "Please, do excuse me." And she swept up the sidewalk to the shelter of Mrs. Scott's front porch. She had barely tucked her hair back under her hat before Lizzie, Mrs. Scott's parlor maid, swung the door open. The assembled ladies greeted her, and the discussion began.

Jenny's mind wandered, returning again and again to the encounter on the street. A warmth stole over her cheeks again, and she impatiently dismissed her foolish wanderings.

"But was Agnes truly repentant when she approached Saint Elmo at the end?" Mrs. Wright could discuss each phrase of the book in excruciating detail. She often did.

Jenny glanced out the windows. The clouds were thick, and might bring snow before the week was out. If it had been icy, she might have landed at the stranger's feet.

"Do you think Agnes was sincere, Jenny?" A voice boomed to the left of Jenny's chair.

She snapped to attention, turning to face Mrs. Allen. "I, ah, I was just looking at the snow."

"What? Did it start snowing already?" Mrs. Allen, a formidable matron, heaved her bulk out of the chair to peer out the window.

"No, I mean, I was thinking it looked like snow," Jenny explained weakly. She seemed to do nothing but embarrass herself and her father lately, she thought with despair. All the ladies were now clustered around the window, looking for a telltale flake.

Mrs. Scott clapped her hands. "Let's have refreshments now, ladies, shall we?" Lizzie scurried into the room with a tray of tea cakes and the teapot.

That night, Jenny and her father had just finished supper when someone knocked at the front door. Jenny, too curious to sit patiently in the parlor, followed her father to the foyer as he opened the door.

"Good evening, sir," said a young man, taking off his hat with a bow. "My name is Joseph Brooks, and I had the pleasure of, ah, meeting your daughter this morning when I accompanied my cousins, the Misses Lavender, to their literary club."

"Yes?"

"She left this behind, and I came to return it."

Jenny's heart jumped when she saw her muff in his hand. Her father accepted it and bowed, ever so slightly, to the visitor.

"Thank you, sir, and good day." Her father closed the door with a soft and final thud.

"Papa," she moaned.

"What?" He turned around to face her, more quickly than you might expect from a man of his bulk.

"You might have invited him in since he was kind enough to return my muff," she protested.

"You didn't tell me you had met a young man," her father rumbled.

"Well, I didn't, really, that is, we weren't introduced."

"Do not forget, young lady, how important it is for me to maintain a certain decorum in my own and my family's life." He stalked into the parlor, leaving her muff lying on the bench in the foyer.

Jenny followed behind him, struggling to maintain her composure. "Shall I read to you, Papa?" She reached for the black, leather-bound Bible which lay in its usual place on the table beside his chair.

"Proverbs 31." He leaned back and closed his eyes.

"Who can find a virtuous woman? For her price is above all rubies," Jenny began. "The heart of her husband doth safely trust in her, so that he shall have no need of spoil. She will do him good and no evil all the days of her life."

As she read, she couldn't help but think of her mother and wondered if her father thought the same. This was one of his favorite passages for her to read aloud. He had always said she looked like her mother.

After less than an hour of reading verses her father selected, Jenny excused herself and drifted upstairs. As she passed through the foyer, she slipped her hands in the folds of her muff, imagining they were still warm from the stranger's hands. She was nearly upstairs before she realized her fingers had closed on a scrap of paper.

She closed the door to her room and sank onto her bed, unfolding the note with uncertain fingers.

"I do not know your name," it read, "but I hope one day I will. Do you read poetry as well as novels? Perhaps you will recognize this:

How say you? Let us, O my dove,
Let us be unashamed of soul,
As earth lies bare to heaven above!
How is it under our control
To love or not to love?

Jenny kept the note and the muff beneath her pillow that night. She heard the nine o'clock train pull out of the station, its lonely cry trailing it west toward Omaha. She heard the late express go through without even slowing down, headed east as fast as coal and steam and modern engineering could take it. That train also howled in protest at the solitary, cold Iowa night, and Jenny felt an answering cry fill her heart.

"Did you sleep well, Papa?" she asked at breakfast.

He threw her a sharp glance. "Of course. I always do." He ate a few more bites of egg and ham before continuing. "What are your plans today, Jenny?"

"I thought I might help Sarah make an apple cake for the church supper tonight," she answered casually. "Then I have some calls to make."

"Not to the Misses Lavender, I'm sure." He did not even bother to look at her. He got up from the table and stretched. "I'm going to my study now. See that I'm not disturbed until dinner."

Jenny kept her eyes on her plate. "Papa, I. . ."

"If the young man wants to meet you, he can surely come to church," he interrupted her. "If he has any objections to church, then he's certainly not a suitable caller."

Jenny rang the little bell to summon Sarah to clear the table and then snatched up her coat and muff and went outside. She dared not leave the garden, but she strode round and round its perimeter until her cheeks were flushed with the cold. It took her nearly half an hour of walking before she realized it was a hot, flaring anger that drove her. She marched back inside and sat down at the writing table in the parlor.

"Dear Caroline," she wrote. "Sometimes I believe Papa never intends for me to marry. And, sometimes, I believe it is for entirely selfish reasons. As long as I remain in his home, he never has to worry about meals, or clothing, or entertaining the often dreadful women in his congregation. I do it for him! Although I cannot be entirely in agreement with those dreadfully strident suffragists like Mrs. Bloomer, I can certainly see the value of independence every now and then!"

Jenny took a deep breath, laid aside her pen, folded the letter, and thrust it deep into her pocket. She would reread it later and possibly mail it. Her best friend in Cleveland was still unmarried, like her, but had no lack of callers. In Iowa it seemed there were no unmarried men, except perhaps the one man her Papa refused to let her see.

Jenny went to the cellar and fetched a few jars of applesauce. She and Sarah spent the better part of the morning making apple cake, and before she knew it, it was time for her to dress for church.

"You look lovely this evening, my dear," her father said, ceremoniously lending her his arm for the walk next door to the church. "I am sure everyone in Winterset feels blessed to have you in their midst."

Jenny shook her head slightly, feeling the unaccustomed weight of her mother's diamond ear-bobs on her earlobes. "Do you mind that I wear them, Papa?" she asked tentatively.

As he shook his head, she saw the muscles of his jaw tighten momentarily, perhaps to suppress some emotion like sadness. Or, she thought suddenly, anger.

Jenny took her customary place in the front, just to the right of the pulpit, and tried to read her Bible as she waited for the service to begin. Her back seemed curiously exposed, and she fought to keep herself from turning and gawking as the congregation gathered behind her.

The sermon seemed tediously long, although she tried loyally to follow her father's complicated train of logic. Afterward, the congregation assembled in the little frame Sunday school hall, attached to the church with an open dogtrot.

"My, doesn't this look wonderful!" enthused Mrs. Allen. Her diminutive husband followed at her heels. He was the county sheriff and seldom spoke when his wife was around. They both filled their plates and moved on.

Jenny's eyes scanned the crowd, searching for a tall, scarcely remembered figure, or the lean, wrinkled forms of the Misses Lavender. She had just about abandoned hope when a touch on her elbow made her jump.

"Miss Cooper?" It was the younger Miss Lavender, followed closely by the older. "We have been so fortunate to have a guest, you know, our cousin from Chicago,"

"Really he's our second cousin, dear," the other interrupted. "Now, where did he go?"

At last Jenny's eyes latched onto a figure in black moving through the crowd toward them. Her mouth became mysteriously dry, and her heart pounded so loud she wondered if perhaps she was having palpitations. At last he arrived and took her hand in his.

"Miss Cooper," he cried, bending low over her hand. "I have heard so much about your astonishing powers of literary criticism."

She giggled.

He stood and his eyes gleamed, reflecting her amusement. "May we join you for supper, Miss Cooper?"

"I would be delighted, Mr. Brooks, is it?" It all seemed such an intriguing little charade, pretending that their encounter on the sidewalk outside Mrs. Scott's house had never taken place. As they talked, largely ignoring the food on their plates, it was as if they were only reacquainting themselves, old friends after a long absence.

"What do you do in Chicago, Mr. Brooks?"

"Oh boring things, mostly to do with trade and agriculture. I am trying very hard to establish myself."

"I would follow you anywhere," thought Jenny, and then she wondered where that wild thought had sprung from.

"You enjoy poetry, sir?" Her mind had flown just as quickly to the captivating scrap of verse he'd tucked into her muff.

A fugitive and gracious light he seeks,
Shy to illumine; and I seek it too.
This does not come with houses or with gold,
'Tis not in the world's market bought and sold.

His half-smile caught her heart just as a shadow fell over them.

"The best poetry ever written is found right here, young man," her father growled, shaking his Bible at eye level. "And the best stories, too, for that matter. I could have nothing else to read for the rest of my life and be content."

"I couldn't agree more, sir." Joseph Brooks sprang from his chair and began to quote again. To Jenny's delight, he chose a passage from Proverbs.

"She openeth her mouth with wisdom, and in her tongue is the law of kindness. Her children arise up and call her blessed; her husband also, and he praiseth her. Many daughters have done virtuously, but thou excellest them all."

He made a little bow in Jenny's direction, which prompted another scowl from her father. "Where is your family from, Mr. Brooks?" The two men faced each other, standing in the center of the room.

"Mostly from right here, Reverend Cooper, these fine fields and homes. My father, rest his soul, came from Chicago, and I work with his brother now. My mother was cousin to the lovely Misses Lavender."

"Any brothers or sisters?"

"No sir, my mother died along with a baby sister, 20 years ago."

"An orphan, then."

"In a manner of speaking, yes sir, I am."

"Well." Reverend Cooper nodded curtly and turned to speak to some church members who were leaving.

"I'd like to call on your daughter, sir," the young man called after him.

"We'll see," said the minister, without turning around.

Jenny had flushed again when the young man had spoken. He sat down again, next to her, and spoke very softly.

"May I? Call on you? You set more than my hat spinning Tuesday morning, Miss Cooper. I've been so distracted that the Misses Lavender tried to dose me with castor oil."

She stifled a giggle and then saw that he had intended to make her laugh. "I'd be honored, Mr. Brooks, but I really can't say for myself. You'll have to get permission from my father."

"Anything." His eyes locked on hers with such sincerity she felt her heart constrict again.

"You be a good boy and fetch the buggy for us, Joseph." Miss Lavender the elder swooped down, fracturing the moment.

The quarter moon shone so brightly that night Jenny could barely keep her eyes closed. Again she heard the nine o'clock train and then the late express, but this time their songs seemed full of hope as they rushed across the fields.

"That boy's a Catholic," her father roared as soon as she entered the dining room for breakfast. "Penniless, too!"

Jenny recoiled from the force of his words.

"Papa," she began.

"Don't you start," he warned. "If I let him call on you, you'd just get your hopes up. He's not suitable at all, and that's the last word."

Too stunned even to cry, Jenny turned and walked stiffly back up to her room. She threw herself across her bed, heedless of her dress, and buried her head beneath the pillow.

Her mind raced from one thought to another, sometimes alighting on reckless schemes to circumvent her father's will. "I'll run away," she thought, "and live with Caroline in Cleveland!" But she knew she never would. At last she began to sob, with a fury that first surprised her and then drained her of her energy. Near noon she fell asleep, too deeply to hear Sarah's timid knock and call to dinner.

When she awoke, she slipped downstairs for pen and paper. Once she returned to the privacy of her room, she began to struggle over the composition of a letter.

After many false starts, she finally had a draft she felt she could send.

"Dear Mr. Brooks," it read. "Please forgive my boldness in writing you, and I pray that God will forgive me for disobeying the deeply felt wishes of my father, whom I respect and love.

"My father believes the barriers between my upbringing as a Protestant and your own as a Catholic are too great to overcome. He is further concerned about your ability to secure an adequate livelihood to support a family.

"I cannot express how profoundly your presence in Winterset has affected me. These circumstances bring the great poet Coleridge to mind:

For hope grew round me like the twining vine,
And fruits and foliage, not my own, seemed mine.
But now afflictions bow me down to earth;
Nor care I that they rob me of my mirth.

I cannot ask that you abandon religious habits you have formed from birth. Yet I recall your sincerity when you expressed a desire to call upon me. If there is hope, please acquaint me with it. I fear dejection will not turn me into a poet, but merely a bitter person."

Having finished the letter, Jenny sealed it and carried it to the kitchen, concealing it in her pocket.

"Sarah, are you about to go home?"

"Yes'm."

"I need you to carry these preserves to the Misses Lavender on your way." Jenny hastily put a few jars into a basket and then scribbled a note to tuck in with them. As Sarah turned to put on her hat, Jenny slipped the letter to Mr. Brooks beneath the jars. "Leave the basket there," she called as Sarah left. "I'll collect it when I see them on Tuesday."

At supper that evening, she and her father barely exchanged three words. Just as she was excusing herself, he spoke.

"I trust you will obey me in this matter, Regina," he said gruffly. "I am acting with your best interests at heart."

She nodded, too filled with a stew of conflicting emotions to trust herself to speak.

When she heard the nine o'clock train pause at the station, she rested her forehead against the cold glass and wondered if Joseph Brooks was boarding. She read fragments of poetry until late into the night, only falling into an restless sleep when her lamp flickered and went out, its supply of oil exhausted.

Sarah lightly tapped on her door the next morning.

"I'm coming, Sarah," Jenny called, struggling out of the twisted sheets that had tried in vain to contain her sleep.

"Oh, Miss, breakfast is over. Your father said to let you sleep. But I had something for you," the girl continued.

Jenny yanked open her door and restrained herself from covering Sarah's mouth. If her father heard anything, he would be most suspicious.

"What?" she whispered.

"A gentleman at the Lavender house gave this to me when I left the preserves," Sarah whispered in reply, pulling an envelope from her apron pocket. "Should I not have accepted it?"

A flying kiss on the cheek was the only response from Jenny, who snatched the letter from Sarah's fingers and closed the door in the surprised girl's face.

"My dear Miss Cooper," the letter began. "I have received with a heavy heart the correspondence of your father. I will with joy become a member of his congregation, if that were all he required to pay suit to you. Of my financial situation, I can make no amends, save that to assure you that the future holds much promise. I am afraid that will not satisfy your father.

"I dare not hope that the strength of your affections for me would cause you to receive this letter with happiness. I will accompany my cousins again to the literary club on Tuesday, and if fate is kind I will glimpse your lovely face. To hear your voice again is beyond all hope.

> Far off thou art, but ever nigh;
> I have thee still, and I rejoice;
> I prosper, circled with thy voice;
> I shall not lose thee though I die.

The next three days were interminable. Her father's watchful, brooding presence weighed heavily on Jenny, and as she had so many times over the past five years, she ached for her mother's bright countenance and calm disposition to lighten the gloom.

Tuesday morning the light waking her was so muffled and diffused that she feared the worst. Crossing to the window, she saw that big, fat snowflakes were spiraling down steadily. She dressed and went downstairs.

"Sarah," she called, glad to see the girl already in the kitchen preparing breakfast. "How bad is the snow?"

"Well, not bad at all, Miss," Sarah responded, "if you're a farmer. It's this kind of snow that makes the corn grow come spring."

Exasperated, Jenny left the kitchen to join her father at the table.

Her father intoned the blessing, and then asked, "Do you have plans today?"

"Just my literary club, Papa," she said, spooning some eggs on her plate.

"Snowing pretty hard this morning," he commented.

"It will stop soon, I'm sure. Would you like me to drop by Mrs. Simpson's house on my way home? I hear she's still feeling poorly."

"That would be a kind thing to do, daughter." They finished their meal in silence.

By half past nine, the snowfall had mercifully slowed to a few lazy flakes circling to the ground, and the dark gray clouds were thinning. Jenny wrapped up tightly in her coat and muffler, stopping at the last moment to slip her mother's ear-bobs on her ears.

Sarah dropped a plate in the dining room, and Jenny let out a little shriek. Sarah came running, full of apologies, and held the door for her.

Jenny's nerves were strung to a high pitch, and she nearly flew out of the house to avoid her father. He would surely comment on her ear-bobs, a sign of increased vanity on what was to him an ordinary Tuesday morning club meeting.

Her steps slowed as she turned the corner to Mrs. Scott's house. She didn't know how she would contrive to speak to Mr. Brooks without risking discovery by the whole circle of ladies inside the parlor.

The muffled sound of hooves on the soft blanket of new snow made her jump and whirl around. A brown horse with white stockings was pulling an unfamiliar buggy.

"Miss Cooper?"

"Oh, it's you, Mr. Brooks!" Jenny was relieved to recognize his lively brown eyes between his hat, pulled low, and a muffler that covered his mouth.

"I know it's most unusual, but would you care to take a short ride with me?"

With a surge of courage, Jenny took his outstretched hand and climbed into the buggy.

"That's the Misses Lavender's horse, isn't it?" she asked. "Where did the buggy come from?"

"The livery stable." He turned the buggy left, and within a few moments they were out of town, surrounded by fields on all sides, glowing with their fresh covering of snow. "The ladies decided that since it was snowing, a covered buggy was called for. I was happy to oblige."

Jenny became suddenly shy, and neither spoke until the road began its gentle slope down to Middle River.

"I shouldn't have done this." The words burst out of her.

"I've loved you since I saw you," he said at the same time.

They were quiet again.

The horse slowed to a standstill on the middle of the bridge, glad of the shelter and forgotten by the man who held the reins.

"I have a plan," he said urgently, aware of Jenny's discomfort in the darkness of the bridge. "My uncle knows a man who is selling a new kind of corn—a hybrid that grows faster and doesn't get the rust. If I invest in his idea, we could be married in a year!"

"I don't understand," Jenny stammered. "What can you invest?"

"I'll work for him for free, or something. Please say you'll marry me, Jenny."

He touched her hand, and even through the wool of her gloves she felt the intensity that sparked between the two of them.

"It's dark now," he continued. "But if we go on, just a little further, see how bright it could be!" He pointed to the opening of the bridge, where the snowy fields shimmered with an uncommon light.

Quickly, without speaking, Jenny stripped off the ear-bobs. She took his hand and turned it up, dropping the diamond jewelry in his open palm.

"Take them," she said breathlessly. "Invest them. I'll be in Winterset until you can come back."

"Are you sure?"

She nodded, and he raised the ornaments to his lips and kissed them gently.

"Take me back," she whispered. "I'm late."

Jenny sat through the discussion of *Saint Elmo* in a daze, barely responding even when her fellow club members spoke directly to her. She relived those moments alone in the carriage over and over, until the whole episode began to feel like a dream.

At home, her silence was so pronounced that her father commented on it. "You're not taking ill, are you? We would miss your company at the church supper tomorrow night."

Listlessly, Jenny assured her father she was fine and excused herself to go to bed. She fell right to sleep, but her dreams were tortured, with odd fragments of poetry spinning from the mouths of incongruous people and pierced by shrieking train whistles.

Wednesday morning her bones felt leaden. She missed breakfast and only appeared downstairs a few minutes before dinner. She had only pulled a comb across her hair and barely fumbled with the row of buttons on her dress. Her father frowned as she sat down at the table.

"I hope you will take more care with your appearance this evening, Jenny," he chided her. "Good grooming is the mark of a good upbringing."

"Yes, Papa," she said dully.

She knew without a doubt that Joseph Brooks would not be at church this evening. Jenny could not even grasp how to make it through the afternoon without sinking into the black despair that threatened. To contemplate a full 12 months of this deadening, thick melancholy was beyond her comprehension.

At last it was half past five, and she and her father were bundling up for the short walk to the church.

"You're not wearing the ear-bobs tonight?"

"No, not tonight, Papa." Her brain moved so sluggishly she could not think of an appropriate response.

"Come along, then." He grasped her elbow, rather too tightly, and they proceeded through the door.

Thursday morning Jenny was struggling to finish a letter to Caroline without mentioning recent events. Sarah appeared at the parlor door and dropped an awkward little curtsy.

"Your father would like to see you in his study, ma'am," she said, avoiding Jenny's eyes. Her father rarely invited her to interrupt his workday. Curious, Jenny tapped at his half-open door.

"Come in," he said, bent over his work. After a moment, he laid down his pen and motioned for Jenny to have a seat in the leather arm chair in front of his desk.

"Sarah tells me she delivered a basket of preserves to the Misses Lavender last week," he said without preamble.

Jenny studied her hands, laid neatly in her lap.

"And she says a young man gave her a letter to carry back to you," he continued. His voice was so calm it terrified her. She made no reply, but a great shudder tore across her torso, and she seemed to shrink.

"She has been dismissed. Bring me the letter."

Jenny rose and turned to go, too numb to feel compassion for poor little Sarah.

"Jenny, what did you do with your mother's ear-bobs?" The whisper blasted her with more force than a hurricane. She could only shake her head and hurry from the room.

His heavy footfall sounded on the stairs moments after she reached her room. She heard a telltale jingle, and then a click as the tumbler fell into the lock.

"When you're ready to speak, you may come out. In the meantime, I shall summon Sheriff Allen to recover my stolen property."

"No," she whimpered, but too quietly for her father to hear.

She held out until nightfall, when she pounded on her door and shouted until she was hoarse. Her father came upstairs to unlock the door.

"The thief is now in jail," he announced with satisfaction. "We shall recover your mother's ear-bobs soon. Will you give me the letter now?"

"No, Papa, I can't," she whispered. "Please, don't make me."

"Then you shall stay in your room. I will not have my child flaunting my authority."

Jenny paced the parameter of her room, frantic. At last, when she heard the nine o'clock train leave the station bound for Omaha, she opened her window. Holding her skirts scandalously high, to free her legs for the climb, she clambered out of the window and dropped, praying wordlessly. Her feet slammed into the roof of the porch and she began to slide, slowly at first but then with growing speed, hurtling toward the edge of the roof and a 10-foot drop to the ground.

Jenny landed with a grunt in the abundant foliage of the holly bush outside the kitchen door. Scratched on her face and hands, she was otherwise uninjured. She picked herself up and began to walk resolutely to the east, the center of town, to the small county jail next to the Winterset train station.

It was a simple, square building, solidly constructed of stone with iron bars across a single, high window in the back. The streets were deserted. After the nine o'clock train, there was no reason for anyone to be out.

She did not know why she had come or what she could do, but she seized the doorknob and rattled it just the same. To her amazement, it opened.

"Mr. Brooks?" she whispered.

"Miss Cooper?" The familiar voice cracked in surprise.

As her eyes adjusted to the gloomy interior, she saw that the space she occupied was a tiny little anteroom to the jail cell itself.

"I'm sorry," she said, ineffectually.

"You didn't do anything," he pointed out, his voice gaining strength.

"I want to help you get out," she said.

"There's the key." He pointed to a nail in the wall to the left of the door. It held an iron ring with a solitary key attached.

She unlocked the door and swung it open.

"Where will you go?"

"West, I suppose." He shrugged. "Why are you doing this?"

"I, ah, I love you, Mr. Brooks."

"Will you come with me?"

She shuddered involuntarily, a great, encompassing motion that shook her as fully as a mother cat shakes her kitten.

"Yes," she whispered.

"Meet me on the bridge, then. I'll get a horse."

Suddenly he was gone, and she looked around in surprise. She had just made a decision to turn her life upside down, yet the world looked oddly the same.

She was half a block down when she heard voices in the jail behind her. "He's gone, dammit," someone shouted.

"He must've broke out and then gone and kidnapped the girl," someone else yelled. She realized it was Sheriff Allen.

"Get your horses! They can't have gone far!"

Five men galloped past her, heading west, as she cowered behind the corner of a house. She turned right and began to run toward the livery stable.

In a matter of minutes, she had grabbed a horse and led it outside. Perched precariously on its side, clutching the mane for support, she urged it west, out of town to Roseman Bridge.

A mile ahead of her, the moon illuminated a black speck against the snow, a solitary figure on horseback. Behind her she heard the shouts and calls of the posse, swollen now to nearly a dozen men.

The wind picked up and snatched a sentence or two from the sheriff's mouth, sending it flying down her way. "He's headed down the bridge road! You and Frank go round and ford the river. We'll get him on the bridge."

The gait of the horse threw her up and down, jarring her roughly with every step. Still she rode, trying to catch up with Joseph before he fell into their trap.

At the crest of the hill, she turned off the road, onto the river path, in a desperate attempt to make it to the bridge before Joseph. Her horse, confused, shimmied back. She slid off and hit the ground.

Dazed, she heard the horses from the sheriff's posse thunder past. Moments later, gunshots split the night.

Jenny staggered to her feet in time to see a riderless horse dance out from the mouth of the bridge.

****

The men greeted each other with few words as they settled into their accustomed spots on the banks of the Middle River.

"You hear Reverend Cooper's daughter died?"

"Yep." They cast their lines and sat in silence again for a while.

"How old was she? Fifty?"

"'Bout that."

"She never was the same after that Brooks boy."

"I dunno why they never caught him."

"He disappeared into thin air, my daddy said. Right there off that bridge." He pointed to the bridge wreathed in mist a few yards down stream.

"I dunno," said the other man doubtfully.

"Reckon she went crazy?"

"Who?"

"Miss Cooper."

"Dunno." The fisherman reeled in his line and slipped another worm deftly onto the hook. After casting out his line once more, he spoke again.

"I heard her mama was crazy. Locked up somewhere back east."

"Huh."

The weight of the mist-shrouded morning again took its toll. It was a good five minutes before either man spoke.

"What's that, Stephen?"

An odd little susurrant sound seemed to mock the gurgle of the water flowing unseen in the fog below the bank.

"Dunno," the other man said softly. "Sounds like somebody whisperin'."

"You 'spect it's Michael, come along to play a trick?"

Something cold and wet pushed its way into the first man's side and he yelped.

"Damn," he swore. "Dog snuck right up on me, didntja, boy?" He rubbed the dog's ears as the creature whimpered.

The whispering sound continued, a little louder now.

"It's comin' from the bridge, Stephen. Let's go see if ol' Michael's playin' a trick on us."

They heaved themselves to their feet and walked slowly through the swirling vapor to the mouth of the bridge.

The dog whined again and pushed its belly flat against the ground.

"Whatsa matter, Sport?"

The dog just cried again, its fur standing up.

"Go on in and look for Michael, Stephen," the other man urged.

"I dunno," his friend said doubtfully. "Listen. It almost sounds like poems. Michael don't know any poems, does he?"

The two men walked slowly into the bridge, side by side, leaving the dog whining softly outside.

"Boy, it's cold this mornin', ain't it?"

"It's June, you idiot." He playfully shoved the other one, inadvertently placing his feet in the center of the bridge.

"It is cold here." They looked at each other, their features indistinct in the gray light of dawn.

The whispering grew louder, so that words were almost distinguishable. It sounded like a man and a woman, murmuring their pledges, safe within the sheltering darkness of the bridge.

The whispers died away. But when raucous laughter rang out from unseen lips, its reluctant audience hurried out of Roseman Bridge, glad to return to the light of day.

To visit Roseman Bridge, go to Winterset in the southwestern corner of Iowa. Take Iowa 92 west out of town. A few miles down the road, you'll see a sign directing you to turn left for Roseman Bridge.

FOOL'S GOLD

California still haunts me. In fact, there is no part of my day, waking or sleeping, that is not populated with shades of those long dead, and memories of my life when it was full of hope and the promise of love.

I have been evicted from yet another boardinghouse for waking the occupants in the dead of night, screaming and wrestling with one of my many ghosts. Although it is barely October, there is frost every evening, and soon I must find a place to stay or risk death by exposure.

Exposure. Perhaps that would not be an undesirable end. After all, it is the hiding of events and facts that has brought me across the continent to this cold, forsaken state of dour, pale people. October in California is a time of bright sunshine and even brighter company; the people there are not forced to abandon their outdoor pursuits until the rains come in late November. Even then, the rains are welcome, for their random action often uncovers new and profitable sources of great wealth.

But the wealth I speak of is a false one. I would happily trade every pinch of gold dust ever found in California for a return to my former state of relative poverty and happiness. Even though I have nearly five pounds of the treacherous substance, secreted in various hidden pockets and seams of my coat and pack, I cannot find a place to stay or even buy a home, for these demons pursue me night and day.

I know there is a reckoning to come, and I fear it even more than the specters who appear before me at every turn. Perhaps I should make my way down South for the winter, plying my trade and trying to settle some part of my soul. No matter where I travel, though, I must cross water, and everyone of those streams and creeks and rivers are spanned by the damnable bridges, identical to the one that became the instrument of my downfall.

I was not, you see, born to become the itinerant peddler I am today. My parents sent me to college in the year 1843, at a great personal sacrifice. I then became a teacher, married my sweetheart, and produced two offspring in short order. One daughter and one son, a tidy little balance to match my tidy little life.

Then in 1849, I was struck by an illness so profound that it left my life—and most probably my afterlife—in ruins. That many others succumbed to this fever gives me no comfort. Those other victims do not give me any companionship, or ease my fears of what is to come, or soothe me when my terror strikes.

My wife had been petitioning me to purchase a carriage. It was not seemly, she said, for her to ride in a rude wagon when her husband was such a person of importance in our little town. But I saw no means of financing such an extravagance. Her nagging irked me. The cries of my two young children made my skin crawl. The local children, whom I was supposed to enlighten, seemed a dull and loutish bunch. Their parents, whose support I must maintain in order to keep my position, seemed equally as tedious, if not more so. So the fellow who appeared at the tavern one evening, slim and well-muscled and bursting with vitality, had found in me a most receptive audience.

"There's gold just lying on the riverbanks, waiting to be picked up," he explained. "You take a flat pan, swirl the water and stones around, and pick out the gold." He pulled out a little pouch. "It looks like this." The pieces scattered on the polished bar top, some smaller than the head of a pin but others nearly the size of a pea, gleamed and glittered wickedly.

"When I left, my daughters were panning $15 to $25 a day in gold dust. It's easy work."

I shouldered my way up through the crowd to study this man more closely. Like me, he appeared to be a gentleman. He spoke well, and I listened with growing excitement as he described the principal routes to the gold fields.

"You can go by ship, but I hear there's so many people waiting for a ship in Panama that it takes longer than the overland route. And people are dropping left and right from scurvy on the ships, too."

"How long does it take to get there by land?" My neighbor, a bank clerk by trade, was as captivated as I.

"It depends. You can get to the mountains in eight weeks or so, even with a loaded wagon. Then you can go through the Sierras by Peter Lassen's trail, which might take six weeks, or take the Truckee River crossing, which could take four or five weeks."

"Isn't that the route the Donner party took?"

The stranger nodded somberly, and the crowd surrounding him recalled the grisly tale of cannibalism and death by the group caught in an early snow.

My dreams that night were filled with visions of great riches, towering, snowcapped mountains, grand mansions, and elegantly clad women, none of whom, I am ashamed to report, bore the slightest resemblance to my wife. The next morning, I hurried to the tavern to speak in private to the man from California.

"How much will it take to get me there?" I was already determined to go at any cost. It seemed the perfect solution.

"You going alone, without your family?" His brown eyes swept over me, assessing, I thought, my physical stamina and courage.

I nodded eagerly.

"You'll need at least $100 once you're there to buy your equipment and such. It'll take another $50 to get there, but only if you're starting out with a good horse."

I asked a bit timidly, if he was returning to California soon himself.

"Matter of fact, I was thinking of leaving next week," he drawled. "I'm taking Pete Lassen's trail 'cause it'll take me around some of the highest mountains instead of through them. May's late to get started, and I don't want to get caught by the snow."

"I could pay you to be my guide, if you would permit me, sir."

"There are a few other adventurers here who are interested in a guide," he said. "If you're ready to go by next Thursday, I'll have you in the gold fields by September 10th. You can pay me $15 just like everybody else."

Fifteen dollars was half a month's salary for me. But, I calculated, if his daughters found $15 a day in gold and I could work twice as hard, his fee was negligible.

I returned home and informed my wife of my decision. She was stunned but could see that argument would be fruitless. Those ridiculous women at Seneca Falls notwithstanding, my wife knew her place. She began to pack hurriedly for a temporary return to her parents' house. She would live there with the children until I came home, within 15 months, I assured her, leading a horse laden with my newfound wealth.

I arranged in a few short days for the sale of our meager furnishings, with the bulk of the proceeds going into my pocket for a grubstake, as the stranger from California so quaintly phrased it. All but one of my fellow townsmen dropped out of the expedition, so we were a group of three leaving Illinois one late May day.

We were only two weeks into our journey when my neighbor, the bank clerk, decided to turn around. The journey was tedious and long, but my guide convinced me that we were making good time, being on horseback and unencumbered by families, wagons, or live-stock. As we labored through the Rockies, we saw many household items by the side of the trail, abandoned by travelers who had overburdened their wagons. Barrels of china, chairs, tables, even a piano were all left to rot in the sun and be buried by snow from September to April or longer.

My first sight of the Sierras gave me such a shock that my guide laughed. It had taken several days' riding to come close enough to comprehend their size, but when I finally did, I nearly lost all courage. I felt so puny on my horse that I thought we would be forever lost among those massive peaks. We pushed on, though, and I was glad for the route that en-abled us to avoid the most difficult climbs.

We left the mountains on September 1st, and my excitement began to mount steadily. Here at last was the promised land. The site of my future prosperity, the night we crossed Deer Creek and camped, the gold fields an easy day's ride south, I proposed we celebrate with a bottle of brandy I had carefully hoarded during the long journey.

I fell into a drunken stupor before midnight and woke before dawn, queasy, cold and stiff. I soon realized my bedroll was gone. Panicked, I stood to look for my horse and pack. All gone. My guide had stolen everything but the clothes on my back, even going so far as to remove the wallet from my pocket while I slept.

I leaned over and vomited violently. Even now, I will not touch brandy for the bitter memories it invokes. But in September of 1849, I still had the courage to continue my quest, and struck out on foot for the gold fields.

I didn't get far. Before dark I found myself on the banks of a large river blocking my access to the future, with only one apparent crossing. The bridge looked dilapidated, although the tollkeeper assured me it had been built at great expense only two years ago.

"I get 10 to 15 people an hour crossin' sometimes," he cackled. "Comin' and goin', but mostly goin'. You lookin' to git rich too, young man?"

I allowed that I was, but that I'd suffered a temporary setback in my financial affairs.

This made him hoot with laughter. "Welcome to California, boy! Don't you trust nobody, 'cause nobody's gonna trust you!"

I found it difficult, at that point, to ask for the privilege of crossing on credit, but I did my best.

He shook his head emphatically.

"No, sir, no credit, no free passage." He cackled again. "Unless you're a man of the law, why, then I'd have to let you pass!"

Discouraged, I retreated a few hundred yards back along the trail and prepared to spend a cold, hungry night considering my options. A family party of about six set up camp next to me right at dusk, and I hurried over to their campfire to introduce myself.

They were kind enough to tell me that passage over all bridges in California was free on Sundays, to allow the faithful to attend church. I was surprised to hear of such civility in such a wild country, but it seemed like Providence was smiling on me. Tomorrow, my fellow travelers told me, was Sunday. I had lost track of the days during my passage through the terrible Sierras.

I was hungry, cold, and discouraged when I arrived at Marysville. The little town was a stew of mud, men, and mules. I had to provision myself, so I asked for work at several establishments.

"A schoolteacher?" The storekeeper thought this was quite a joke. "Look, Samuel, here's a schoolteacher from . . . " He turned back to me. "Where'd ya say you was from?"

"Illinois." I didn't appreciate being the source of his amusement, but I hadn't had a meal in three days.

"Illinois! He wants to work!" A man half as large as a house came lumbering over. Samuel, I suppose.

"Illinois, you'd better git yourself some gear and git out to them fields," he told me. "You won't find any work in town 'cause nobody's gonna hire you for fear you'll run off after that gold as soon as you can."

I had to admit he had a certain logic. I begged him for a job anyway.

"Look, in Illinois, I gits $1 a pound fer flour, $2 fer a pound of bacon or dried beef, $30 fer a shirt, and $100 fer one a them serapes over there," he gestured toward a bright garment tightly woven out of wool. "Now, am I gonna trust a complete stranger with all these things that are pretty near worth their weight in gold?"

They did give me a few slices of bread in exchange for sweeping the floor. I headed east, out of town, since I could not go either south or west without crossing a toll bridge. Already the covered, barnlike structures were becoming a symbol of my desperate state of mind. Through their shadowy depths, I was sure, lay my salvation. I could not have been more wrong.

I walked until nearly dark, parallel to the Yuba River, a wild and ferocious torrent that roared out of the Sierras, which brooded over the landscape some 50 miles east. I saw little activity on either side of the river until I reached yet another covered bridge.

A little knot of men had gathered at the mouth of the bridge, shouting and gesturing. On the other side, I could see tents pitched all across a field and men hunkered down by the side of the river, washing dirt or building elaborate contraptions to wash greater quantities of dirt. Again, as at Marysville, there was a confusion of men, mud, and mules, but there was no air of carnival here as there had been in the town. This was deadly serious work.

"You can't get away with that, Jim Cooper!" A burly man with crossed forearms seemed to be the center of the storm. He stood squarely in the center of the bridge opening, while another smaller man hovered around him.

"You took at least $5 worth of gold dust, and now you're saying I owe you for crossing back? That's robbery, and you know it!"

"I weighed that dust, and it was less than a quarter of an ounce. You left with a loaded mule, you're comin' back with a loaded mule, it's a dollar each way. See there?" The big man pointed to a sign nailed to the side of the bridge.

To my dismay, tolls here were higher than any I'd seen yet. It cost 25 cents to cross on foot, 50 cents with a mule, and a dollar if your mule had a pack. I had no desire to argue with the formidable man guarding the mouth of the bridge, but the first sign of any gold mining I had yet seen was on the other side of the river, so I had no alternative.

Just as I approached the man, I sensed some movement underneath the bridge out of the corner of my eye. I looked, and there was a young man, swinging by his arms from one crisscrossed support to the next, across the river, going to desperate measures to avoid the toll.

I walked up to the tollkeeper with as much dignity as I could muster.

"Sir," I said, "Is there a penalty for cheating the tollkeeper out of his toll?"

"Damn right," he roared. "Who the hell are you?"

"Should you collect such a penalty, would you be obliged to reward the person who led you to catch such a scoundrel?"

"No!" He scowled at me so fiercely that I began to think I should follow the young man under the bridge, instead of reporting him.

"Well," said another man, "we would certainly be most grateful. You wouldn't believe the lengths some people go to avoid our toll, which is, I think, quite reasonable." It was the smaller man who had been hovering around earlier.

"Then sir, cross the bridge with me and I shall show you your culprit!" I decided I was not agile or foolhardy enough to swing across the underside of the bridge.

The three of us crossed, but not before the burly man picked up a shotgun from the inside corner of the structure. When I saw the gun, I was well satisfied with my decision not to cheat them of their toll.

"You there," he shouted at the figure, who had just dropped off the last support and was clambering down the stone pier to reach the riverbank. "The toll is a quarter, whether you cross over or under, and now you'll pay triple!"

When the agile young shirker appeared before us, I saw he was little more than a boy.

"Aw, Mr. Cooper," he said. "I've been at Marysville, and I lost all my money. I've got a little dust in my pack, back at camp, and I'll pay you, really I will!"

"But you didn't intend to, is that right, Jack?" The other man, Mr. Cooper's partner, could also put forth an intimidating stare.

"Of course he wasn't going to pay us!" Mr. Cooper—the burly man—grabbed the young man's arm and twisted up until the boy's face went white.

"I'll pay you now, really—come with me, we'll go get it!"

Half carrying the boy by his upper arm, Mr. Cooper marched off in the direction of a little cluster of tents. I tried to melt into the crowd that had gathered, but Mr. Cooper's partner grabbed my arm.

"Didn't fergit about the toll, didja?" He grinned, and the awful stench of his breath wafted over me.

"Ah, of course not!" I cast about in my mind for an explanation, but found none. "I was, actually, wanting to know if you would have some employment for me since I was the unfortunate victim of a swindle just three days ago."

He laughed. "The swindle started the day you left fer California, man, haven't you figgered that out yet?" We walked back across the bridge, which creaked and moaned with the rising evening wind. "All those men over there, they'll not make more than they need to buy more supplies, and then that deposit'll run out and they'll need to build a stamp mill to git the gold out or have to move on to another deposit." He leaned over to me, confidentially, and I had to force myself not to withdraw from his offensive odor.

"You wanna get rich, you build yerself a bridge. That's the way to make a livin' and not break yer back in the process!"

It seemed as if he were right. When we emerged, there were three more men waiting to pay their toll, and a farmer with a wagon drawn by two oxen. Nearly two days' wages for me in Illinois, and all in the space of a few minutes.

After collecting the money, my companion turned to me again. "You've got long legs," he said. "Ain't afraid to climb, are ya?"

In fact, I am afraid of heights, but I saw no other reply was wanted, so I said no. He handed me a hammer and a canvas sack of shingles, and told me to attend to the roof where some shingles had blown off during a recent storm.

With some difficulty I ascended to the roof. A few rough boards had been nailed to the side of the structure to aid in my climb. Apparently these repairs were frequently needed. Once on top, the river was so far below me and rushing at such a speed that I felt near fainting with fear. I could not stand up but lay on the roof, clutching the shingles and praying that the shingles I held would not come unstuck from the bridge and send me tumbling to my death in the torrents below.

After a time, my senses steadied. I studiously avoided looking down at the water and crawled on my hands and knees across the structure, looking for places where shingles were missing. I nailed six or seven new ones into place before I heard a shout from below.

"Hey, you! You gonna spend the night up there?"

I crawled to the edge and awkwardly climbed down. Mr. Cooper and his partner were standing there to greet me, both smiling broadly.

"Fun, huh?"

"I did not come to California for fun, sir," I replied stiffly. "May I ask what wages I will receive for my labors?"

"When you're finished, we'll pay you, oh, I dunno, what do you think, Joseph?"

"Two bits?" suggested the smaller man.

"Since that is the price of passage over your bridge, I would expect a slightly higher renumeration."

"My, he do talk fancy, don't he?"

Mr. Cooper laughed and slapped me on the back. "Hungry?" he asked. "I think we owe you a plate of beans for catching young Jack at his tricks again."

I was, of course, famished, and ate not one but two plates of beans for supper. They suggested I bed down in the bridge for the evening, in a corner. I was glad for the shelter.

The next morning I forced myself to climb back up to the rooftop. It took me all morning to finish, and then I crawled over the roof twice to make sure every missing shingle had been replaced. When I looked south, toward the gold field, I saw hundreds of tents dotting the landscape, some on the edge of little streams, others dwarfed by huge mounds of dirt, stripped of their value by the industrious miner. Everywhere was squalor, men toiling with a single-minded purpose that boggled my mind. I had no idea how to apply for a claim, how to work one if I got it, and for the first time I began to seriously question my ability to succeed.

I clambered down and presented the hammer and depleted sack of shingles to Joseph Kyle with a flourish.

"I hope I have proved my worth to you, sir," I said. "I believe my labor is worth a dollar at least."

To my surprise, he agreed at once. I followed him inside to the safe, which he carefully unlocked before handing me a coin.

"You gonna go try yer luck?"

"I do not yet have the means to equip myself, sir."

"I've got to go to Marysville tomorrow. Stay here and watch the bridge with Jim. We'll pay you two bits."

I hesitated, but felt I had no alternative. After agreeing, I stepped back outside in the bright sunshine. Jim Cooper was arguing fiercely with a bent old man, heading south across the bridge. His mule was loaded with gear. This, I came to see, was Mr. Cooper's primary sport—abusing travelers who had no other choice but to cross at his bridge.

"I'm no storekeeper! I'm no miner! Your gear is worth less than nothing to me! I'll have cold, hard cash or you'll not cross, old man!"

Seeing an opportunity, I stepped up to the miner.

"I'll purchase your spare pick for two bits, sir, and solve your dilemma."

He grumbled a bit, claiming that he'd paid $3 for it in Yuba City, but he needed the toll and gave in.

After the miner had crossed, Mr. Cooper clapped me heartily on the back. I winced. The man had hands like hams.

"You've caught the right spirit, now," he shouted. "Pin 'em down and squeeze 'em till they scream for mercy!" He called to his partner. "Hey, Joe, this one's got the makin's of a real California businessman!"

I didn't want to spend what little money I had to cross the bridge, so I positioned myself beneath a massive pine tree to watch the travelers come and go. Toward the end of the day, another miner appeared who had been drinking rather too zealously in Marysville. He had no mule and no money left, but tied to his pack were three flat miner's pans. I again offered to help him cross the bridge by purchasing one of the pans, and we struck a deal.

"Didn't I see you up there, repairing the roof yesterday?"

I admitted that I had been.

"I hope that old skinflint paid you well," he grumbled. "The last man who took that job fell and died for these greedy bastards."

I was shocked to hear that my feelings of danger had been so well justified and resolved to make as much profit as I could from this infamous team of tolltakers.

The next day I watched over the south end of the bridge, while Mr. Cooper assaulted travelers making their way back to the gold fields. My job was relatively easy because most miners leaving had at least a little gold dust, being on their way to buy supplies or find amusement at Marysville, Yuba City, or even on their way to San Francisco or home to their families. On the north end of the bridge, travelers were either newcomers to the fields or miners coming back, usually penniless.

Once Mr. Cooper suspected me of holding back a toll, having miscounted the number of miners who crossed. He lifted me up by both forearms and shook me until my teeth rattled. The thought had crossed my mind, since 15 men, 6 with mules, 1 buggy and 3 wagons made their way across heading north, just in one morning.

I assured Mr. Cooper I had given over every pinch of gold dust and every coin, and I turned my pockets inside out as proof. Somewhat mollified, he took me across and showed me where he scratched a tally in the dirt with a long stick.

"I don't trust nobody," he growled. "You'd be wise to do the same." Between us that day, we caught three people trying to steal across without paying. From one I extracted a serviceable tent, after escorting him to campsite to retrieve the toll. Mr. Cooper agreed to let me have the tent in exchange for my day's wages—a true bargain, he told me, as I was well aware.

That night I pitched my tent near the river, almost underneath the south end of the bridge. In secret, I began to chop gingerly at the rocky, sandy soil of the river's edge. For weeks, I worked only after I was certain that Kyle and Cooper were asleep.

Almost immediately I began to find small particles of gold, which I sewed into the seams of my tent. By day, I worked with either Kyle or Cooper, ensuring that every person paid their toll, and squeezing triple tolls from those reckless enough to try to sneak by our vigilant gaze.

One morning, several hours before dawn, I was wakened by the sound of hoofbeats on the bridge above. I scrambled up the bank and stood at the mouth of the bridge, blocking the horse and its three riders.

"Is that you, Cooper?" The man squinted through the darkness at me.

"No," I said gruffly. "But the toll's a dollar just the same."

"My baby's sick," came a woman's voice from behind the man. "She's got a fever and I've got to get her to Yuba City."

"Toll's a dollar." I was stubborn. The baby set up a thin wailing cry.

"Please, please let us by," the man begged. "I can bring you a dollar in the morning."

I was obstinate. I turned them away. I suppose they tended the brat themselves or forded the river three miles down, although it was a dangerous crossing. No one deserved mercy from me, least of all a man wealthy enough to own a horse.

Kyle and Cooper were scouring the area for other likely bridge locations, and one or the other was absent almost every day. It took two men to guard the bridge, and I had apparently proven my loyalty. Soon my wages were increased to 75 cents a day, and I had collected all the gear I needed from desperate travelers at greatly reduced prices.

I felt not a single twinge of compassion. These travelers were no more deserving of pity than myself, and I had certainly not received any kindhearted treatment from tollkeepers or merchants, fellow travelers or miners since I had left my home months ago.

Every night I covertly scratched in the dirt at the river's edge. The piles of dirt in my tent were so high there was barely enough room to turn around, much less stretch out and sleep. But I barely slept, so feverish was my desire to wring wealth from the unwelcoming California soil. At last I felt like I had removed every possible scrap of gold without calling attention to my labors. I spread the dirt back around, packed it down tightly over the course of a week, and moved my tent downstream a few yards.

"Movin', Teacher?"

The nickname they had attached to me rankled somewhat in view of their illiterate scorn for learning, but I accepted it. I had no choice, really.

"I thought the mosquitoes might be better if I moved."

"As long as you can still hear footsteps on the bridge at night, you can pitch that tent anywhere you like." Kyle grinned at me, exposing his mouth full of rotten, stinking stumps, and I forced a smile in return.

One day, a family approached the north end of the bridge while Cooper was eating his lunch or, more likely, toting up the week's earnings. Their oxen were bone-thin, the wagon nearly empty except for a half-empty barrel of flour, and the children's faces were pinched and wretched. The man wouldn't speak, and his wife approached me about the toll.

"We've only just made it here," she began in a low voice. "We were snowed in for a week in the mountains, and the tollkeeper at the Feather River Bridge took our last dollar. I've got two picks left, and a miner's pan, and some flour. You can have it all, if you'll just let us through."

"Now what'll you do over there with no pick?" I pretended kindness as I walked her to the river's bank and gestured toward the fields. "You think one of those miner's gonna lend you a pick?"

The last glimmer of hope in her eyes died.

It was Saturday. Near sundown. All the woman had to do was make camp for the night and tomorrow morning we'd have to pass her through, free. It was a law Cooper and Kyle didn't dare break, for their bridge charter would be revoked immediately as penalty. New-comers to the state were seldom aware of the law.

"Nice ring," I commented. She was twisting a ring savagely around and around on her finger. It was quite loose. Her fingers were long and elegant, and I could see that she had once been an attractive woman. Of course, out here, any woman was attractive. I had not seen a woman since that early morning rider a month or more ago.

"Here," she said bitterly, thrusting the ring in my hand. "Take it. I hope you rot in hell."

The next day I noticed my tent was sagging in the center. I took some extra poles and shored it up. I had sewn so much gold into the seams the weight was pulling it down. I decided to begin hiding my gold in the seams of my clothes.

I was working that night, systematically digging up the dirt and sand that made up the floor of my tent and taking it to the river to wash away the silt, when I heard a floorboard on the bridge above me creak. Living under the bridge and working on it day after day, I had come to know all the different kinds of noises it would make. This was definitely the sound of someone, probably small, trying to creep across unnoticed. I set my pan under my cot and stole up the bank to the opening of the bridge.

There was a full moon that had helped me as I worked, but its light now threatened to expose me to the prowler on the bridge. I slipped through the shadows as best I could and hugged the walls as I followed the intruder. Two-thirds of the way across he froze, sensing a presence near him. I threw my arms around his neck and pinned him roughly to the ground.

He was thirteen at most. He lay there and tried not to cry as I glowered at him. "Where do you think you're going, you rogue?"

"I was just headed back to camp, sir."

"Toll's twenty-five cents." I held out my hand, knowing full well he didn't have a penny.

"I don't have it, sir." A tear slipped down his face, and he lay there, immobile, too frightened to wipe it away.

"Get off the bridge, then." I kicked him and then waited till he struggled to his feet and trotted back out the south end of the bridge.

I went back to my tent and retrieved my pan from under my cot. I was quietly washing a pan full of silt and pebbles when I noticed movement on the river. It was that damn boy, attempting to get across. He'd dragged a log to the water's edge, found a tent pole, and was trying to perch on the log and pole his way across the current. I watched him, curious. He would move forward a few feet, then the current would catch him and pull him sideways, downstream. Sometimes the current would turn the log completely around, and he would get a dunking.

The whole scene was washed with a silvery, mystic light, and the boy never made a sound. Only the endless rushing clamor of the water accompanied his struggle. At last, when he had about 30 feet left to go, the log rolled over and the boy didn't come back up. I studied the surface of the water for a long minute, waiting to see his head break through, but it never appeared.

A big hand clapped on my shoulder. I jumped, and nearly screamed. It was Mr. Cooper. "Any luck tonight, Teacher?"

"I, I don't know what you mean," I stammered.

He sighed. "You're not as smart as I thought. I told you, never trust anybody. But you thought I trusted you."

A second figure appeared on the river's edge, it was Mr. Kyle. "What have you got? About $2,000 in dust? Your tent nearly collapsed with the weight."

"You think we're stupid?" sneered Mr. Cooper. "We thought we'd see how much you could dig up before we stopped you. Tomorrow, you'll go to jail. It's illegal to jump somebody's claim, you know."

"They hanged that miner down on the American River, didn't they, Jim?" Mr. Kyle was idly fingering the collar of his shirt.

"You can have it all," I stuttered. "I meant to give you your share, really, I was going to."

"I'll tell you what, Teacher," Mr. Cooper said softly. "You just take it all out of your little hiding place and bring it up to the tollhouse. We'll talk about it then."

They both turned and walked back up to the tollhouse in silence.

I ripped out all the seams as quickly as I could. In my pack (I got it with a cup and plate for a quarter), I put the gold and about a dozen smooth river stones. I grabbed my pick and slipped up to the bridge.

I hid in the rafters on the south end of the bridge and threw the rocks with great force onto the wooden planking. As I expected, Cooper came running to the bridge with his gun, shouting over his shoulder.

"I'll shoot the little bastard, Joseph, with great pleasure!" He stopped at the opening of the bridge, expecting to see me silhouetted against the moonlight pouring in the other side.

With a banshee scream, I jumped from the rafters down onto his neck. When he lay still and quiet, I headed inside for Joseph Kyle.

The sun came in a pleasant little pattern on my face, through the stitches I had hastily sewn last night to repair my tattered tent. I lay on my cot, contemplating the soothing sounds of a Sunday morning. It must have been nine o'clock before the first miner crossed the bridge.

"Oh, my God! Murder! Help!" He ran back toward the camp, and I waited until several witnesses returned with him before emerging from my tent, stretching and yawning.

"What's happened?" I asked.

James Cooper lay face down in a pool of blood. His body was mangled, face and torso cruelly torn with vicious stabbing blows from a pick. His sightless eyes glared up at the rafters when the miners rolled him over.

"He was a ruthless bastard, but he didn't deserve this," one miner commented. "Didja hear anything last night, Teacher?"

I shook my head. "I'm afraid I drank too much last night," I said. "I passed out around ten."

When the lawmen came, they found Joseph Kyle in front of the open, empty safe in the tollhouse. They questioned me at great length until I remembered some of the events of the previous night.

"I was really drunk," I broke down and began to sob, the strain telling on me. "I heard two horses crossing, going north. If I'd only gone up to see, I might've. . ."

A lawman patted me roughly on the shoulder. "The thieves would've probably murdered you, too," he said. His foot struck a bottle that had rolled under my cot. "What's this?"

"Brandy," I said with a rueful little smile. "I drank it all."

They let me stay on at the bridge. I moved into the tollhouse. But livestock were spooked by the bloodstains on the floorboards at the mouth of the bridge, no matter how many times I scoured them clean. Some horses would only pass through the bridge if they were led blindfolded around the irregular splotch that marked the end of James Cooper.

Soon, to keep from losing all my trade, I was out there scrubbing every day. I even tore the boards up and replaced them, but the stains came back. No matter how I washed and rubbed, the blackish-red blot reappeared, about two feet across, with trails and spatters in every direction. I put a box outside, for people to drop the toll in, so I wouldn't be distracted from my chore. It didn't matter how many times I cleaned the floorboards, the stains returned.

The wind began to moan around the bridge all the time, too, and the hushing of the water's current sounded like the laughter of a young boy. I finally left Yuba River Bridge and wandered south.

I had plenty of money. But one day when my landlady put on the face of the woman whose wedding ring I took in lieu of the toll, I began to scream. I left San Francisco after that and wandered east. I bought a peddler's pack, because peddlers are supposed to wander, but I'm not a very successful peddler because I do not chat for long before the customer begins to look like my wife. Or a 13-year-old boy in the moonlight. Or a desperate woman clutching a baby.

Today I am in Kentucky. It is warm here, but a different kind of warmth than California. On the road out of town there is a bridge with wooden shingles on top, just like a bridge I used to know. I plan to climb on the bridge.

My seams are heavy with gold. If I change my mind once I am in the water, my treasure shall carry me down. It is the best use of that treacherous metal I can devise. How far down it shall carry me, I cannot say. How far down I deserve to go, I do not know. I can only hope that somewhere I will find the mercy I lost so long ago.

Yuba River Covered Bridge fell long ago, but there are still many interesting covered bridges in northern California. You can find directions to them in the International Guide to Covered Bridges, *a publication of the National Society for the Preservation of Covered Bridges.*

Business is Good

The rain struck the bottom of the pail with a rhythmic ping, ping, ping. Across the dark room, an iron kettle was full, each fat drop threatening to send a cascade of water flowing over the edge. Another bucket and a battered saucepan had also been pressed into service.

Three tousled heads—one fair, two dark—were just visible, nearly hidden by a thick layer of quilts piled high on a bedstead set askew in the center of the room to avoid the rapidly falling drops of rain. A pallet near the foot of the bed held two more figures, mouths open, long limbs tangled in sleep.

A small woman stepped over and between the sleeping children. Her hair was pulling loose from a hastily-pinned knot. Bone-weary, she hauled the brimming containers one by one to the window, tugged open the reluctant sash, poured out the rainwater, and repositioned the container.

The drumming of the rain on the roof and the soft musical counterpoint provided by the raindrops in their receptacles made a soothing sound as she settled into her chair by the fire in the next room. Pulling the mending basket close to her feet, she drew out a shirt that needed patching on the elbow—it was Benjamin's. As if to compensate for being the youngest, he always had to climb higher in the tree, jump farther out into the brook, or run the fastest down the road to meet his father. His clothes showed it.

Above the noise of the deluge she heard the steady thrumming of hooves on the road. No doubt to escape the downpour, although, she thought with a small smile, it could be he was riding hard to catch up with that good fortune that always seemed to elude him.

Seth Allen burst into the door, spreading a hail of drops as he opened his arms wide to encompass his little house and not-so-little family.

"Mary," he boomed, "All my hard work has now come to fruition. I have been awarded the contract to maintain every bridge in the county."

"Sshhh," she said, nodding her head toward the next room. "They've only just gone to sleep."

"I will begin tomorrow by mending the roof of Scott Bridge west of town," he continued in a slightly lower voice.

Mary burst out with a long and delighted peal of laughter. The cat that had been dozing peacefully on the hearth woke, stretched, and stalked out of the room in high dudgeon. Seth only stared at his wife, bewildered.

"Well," he conceded, "It isn't really a contract for all the bridges. It could be, though, in time!"

Mary, shaking her head, laid the shirt back in the basket and stood. Taking her husband by the arm, she led him to the door of the little room where the children slept.

"What do you hear, Seth Allen?"

"They haven't got the croup again, have they?" he whispered anxiously.

"No. Try again."

He tilted his head, straining to hear something unusual in the darkened room. Finally he shook his head, admitting defeat.

"The rain, husband, the rain," she hissed. "This roof's needed mending for six months now, and you've not found the time!" The drops clattered and spit as they landed in their various receptacles. Her voice climbed in intensity. The oldest child, asleep on the pallet, stirred uneasily.

He pulled her back from the door and swept her tiny form into his arms. "Now, now, my Mary," he crooned. "I've always taken care of you before, haven't I?"

Stiff in his embrace, her humor turned sour with the memory of broken promises. "The fence for the chicken run," she began to list. "The extra room for the older boys. The floorboards on the porch. The door to the barn. And now the roof. All promised. And nothing, nothing finished!"

She stepped hard on the side of his foot. Wincing, he released her arm and sat in his chair to rub his foot thoughtfully. "You have a point, Mary," he acknowledged at last. "And you have my solemn pledge that I will be up on the roof at first light, making those repairs."

Only slightly mollified, she reached back into the basket for the shirt. "Mrs. Harrison sent her son over today." She squinted as she tried to thread the needle by the wavering light of the fire. "He said his pa wanted that barn painted by Friday or there wouldn't be another penny in it for you."

Seth threw up his hands. "For what that skinflint is paying me, they should be a little less particular about when I can get to it."

"I could use a penny or two, Seth," Mary said gently. She held the shirt up. "More patches than shirt. And we're down to the bottom of the barrel on the cornmeal."

"It won't take me but a few hours to finish that barn. I'll take Jacob and Joshua with me."

"I hope the rain stops."

"Mary, Mary, Mary," her husband sang as he swooped across the room. "You would make the sun shine his very self, you would, with that bright smile."

She shook her head, but a smile was growing on her lips. She did not protest this time as he drew her into his arms, crushing the half-mended shirt between them.

"Ouch," he exclaimed, jumping back. The needle, neatly threaded, had pierced his forearm. Mary stood on her tiptoes to give him a peck on the cheek before sitting down again to resume her mending.

"There's some supper on the back of the stove," she said.

"Oh, I ate at the tavern." He slumped back into his chair. "I should finish the barn about noon, and then I'll get started on the roof." His voice softened. "I know I've made you many promises before, Mary, but this one I'll keep. I swear it."

"I believe you will, Seth. I know you intend to." She bent over her task again, firmly stitching the patch in place. Finished, she folded the shirt neatly and tucked the needle into the side of the basket so it wouldn't get lost.

"You'd best get on to bed, so you can get up early in the morning."

The two made an incongruous picture, one tall and the other one short, as they walked to the little room tacked on behind the fireplace. But the tenderness was unmistakable as Mary slipped her hand in the crook of her husband's elbow on the way.

"Mamaaaa!" Next morning a little girl flew into the shelter of her mother's skirts just as two of her brothers reached out to grab the white-blond braids that trailed down her back. They skipped up and over the bench by the table, tumbling it to the floor.

Mary slapped at the arms and legs within reach. "Stop that," she said crossly. "Stop tormenting your sister and sit down and do your lessons!"

The older boy, Joseph, obediently turned the bench right side up and sat down. Benjamin sidled up to his mother.

"When we're done can we go help Pa, please, Mama?" He mustered up all the charm in his five-year-old body.

"I reckon," she relented, smoothing his thick, dark hair. "If he goes to work at all today, which I don't know." The rain still came down, the drops singing in the next room as they danced into the buckets and pans.

"I feel sunshine coming," declared Seth from his post in the chair by the fire. "When I went to go check on Josh and Jacob, I think I saw a patch of clear sky over to the west."

"I want to help Josh and Jacob, Pa!" Joseph jumped up, overturning the bench again.

"Only have two axes, son, and besides, making shingles is a man's job," Seth said. Mary added a little more water to the corn mush and decided not to comment.

"At least it's not cold," she sighed as she cleared the table for their meager dinner. "Can't patch an icy roof."

"Ah, Mary, what'd I tell you?" Seth crowed as his oldest sons came in from their work in the barn. A golden rectangle of sun spilled into the room from the open door. The storm had finally passed.

Mary had just seen her husband and four sons off down the hill when a rider approached their house, coming from town.

"Good afternoon, Miz Allen," he said as he dismounted. "Mr. Allen here?"

"No, you just missed him, Mr. Watson." She shooed the chickens back toward the barn. "Care to leave a message?"

"Well, I think it's time we added that room," he said. "Seth told me last summer he could put a room on behind the kitchen."

"I'm sure he'll do a fine job, Mr. Watson, and I'll have him come right over," Mary said. "He's got a barn to finish painting and a couple roofs to mend, but maybe he'll get you fixed up before snow comes."

"Tell him to come as soon as he can," Mr. Watson said as he remounted the horse.

"Tell Mrs. Watson I said hello," called Mary. The man waved and trotted down the hill.

It was well past dark when Seth and the four boys returned, paint-smeared and hungry.

"Remind me, Mary," Seth said wearily as he sat down to warmed-over corn mush and milk, "not to ever offer to paint a barn again. It's too much work and not enough money."

"Mr. Watson came by," Mary said, spooning out supper. "He wants you to get started on that spare room you talked with him about last summer."

Seth bowed his head and the rest of the family followed. "For this food and for thy many blessings, we are most grateful, Almighty Father. Amen."

He put a spoonful of food in his mouth and swallowed before he continued.

"I saw Mr. Lamson today on the way to the Harrison's. You know, he built the West Dummerston Bridge? He wants some help repairing some other bridges, and he says he needs somebody with experience like me."

"That's welcome news, Seth." Mary watched as Josh and Jacob finished their portions in four or five bites. They knew better than to ask for more. She pushed back her chair to go to the stove. All eyes watched as she bent to pull a pan from the oven.

"Baked apples for dessert. We didn't have any sugar left, but I put plenty of honey in." She placed one small, wizened apple on each plate, smiling at their surprise.

"Mary, you're a wonder." Seth set his fork down for just a moment and smiled back at his wife. "Can you and Anna spare the time to go to the store tomorrow? Mr. Harrison paid me today."

"I think we can manage."

"Can I come, Ma?" Benjamin decided to take advantage of his status as the youngest child.

"If your Pa can spare you."

Seth winked at Mary.

"Let's clear up, now. It's getting late." While Mary and Anna started on the dishes, Seth and the two older boys stepped outside. In just a few minutes, an enormous clattering noise filtered down into the main room of the house.

"What on earth?" Mary, drying her hands hastily on her apron, ran outside to peer up at the roof of the house. Silhouetted clearly against the starry night sky was her oldest son.

"Joshua Allen, what on earth are you doing up there?"

"We're mending the roof, Mary Allen." The voice of her unseen husband floated over the peak of the roof.

"That is the most ridiculous thing I have ever heard!" With her hands on her hips, she looked no more intimidating than her daughter Anna. But her husband knew better. With a few short words, he directed Joshua and Jacob down the ladder and back into the house.

"I promised you I'd start mending the roof today, Mary." He took her hands up in his own and squeezed them gently. "I wanted to keep my promise."

He looked so woebegone Mary had to laugh. "You are a big silly goose sometimes, Seth Allen."

"The moon will be rising soon, won't it?"

"I don't know. You should check the *Farmer's Almanac*." She caught herself. "No, don't check it because the children won't get to sleep with you up there pounding and walking around."

"You're right, Mary. But I will get that roof mended. You wait and see."

"I know you will, Seth Allen. You're a man of your word—most of the time."

As Mary bustled about getting one child's face washed, settling squabbles here and there, telling stories and tucking in, Seth wandered restlessly through the rooms. At last, when Mary sat down in her chair by the fire and pulled the mending basket close, Seth snatched his hat off the hook by the door.

"I'm going to the tavern, love," he announced.

Mary looked up in surprise, but only told him goodbye as he pulled the door shut behind him.

He came in so late she barely stirred as he threw his arms around her. He struggled out of bed at cockcrow the next morning, joining her and the children for a small breakfast of bread and honey. He and the older boys climbed cheerfully to the roof to begin the mending job in earnest.

Joseph, Benjamin, and Anna set to work on their lessons, their recitations and songs punctuated by the irregular tapping and pounding of three hammers. Seth often bellowed a verse or two of song as he worked, until Mary stuck her head out the door and called up to him.

"Seth, your music makes my heart glad, but we can't hear our lessons when you sing so loudly."

"Yes, Mary Sunshine," he called back down. "I'll hold my tunes until you go to the store this afternoon."

The sky was the shade of blue common to autumn, achingly pure, and there was a crisp breeze that hinted at the weather to come. Mary checked the garden as she and her two youngest headed to town.

"The pumpkins will soon be ripe," she commented. "Anna, tie your bonnet on."

They walked down the hill, Mary allowing Anna to skip and run with Benjamin until they reached the bridge on the edge of town.

"Anna, walk with me," she commanded. "You're almost a young lady now."

"I'd rather not be," the little girl grumbled under her breath, so her mother couldn't distinguish the words.

"Benjamin!" Mary called through the bridge opening. "Don't go down to the river, now!"

They were halfway through the bridge when a buggy clattered through. "Hello, Mrs. Chamberlain," Mary said politely after she had discerned the familiar face in the gloom.

"Mary and Anna Allen!" exclaimed the buggy's sole occupant. "How are you?"

"Very well, thank you. We're on our way to the . . . "

Her sentence was interrupted by a wild banshee shriek as a small figure leaped through the air and landed with a thump on the wooden floor.

Mrs. Chamberlain's horse screamed in fright, followed at once by cries from the two ladies and the little girl. With some difficulty, the woman managed to restrain the terrified horse, whose hooves danced and clattered loudly in the dim space.

"I'm sorry, Mama." The figure picked itself up, dusted off and proceeded to place a small hand in Mary's. "I was climbing, and I fell."

"Mercy, you gave me such a scare I thought I would just die right here on the spot!" Mrs. Chamberlain held a hand to her chest, breathing rapidly. Mary glared at her son, too angry to find words.

"I'm sorry, Mama," the boy repeated.

"Don't you ever do that again, you hear me, Benjamin Allen?" She shook him by the shoulders.

"Yes, Mama."

"Well, I'll tell you why that gave me such a terrible fright." Mrs. Chamberlain adjusted her hat. "Our hired man, Henry? He was bringing in the cows last night and he looked down the hill and saw a light, moving around the bridge!"

"Must've been someone coming home late. Sometimes Seth carries a lantern if he's out late, especially if the boys are with him."

Mrs. Chamberlain shook her head. "No, the light didn't pass through the bridge and up the road. It hovered all around the bridge, he said."

"Isn't that odd?" Mary was distracted by a movement she caught out of the corner of her eye.

"Then he came down here and looked all around!" She paused and waited for Mary to respond. Mary was straining to see deep in the shadows of the bridge. She thought she had glimpsed a flash of white. "Uh-huh," she said vaguely.

"There was no one here!" Mrs. Chamberlain said triumphantly.

"Oh, my!"

Mary had made out the mystifying shape at the far end of the bridge. It was Anna, and the flash of her white petticoats as she clambered up the latticework of the bridge, trying valiantly to reach the rafters.

Pleased with the astonished reaction of her audience, Mrs. Chamberlain nodded in satisfaction. "I'll be going then. Give Mr. Allen my regards."

Mary recovered enough to answer. "Oh, yes, and you do the same. I'm awfully sorry about Benjamin falling out from the rafters!"

The woman raised her hand in response as she urged the horse forward and off the bridge.

"Anna Allen, you get down from there! Right now!" Mary advanced across the bridge to gather her children and continue their trip to the store.

That night after supper, Seth left the house. It wasn't Mary's place to protest or even comment, but she did feel a twinge of resentment as she began to let out the hem to Anna's dress again. In a month, at least, she'd need a strip of cloth to sew across the bottom to hide Anna's growing legs. Instead of spending money at the tavern, Seth should be spending money for clothes for his children, she thought irritably.

Again, Seth arrived home so late that she barely woke up. They all awoke at the usual time, and Seth and the big boys climbed up to the roof. Mary heard pounding and stomping and shouted commands, but Seth wasn't singing today. Clouds were gathering to the west as she and Anna and Benjamin picked butter beans in the garden. Dinner at noon was a bountiful meal compared to the meals of the past weeks: cornbread, butter beans, and boiled potatoes.

"We'll be finished with the roof in another hour or two," Seth said after accepting a second helping of butter beans. "Then I thought I'd go over to see Mr. Watson."

"When will you start on the roof of the bridge?"

"Oh, I'll get to it, never fear." He smiled broadly at her.

"Will the boys work on the shingles for it this afternoon?"

"That would be a fine idea."

"I know how particular the county is about getting jobs done quickly."

"Yes, yes, Mary, no need to worry." He was getting a bit testy now.

"We're fortunate you have so much work to do. When will you start on the other bridge repairs?"

"I told, you, Mary, I can mind my own affairs!"

Mary averted her eyes. "Yes, Seth."

Mary was relieved to hear him whistling in a pleasant mood as he came up the hill that evening, returning from the Watsons' house. She hoped he would stay home after supper, but he grabbed his hat again and slipped out the door, kissing her and telling her he might be late again.

"Be careful," she called, but he had already closed the door.

The next afternoon she and Anna had just finished the washing when her neighbor came to call.

"Good afternoon, Mary, Anna. I had some fresh pumpkin and I thought you might like to make a pie tomorrow." Elizabeth Saulter's children were grown, and she often looked for company at the Allen house. Anna, relieved by her mother's preoccupation with the visitor, slipped off to the barn with Benjamin.

"That's most kind of you, Elizabeth. Our pumpkins aren't quite ripe yet, but when they are, I'll bring you some."

The older woman waved the offer aside. "We have more than we need, Mary, and goodness knows you have plenty of mouths to feed."

They sat on the porch in companionable silence for a while before Elizabeth spoke. "Didn't you tell me Mr. Allen was working on the bridge?"

Mary sighed. "Yes, well, he's going to start on it soon, I hope."

"There've been some strange goings-on over there lately, I hear."

"Mrs. Chamberlain told me all about it." Mary smiled. "Their hired man saw some lights or something. Did I tell you what Benjamin did?"

"No."

Mary related the incident, and Elizabeth shook her head with a rueful laugh. "Henry's not the only one to have something strange happen at the bridge." Elizabeth leaned conspiratorially toward her friend. "Leslie Lowe swears he heard the devil on the bridge last night."

"Oh?"

"He was riding along through the bridge, oh, it must've been about ten last night. It was just as quiet as it could be, when all of a sudden, he heard such a banging and a clattering that his old horse, Jerry, took off running as fast as he could. It was all Mr. Lowe could do to hang on!"

Elizabeth nodded at her friend, her eyes wide.

"Mr. Lowe says it was the devil, knocking on the roof of the bridge or maybe a witch, since there was a full moon last night."

Mary closed her eyes for just a moment, thinking. She opened them and asked, "Did you say Scott Bridge?"

Elizabeth nodded again.

Mary's laughter rang out across the yard, bringing the children running. When she caught her breath, she spoke.

"Elizabeth, that wasn't the devil! That was plain old Seth Allen, trying his best to keep his word!"

Scott Bridge is in Windham County in southern Vermont. To visit it, take Vermont 30 north out of Townshend. About 4.5 miles after the junction with Vermont 100, take a right onto Back Side Road. The bridge is closed to traffic.

Windham County has many delightful covered bridges, all of them well worth visiting. For information, check the World Guide to Covered Bridges, *published by the National Society for the Preservation of Covered Bridges, or contact the Windham County Chamber of Commerce.*

THE RIVER SPEAKS

anuary 14, 1863

My Christmas package arrived, mostly intact and containing this diary. God's grace alone must have guided the package, for Julia, not knowing where I was, simply addressed it to me by name and regiment number. She is well and the farm all right in spite of the lack of help.

I have not told her much about my injuries. I can hardly bear to think of them myself. But when I remember Sharpsburg, I guess I should be grateful to have escaped with my life. I still dream of it.

My comrades that had been laughing and sharing cornbread with me that morning, I left lying two and three deep in the road, mutilated and torn almost beyond recognition. Some of the wounds were so large I could have passed my fist through them and touched the soldier beneath.

My caretakers here say that I am fortunate to have survived the first few weeks after my surgery. Many, many men died as a result of fevers or complications to their wounds. I do not feel lucky. I feel most times abandoned by God. I have been to Hell.

January 18

The man who buries the dead here must be simpleminded. He wanders through the rows of beds calling "Anybody dead here? Anybody dying?" I have talked to him once or twice. He asked if I were well enough to help him with the burials and I asked him if he really thought I could manage a shovel.

I received another letter from Julia today. She hears of movement in Tennessee by the Yankees and is concerned. I wrote back and told her to hide the seed corn and set the pigs loose to forage in the woods. She'll be fine as long as she doesn't make anybody mad, Confederate or Yankee.

After a week of smelling worse and worse, the man on the bed next to me has finally died. I suppose his wound became infected. Many nights I lay awake worrying that it was my body rotting away. The orderly assured me it was not so, but only until I began to use the crutches and hobble outside, away from the other patients, would I believe him. I am mastering the use of the crutches.

The weather is oddly springlike. I am nearly 500 miles north and east of home, so it should be colder here. I am glad of the warmth, though, because our makeshift hospital, formerly a barn, has gaps of three inches or more between the strips of siding. I feel sorry for the poor animals who will call this structure home in colder weather.

January 23

They have told me I must go home. My regiment has been dissolved. Most of us died at Sharpsburg and I would be better off if I had, too. I told them I did not want to return home. They said they had no further use for me. I approached an officer who had come to check on some of his men and begged him to let me serve the Confederacy again. After some delay, he agreed. I am to go to Jackson, Mississippi, with a small company in the morning.

The weather has turned cold and wet. The rain runs in little rivulets between the cots so that everything is wet and muddy. There is still a shortage of chamber pots. I will be glad to be quit of this stinking hellhole. I saw a surgeon today for the first time since I was brought here. He was enjoying a smoke on the porch of the farmhouse. I began to approach him but the tips of my crutches sank so deeply in the mud I abandoned the idea. Instead, I spit as loudly and voluminously as I could in his direction.

January 30

I marched as best I could before developing festering sores under my arms from the damned crutches. My new company commander, Cap. N—, had me tossed on top of the supply wagon and so I made my way here to Jackson, Mississippi. I am not the only cripple in the company. In fact, between us all (there are 40), we probably total about 20 whole men.

It is downright cold in Jackson and the rain blows today in almost horizontal sheets. I am not sorry to be here. We passed within 50 miles of my home on our march here, but I did not request leave to see Julia. I doubt she would want to see me in the state I am in now.

We are housed in tents on the banks of a river. The Pearl River, they call it. There is a ruined bridge upstream of our camp a few hundred yards. The people of Jackson are very anxious about Grant's armies. I suppose our presence, piecemeal as we are, is small comfort.

I have been sick for four days with diarrhea. I believe the saltback we were issued in Richmond was wormy, but the company cook insists on putting it in the beans anyway. We are all sick to one degree or another. The Cap.'s servant who used to cook ran away on January 2nd after telling the Cap. that Mr. Lincoln had made him free.

January 31

Our Cap. is either very intelligent or crazy. He has ordered us to secure the bridge and turn it into a prison for Yankee officers. The approach on the south bank had completely fallen away, so we took some miscellaneous boards and covered over the end of the bridge. After boarding up the north end, except for a narrow opening, the prison was ready for its inmates. We will have a patrol on each bank and one on the river itself in case one of the officers is desperate or foolish enough to try the river as an escape route.

Since I have had a great deal of experience in small boats, having been raised on a river, I am eager to take on the river patrol. It will be easy for me to row and watch since I will not have to stand up for a long time. Tomorrow the prisoners arrive from Vicksburg. The news from Vicksburg is all bad. The siege is taking a terrible toll. I have heard the civilians there are forced to turn to their horses and even to their dogs for food.

The rain stopped but mud is everywhere. We have taken a few leftover boards to make wooden floors for our tents, so they are more habitable than many other quarters I have found in the past two years. The bridge is quite dilapidated. Working on it today I could swear it was swaying on its foundations. There are large gaps between the boards on the side, wider than those at the hospital barn in Richmond. But at least the prisoners will have a roof overhead.

February 1

Twenty captured Yankee officers marched in today. They looked thin but not any worse off than any of the rest of us, I reckon. One man, near the end of the line with his arm in a sling, looked so much like my cousin Sam Watterson that I went up to him to see his face closer.

"Sam?" I asked. He turned to look at me. I still couldn't tell if he was my cousin. It's been at least fifteen years since I saw him.

"You related to the Wattersons of Tennessee?"

He shook his head and I could tell his arm or shoulder was paining him pretty bad.

"Where are you from?" I was walking alongside them as they filed into the bridge.

"Illinois," he croaked. "Can I have a drink of water?"

Without thinking, I handed over my canteen. He looked at it blankly then spoke again.

"I can't use my hand to unscrew it." I helped him take a drink, then it was his turn to enter the dark bridge.

My comrades gave me a hard time about giving that old Yankee boy a drink. When I told them he looked like my cousin, though, they let up some.

I spent the rest of my shift in a boat on the river. I could hear the floor of that old bridge creak and crack with their weight, but I figured it was strong enough to hold them. Pretty soon one of them called out.

"We want food! We ain't et since we left Vicksburg on Sunday!" They'd been on the road a few days, but it wasn't my job to see that they got fed. I guess that's the sergeant's job. They were still fussing and hollering when I went off to my tent. That idiot Fritch is still cooking for us and he forgot to soak the hardtack this morning. But I guess a plate of beans is better than nothing at all.

The rain is colder now, but the local folks say it rarely snows around here. That's good, because I lost my blanket back at Sharpsburg and I don't think I'll be seeing another one for a while. I have a cough, but it's not too bad. The diarrhea is still awful and I hope Fritch will stop putting that rancid fatback in the beans. I talked to an old man who lives nearby who says his old lady's got a cure for the runs. I hope it works. I promised him a dollar if he'd bring it back to me tomorrow.

February 3

I spent all day yesterday with such terrible cramps I thought I'd die. I couldn't even make it to the latrine so I spent all day lying in piles of my own shit. One good thing about the rain is that I can just hang my drawers from the tent pole outside and they get washed. Sort of. The old man came back right before dark and I brewed the bark to make a tea. It tasted nasty, but it must have worked. I feel all right today, just weak.

February 4

Got a letter from Julia today. Damn those Yankees. They came and made off with both cows and the mule. She had hid the seed corn, so at least she'll be able to start a crop this spring. And the pigs have been out in the woods foraging for a month now, so they are all right as long as nobody else found them. Julia's all right, too. Thank God. But she's mad enough that I sure wouldn't cross her.

Those Yankees on the bridge were still hollering for food today. I hollered back that their friends in Alabama were drinking milk from my cows and that would have to satisfy these bastards in Mississippi, too. I could see them sticking their hands out between the boards, I guess trying to catch a little rain. I wonder what the sergeant has done for provisions for them. We ain't eating much either, but at least we've got more than the folks at Vicksburg.

The sergeant told us to expect some more prisoners soon. Maybe even tomorrow. If it gets much colder, those Yankees are going to need some blankets or something. I know the wind's blowing right through the sides of the bridge. It rained today, all day, letting up to a light drizzle this evening.

Some of the other men told me the Captain left today to go to Vicksburg. I guess that leaves our sergeant in command.

February 5

The old man brought some potatoes to sell and some eggs. Me and some of the boys split a dozen eggs—they cost $3 but they were worth every penny. I'll roast me a potato tonight. The sergeant let one of the prisoners out to cook for the rest of them—can't build a fire on the bridge, so me and one other soldier watched while he boiled some beans. Didn't look like much, but he said they would be glad for anything. I helped him carry the pot back to the bridge and saw the Yankee that looked like my cousin Sam lying on the floor.

"You sick?"

He just groaned.

"Got the Mississippi shits," said the man next to him. "He's been sick for a couple days."

I still had some of that bark left in my pocket. I pulled some out and stuffed it into the soldier's hand. I don't know why. I guess I was still thinking about Sam.

"Give 'em these," I said. "Brew them in some water. Don't tell anybody I gave 'em to you."

It was dark on that bridge, since we'd closed up one end and blocked off all but a little of the other end. It smelled bad, too. I guess they'd made a hole in the floor in the corner to use as a latrine. I asked them what they were doing for water and they said they were catching a little rainwater here and there. I don't think I'd even treat a dog like that. But then again, they're Yankees.

Still raining and mighty cold. The fog off the river in the mornings makes it hard to see sometimes, but if anybody jumped off the bridge into the water, I'd hear it. They wouldn't get far.

February 6

I went and talked to the sergeant this morning and told him that I'd help forage provisions for the regiment and the prisoners. He showed me a 50-pound bag of cornmeal just come in and another barrel of salted meat. I agreed that it looked like plenty for a while and he told me to keep up the good work. He's been watching me, he said.

Then I got outside and saw a whole stream of new prisoners come marching in. They were more stumbling than marching. It seemed like there was no end to the line of soldiers and I asked the boys bringing them in how many there was.

"Two hunnerd and fifty," he told me.

Now I am no genius. But I don't know how you fit nearly 300 men in a space that's 18 feet wide and 90 or a 100 feet long. I guess you can; I saw them go in and certainly none of them came out, but I am glad I have my little tent even if it does leak sometimes.

Their cook came out and I had guard detail again while he cooked some corn mush. It started raining so hard it was putting out the cooking fire, so we rigged up a tarp to keep him a little dry. It's a small kettle and he's feeding a lot of people, so he had to be outside a while.

Jimmy, the other guard, went to the latrine and while he was gone I asked about the Yankee that looked like Sam.

"He's feelin' better," their cook allowed. "But we all need more water. And there's more of us sick than him."

"Just about all of us have the shits, too," I told him. "I wish I knew what kind of bark that old man gave me and I could make a fortune out of the Confederate Army." We both had a good laugh and he told me that before he'd gotten captured his regiment had a lot of diarrhea, too. And fevers and coughs and measles and smallpox.

Jimmy came back and we quit chatting so friendly. Before I left, we'd carried that kettle back and forth about five times and the bag of cornmeal was more than half-empty. I can get along good on one crutch now. Jimmy asked me on our way back to the camp if I worried about going in the bridge without my rifle. It never occurred to me that the Yankees would try to hurt me. Now don't that sound stupid?

I wish it was spring; I'd go find some greens to cook. I've got such a craving for them I could spit. It's raining like it'll never quit. I guess that's what winter's like in Mississippi. I would almost wish for snow, if I had some decent shoes, just to be rid of this damned rain.

I hear some fuss going on over at the bridge but I'm dry and I'll wait and see what's going on in the morning. If they need me they can come and get me.

February 7

Well, I couldn't believe it when they told me. The noise last night was some boys bringing in another 130 prisoners. Nobody knows where they come from but my guess is Vicksburg. They are still surrounded and things don't look too good. I suppose they want to be sure the prisoners don't turn on them.

But I don't know how they'll fit all those men in that bridge. I have been all around its foundations patrolling in the water and it is an old bridge. With that many men they won't even be able to lie down. I suppose our sergeant knows what he's doing or maybe even he has orders to do this. But it seems a very hard thing to treat their soldiers like this. I hope they are treating our boys better.

I was under the bridge in the rowboat today and I looked up. I thought I saw the floorboards sagging and I reported it to the sergeant when my watch was up. He said he thought it would be all right.

Their cook was under the tarp we had rigged for him, cooking some beans. I stopped for a smoke and he started coughing very bad. I looked at him and he had bright cheeks, like he'd been out in the wind too long, but he said he had a fever. Some of the new soldiers were pretty sick and nobody could sleep because there wasn't any way to lie down. Some men were sitting and others were taking turns lying down but it was pretty awful in there, he told me. I believe him.

This tent feels like a palace. The mail has not come through for a few days and the men are starting to grumble. It is mail from home that keeps us from going crazy. Or maybe we are crazy. Sometimes I wake up at night and both my legs hurt like hell.

February 9

Those Yankees that got here day before yesterday must have been pretty sick. Five of them died last night and we had some other prisoners drag them out and put them on the riverbank. Sergeant says he'll get up a burial detail tomorrow, but we're shorthanded ourselves today because everyone, including me, has terrific stomach cramps. I tried to tell him the salt pork wasn't fit to eat, but he won't listen. I guess he didn't give the prisoners any or else I'd have heard them moan when I passed under the bridge on my watch. I threw up four times but the river took it all away.

Haskell had the river detail last night and wasn't paying attention. He stopped the rowboat under the bridge to get out of the rain for a smoke, only he was right under their latrine. Ha ha.

The rain has cleared for the first time in a week and if I weren't so weak I'd jump up and say "Hallelujah!"

February 10

I guess the river air is deadly for Yankees. Four more died. The prisoners are shouting for a doctor. I should tell them how much doctoring I got after being wounded. They would shut up right quick. The doctor couldn't do anything for them anyway, because there isn't any medicine left in all of Jackson, the old man told me. The trains aren't getting through.

There wasn't but a few cups of cornmeal left, but their cook made a thin gruel with it anyway. When I helped him carry the pot to the bridge, I was almost afraid to look in. My God, I have fought in some of the bloodiest battles ever, but there is something even worse about treating men like they were lower than an animal. They were moaning and groaning, packed in there so close that when one man turned, his neighbor had to move too or else get stepped on. That started a chain reaction so they were constantly in motion, taking tiny steps first in one direction and then the other.

It was so dark I couldn't see anything but the first few lines of men near the door. But I could hear their feet moving and feel the heat of their bodies. With so many packed in there, they didn't even need any blankets. Except, I guess, the poor bastards next to the walls.

The sun was shining again today but it has turned bitter cold. The old man from town sold me some newspapers to stuff in my shoe, but I would really like to have my blanket back. I suppose some Yankee at Sharpsburg is wrapped up all warm and snug. I am consoled by remembering the lice I surely left in that blanket. I hope those little bastards keep that Yankee up all night, crawling through his hair.

February 13

Every morning they carry out two or three more men. I can't help with the burial detail because I can't manage a shovel. The sergeant doesn't seem to care. The Yankees are just lying there on the riverbank rotting. I guess there are too many of us sick. There seem to be fewer of us, but I haven't been really keeping track. We don't know each other anyway. We formed up as a company less than a month ago and we're from all over, so nobody really cares about anybody else. I wish I'd get a letter from Julia. It's still cold and our ration of beans is gone. The prisoners don't have anything left to eat either. If the old man would come by, I'd buy everything he had to eat. I'd even eat that maggoty old saltback if Fritch put it in front of me.

Jimmy says it's the air from the river killing the Yankees but I don't understand why it don't kill us, too. Sometimes they get to coughing on the bridge and the whole thing seems to shake. It makes my chest hurt to hear that cough. Maybe all the sick ones that came in last have all died by now. There are about 20 bodies waiting to get buried.

February 14

No one died on the bridge last night. I must've been right. The weak ones died and now everything will be all right.

I figured out why it seems like there are fewer of us now. Men have been slipping off, going home I guess to get some food. It's dismal here and I don't think it'll get any better anytime soon. If I thought Julia could stand the sight of me, I'd go back home, too. But I wouldn't be any use to her the way I am. I should write and tell her to forget about me, but I'm a coward.

I went up to the bridge and poked my head in after I did my watch on the river. It's truly awful and I know it's not right. I wish there was someone I could talk to, but the sergeant doesn't care and I guess they'd call it treason for me to complain on account of the prisoners anyway. I don't know why I care. They're only Yankees and they'd kill me if they had the chance. But God knows I'd rather be dead than packed onto that bridge. Sometimes when the wind blows hard I wonder if it will stand up.

I heard from the old man that Vicksburg is still defying Grant. Good for them. It was cold but clear today.

February 15

What would it be like, I wonder, to be standing elbow to elbow with a man and listen to him cough his life out? To feel his last breath hot on your neck, feel his body turn limp and start to slide to the ground, only to get caught by the arms and elbows and knees of people packed in around him?

Three men died in the bridge last night. I guess it's the same fever because their cook told me the men who cough don't die. It's the ones who start heating up from the inside out who eventually die after getting chills and fever and losing their senses. Sometimes I can hear them from my post down in the rowboat, crying out for their mama or their sweetheart. It gives me a chill and then I start worrying that I've got the damn fever.

We got another bag of cornmeal today and I helped the cook carry gruel to the bridge. I told the sergeant I'd give every soldier his ration and then give the leftovers to the prisoners, but I split it up evenly in half. There's only 30 of us left, maybe 25, and nearly 400 of them. Less the ones who've died, of course. It didn't seem right to keep so much for ourselves when at least we can go out and forage. I found a woman today who sold me half a ham and I ate it till I got sick. Then I gave the rest to Jimmy.

Still no mail. If the Union Army wanted to make us give up, they should start by keeping the mail from getting through. I suppose that's exactly what they're doing.

February 16

Jimmy came to my tent last night and told me he was leaving. They tried to discharge him in November after he was injured, but he wouldn't go. He lost his left eye. Now he says he's scared. He's seen the elephant, faced hundreds of men with rifles whose sole aim was to shoot him down, but this fever has got him scared.

I'm scared, too, but I don't know where I'd go if I left. Four more men died on the bridge last night. If they keep dying like this there won't be any left by spring.

Jimmy gave me his blanket. He says he's going south anyway and he'll get all the blankets he needs. His family is in Louisiana and they'll be glad to see him. I wished him luck.

February 18

It started raining again today and I was sliding in the mud down to the rowboat past the row of corpses and one of them moved. I liked to have died right there. But it must have been a rat or something because I looked very closely and they were all dead. There are more than 40 bodies piled up and the sergeant stays in his tent all day. I think he's drunk. If he's got whiskey rations for us, I wish he'd let us have them. I could use it. On the river it gets foggy and I hear the men call and cry out. God, I get so scared. They sound like they're right there in the boat with me. Their feet shifting and turning to accommodate every soldier's move, whispering on the planks of the bridge and it sounds like they're saying my name.

I sound like a lunatic and maybe I am. That body moving nearly did me in. Why won't the sergeant bury them?

February 19

The old man brought a bushel of apples. I almost cried they smelled so good. He wanted $10 for them and I asked some of the boys for some money and the cook from the prisoners gave me $3. I have six shiny apples lined up by the head of my cot and I will have one a day until they are gone.

How would you divide a half-bushel of apples between 350 men? I don't even want to think about the scrambling and pushing that must have occurred when their cook went in with those apples. Or maybe they are all too weak to fight over food now.

I don't know why I stay. If I were not such a coward, I would leave. If those men were let out of the bridge, though, they would head straight north to get their guns and come back here to kill us. Is it worse to take a gun and shoot a man or put him in the dark and starve him to death? Maybe there will be no forgiveness for me no matter what I do.

I saw the Yankee that looks like Sam lying among the dead today. The sergeant is openly drunk when he bothers to appear from his tent, which is infrequent. Rain has come in from the west and so it blows and rains intermittently. No mail.

February 20

Four letters from Julia. Troops from Huntsville are foraging around the farm regularly. There are no men left in the area so she says the women just let the soldiers take what little is left. Julia has been nibbling away at the seed corn, she says, but there is still plenty to plant. She will try to start planting in another six weeks.

She has been writing me regularly, but the mail isn't getting through. I have heard no good news about the war. Four men died on the bridge last night. The fever is taking them quicker now their cook tells me. We have gotten a 50-pound sack of beans but many of the prisoners are too weak to eat.

Julia asks if I will have any leave at springtime to help her with the planting. I must write to her and tell her that I can no longer do the work I once could. I try to imagine what will happen to me once the war is over, but I cannot.

I can't even imagine this war being over. It seems like I have been moving up and down the Pearl River in that little rowboat with my rifle in my lap for all my life. Has it really only been 20 days?

The rain cleared at midday. It seems a little warmer, but I doubt winter is over yet.

February 21

I talked to the cook today while he was fixing their rations. I asked him where he was from and he told me Missouri. I have never talked to somebody from there before.

"Are you a farmer?" I asked him.

"Yes, sir," he said, all proud. "I raise some of the fattest, finest hogs west of the Mississippi!"

I told him I was a farmer, too, or used to be, before the war.

"How many slaves do you have?" he asked me.

When I told him I didn't have any, he didn't believe me at first. I told him me and Julia had about 75 acres near Huntsville, Alabama, on the Flint River and grew cotton before the war, but then switched to corn to help feed the army.

He scratched his head. "If you ain't got any slaves, why are you fightin'?"

Well, I am not sure I really know the answer to that anymore, but I tried to answer him truthfully. "Because I didn't want anyone telling me what to do," I told him. "You Yankees were always poking your noses in my business."

He just shrugged and said that's why he moved out West, but he didn't see it as a reason for killing anybody.

"Why are you in the army, then?"

He shrugged again, then looked up and grinned.

"Bounty was good," he said. "I stayed drunk for four days before they found me and shipped me off."

He seems like a nice enough fellow and Missouri sounds like it has some good farmland.

Clear today and still on the warm side. The sergeant came out of his tent and stood in front of all those bodies. They stink pretty bad and it will get worse if he doesn't get somebody to bury them.

February 22

I was helping the Yankee cook carry those beans to the bridge today when my damn crutch broke—snapped right in two. I spilled the beans and lay there on the ground, helpless as a baby. Couldn't even stand up and the other guards were inside playing cards or something.

That Yankee quickly disappeared and I lay there wondering what it'd be like to get court-martialed. I could see my rifle propped up against the side of the guardhouse.

He came back with a stout stick to use as a crutch. I lay there with my mouth open until he hauled me back up to my leg and stuck that stick under my arm. I didn't ask him why he didn't run away. I think I know why. It's because he's a better man than me.

I asked him if there were any able-bodied men on the bridge who could bury the dead. He said he could find four or five. Three more Yankees died of the fever last night and one of our men has come down with a fever, too. The sergeant packed him off to the hospital but all the rest of the boys are pretty worried.

February 23

The sergeant just looked at me with his beady little mean eyes when I asked him if some of the prisoners could bury the dead. Then he asked if I had abandoned my post to come bother him with my stupid questions.

"We hang traitors!" he hollered after me as I left. I guess he's still got our whiskey ration hiding somewhere. I wish I could get my hands on it.

The cook didn't come out today—there is nothing for him to cook. It hasn't rained in three days and those prisoners don't have any water. I can't carry a barrel, but I ordered one of the younger boys—I think he's from Georgia—to take them a barrel of water from the river.

February 24

I am so hungry I could boil my shoe and eat it. I don't feel like writing much. No rain, but the weather has turned colder.

February 25

A train must have made it through because we now have two barrels of salted meat and four bags of cornmeal. The prisoners sent a different cook out. While I watched him I asked him where was the man from Missouri.

"Sick," he said, all mad and sullen.

"Fever?"

He just nodded. "You might as well kill us all now," he burst out, after we'd carried a couple buckets of gruel to the bridge and passed them in. "We're all gonna die here, so why not just shoot us here?"

A gunshot came from behind me and I turned around. There was that crazy sergeant, drunk as a lord, barely able to stand up. I turned around and that poor boy that had been cooking was laying there bleeding to death.

"Didja see that Yankee bastard tryin' to 'scape?" the sergeant grinned at me and it was horrible.

I hobbled off as quickly as I could. I couldn't say anything to the sergeant or he'd have shot me, too. The boy was right, anyway. I'd rather be shot dead myself than have that fever. Sometimes they foam at the mouth or flail around like they lost their wits. It's awful.

March 22

Well, I might as well have been shot dead. I don't remember having any convulsions or foaming at the mouth, but the old man tells me I was really sick. I don't know why he took me in, but he came to our camp and everybody was gone but me and I was lying on the ground shivering, so he threw me over his shoulder and carried me home.

I've been out of my head for almost a month and now it's nearly planting time. The sergeant meant for me to die; I know he must've, because he took my tent, my cot, and my rifle and left me on the ground. He put some papers in my bag that said I've been discharged from the Confederate Army because I'm crippled.

I'm tired and the old man says I should sleep.

March 24

I sat on the porch today and watched these two plant their garden. They will have watermelons, corn, green beans, beets, and squash. I want to help them but the old man says just to watch for now. I am awful tired. The sun feels good. If I am out on the porch I can hear the river but I can't see it.

March 30

I walked all the way back to the bridge today. Two months ago I could go for miles, but I am still as weak as a kitten. The old man says it was his wife's herbals that saved my life and I guess I am grateful.

There was no one at the bridge. The door was open and the only sign that the prisoners had ever been there was the barrel they had water in. The bodies were gone, too, but I don't think they were buried there. I didn't see any signs of digging.

The river sounds like the voices I heard when I was patrolling. Men crying for their mamas, wanting a little comfort when they're sick. Even if I do go home, I don't think I can stand to hear the river anymore. It used to sound so sweet but now it just sounds like men being killed for no good reason.

April 15

Jackson is full of rumors. The old man gets around and hears them all. People are saying that Grant has given up, Vicksburg has fallen, Grant's gone west, or that Grant's on his way to Jackson. Most folks are scared and some are leaving town. Me and the old man and the old lady are just staying put, though. There's not much that can scare me now.

April 20

I went down to the river today for a wash and heard that Yankee from Missouri talking to me. I swear it. It was foggy and I couldn't see but I swear I heard him ask me how the farming was in Jackson. He didn't sound mad or anything. I turned around and expected to see him walking to me out of the fog but he never came.

Maybe I did imagine it. If I can imagine that my left leg has taken a bullet again, then I guess I can imagine anything.

The old man's crops are doing just fine. I took a hoe to that garden and did just fine. Balancing is tricky, but I can manage.

May 12

There was a great commotion in town as a brigade of men came through. They were fighting the Yankees at Raymond and were outnumbered, so they retreated. Raymond is only 10 miles from town. Grant is said to be headed here and many folks are leaving in a panic.

May 14

Rain coming down in sheets. Jackson fell today to Sherman and Grant.

May 16

As I am obviously no threat to anyone, I can move freely about the area. I went this morning to the bridge to see if there was any activity. I ran into a Union soldier, alone on the banks of the river.

"Howdy," he said, nodding. "You live around here?"

I told him I did. He asked me where I'd been hurt and I told him Sharpsburg.

"Did you know they kept prisoners here?"

I said I did and he told me his brother had died here in February. I said I was sorry and that the fever had killed a lot of good men.

"They had 400 men packed onto that bridge," he said bitterly. "I'd shoot every last son of a bitch that did that to my brother."

I was quiet. What could I say?

"I hope it haunts them till their dying day," he continued. "I hope they never lie down without remembering what they did."

"They probably will." He looked at me hard and then went away. I sat there and listened to the water a little longer. It's funny how you can hear voices if you listen hard enough.

Then I gathered up as many fallen branches as I could find. I stacked them up against the side of the bridge and lit them. I watched that bridge burn and burn and burn until at last it fell into the water and washed away. The river takes away so much. I wish it could take away my guilt.

If you go to Jackson, Mississippi, today, don't bother asking about the old bridge that served as a prison during the Civil War—no one knows where it once stood. If you had been in Jackson a hundred years ago, they might have even denied such a bridge once stood. If you research the infamous prisons of the Civil War, chances are you won't find even a passing mention of the prison-bridge over the Pearl River—no one wants to re-member. But the river speaks.

COLD FEET

June 1898

"Come on, come on, come on!" She was shooing them into the wagon with no more patience than she showed the chickens in the yard at dusk.

"Mary Ellen, hold Patrick. Toby, take this basket. Lizzie Mae, don't you dare get back out."

Balling a handful of her skirts in her fist, she climbed up to the bench in front and spoke to the mule.

"Gee-up, Patsy!" Obediently the mule began to move.

The sun was hovering just above the horizon as they turned out of the Jackson farm road onto White Oak Creek road. The woman urged the mule to its fastest pace—a walking half-trot—until she saw the dark shape of Alvaton Bridge huddling over the creek ahead.

"Momma!"

"What, Lizzie?"

"Where's David?"

"I thought he was under the blanket. Lift it up. Ain't he there?"

"No, he must've stayed behind at the Jackson place."

"Lizzie Mae, I told you to look out for them."

Lizzie, the oldest child, hung her head, feeling vaguely wronged but knowing all the same that she'd failed her Momma.

With a sigh, the woman coaxed the mule into turning around and heading back the way they'd come. Her mouth set into a tight line, she measured with her eyes the distance of the sun from the horizon. Sunset in about 10 minutes.

Anne Jackson was walking down the road, holding David's hand as he struggled not to cry. "Momma!" He ran to the wagon and threw himself into her arms. "I thought you'd forgotten me!"

"I told you to git in the wagon," she scolded him gently. "Thanks, Anne!" She waved to her neighbor and turned the mule around again.

Now the sun had set, and the shadows of the trees on either side of the road were melting into one another, creating a seamless ribbon of blackness that marched without hesitation to the inky rectangle that was the open mouth of Alvaton Bridge. The woman tried to avert her eyes as she steered the mule and her family toward it, but there was a certain macabre fascination intertwined with her fear.

"I want you to sing with me," she commanded as the wagon came within a few hundred feet of the bridge. "Sing!"

She opened her mouth and began to thunder her favorite hymn.

"Just as I am, without one plea . . ."

Her voice wavered just a bit as the mule's shoes made a hollow drumming sound on the wooden planking of the bridge. "And that thou bids't me come to thee, O Lamb of God . . ."

The girls added their thin voices to their mother's strong alto.

"I come, I come."

Without hesitating, the woman swung right into the second verse, singing as if her very life depended upon it. The song rose to the rafters of the bridge, hidden by the darkness. The wood of the old bridge seemed to muffle the sound of the hymn, soaking up the notes greedily instead of echoing them back to the singers' ears.

At last they were through the bridge, and the woman's shoulders slumped in relief. Their farm was just ahead, up a little rise. It took barely 15 minutes for her to get all five children tucked into their blankets.

She held the lamp up high, showering as much light as she could on their still squirming bodies, wrestling to find a comfortable spot on the big bed they all shared.

"Go to sleep, now. I don't want to hear a peep out of you," she admonished them sternly. "Don't fergit your prayers."

She pulled the door nearly to the frame, allowing just a sliver of light to enter the bedroom from the main room of the house where she would sit for an hour or two longer with her sewing or her Bible.

"Lizzie," whispered Toby. "Don't go to sleep yet."

"What?"

"Why is Momma so scared of the bridge, Lizzie?"

"She didn't even git scared when Henderson's old bull got loose and ran right at her," chimed in Mary Ellen. "How come she hates that bridge so?"

"I don't know fer sure," Lizzie Mae said slowly, pulling together the loose strands of a story that were floating about in her mind. "But mebbe, it could be . . . "

She was interrupted by a wide band of light that burst from the doorway. "I told you to go to sleep!" Their momma stood with her hands on her hips in the open doorway. "You want a switchin'?"

"No'm," they murmured. They lay still as death until she turned and left the room, again pulling the door nearly closed.

Lizzie rolled over and put her mouth near her brother's ear. "Lula tol' me once, somebody was hanged to death on that bridge."

She was gratified by the sharp intake of his breath. "Wrapped a rope around his neck and strung 'im up, until his eyes bugged out like this," she made a face, "and his tongue popped out, all purple and swole up!"

Toby shuddered and Lizzie lay back down, satisfied. Mary Ellen poked and prodded at her.

"Tell me," she whined. "I wanna hear it, too,"

"You're too young," Lizzie retorted in a sharp whisper. "It'd give you night mirrors."

"Tell me," Mary Ellen whined again.

"Hush now, or Momma'll come take a switch to all of us," Lizzie answered and turned her back to all of them. She listened to the soft, even rhythm of baby Patrick's breathing until it lulled her to sleep.

December 1915

Gene McClure cursed again and kicked the side of the truck hard enough to make the whole body shudder. A bale of hay tumbled off the precariously balanced stack that reached a good seven feet above the guardrail, and he cursed again.

His wife leaned around to grin at him. "I know that used to make Nellie go," she said, "But I didn't know kickin' and cussin' made Fords go, too."

His only response was another kick, and she turned around again.

"Least it had the courtesy to break down on the bridge," she pointed out, climbing out of the truck. "We're not gonna get rained on while you get it fixed."

"No, but it'll damn sure git stuck in the mud on the way home," he muttered sullenly, pacing up and down beside the truck. "I was a damn fool to ever buy this contraption."

She shrugged her shoulders and climbed back to wait while he figured out a solution. Eventually he threw open the hood of the truck and stood staring morosely down at the engine.

She wished she'd brought her knitting. She hated to sit still and do nothing. It felt unnatural. "Idle hands do the devil's work." The proverb raced through her mind, and she shifted uneasily in the seat.

"Gene," she said at last. "We're not but a mile from home. I'm gonna head back." He looked up from his tinkering and glared at her. "It's almost dark," she said reasonably. "Might as well go milk the cows."

"Fix me some supper," he called out to her retreating back. "I'll take this hay to town tomorrow."

She waved without looking back, and he returned to his study of the engine. The red clay of the road was fast losing its color, turning a murky gray in the failing daylight.

Gene lay down on his back and inched under the body of the truck. Maybe it was something underneath that wasn't working properly. He looked and ran his hands over all the cables he could see, checking to make sure everything was connected to something. He didn't have any idea of how to fix this truck, and his helplessness quickly transformed into anger.

When he heard a footstep on the wooden planking of the bridge, he tried to sit up before scooting out from under the truck.

"Goddammit to hell," he howled, rolling sideways and holding his head. He finally extricated himself from the undercarriage of the truck and sat up. He'd cut his head. It was now full dark, and the bridge was filled with shadows.

"Who's there?" He strained his eyes to see if anyone stood at the mouth of the bridge. All the stories he'd heard as a child came flooding back to him, and he fought back a little whimper as he felt blood ooze from his scalp and between his fingers.

A slight fluttering noise was the only answer. Bats. That's all it was. He stood up and tried to crank the truck again. No luck. He caught a movement out of the corner of his eye and whirled around. Nothing again. He laughed a little nervously. His fingers ran up to his scalp again, but the cut seemed to have stopped bleeding. What a day.

He kicked the truck again and decided to leave it till one of his neighbors could loan him a mule team to haul it into town. It was blocking the bridge, but there were only four or five families who used the structure anyway. If they needed him, they could come get him. He was going home.

As he walked from the mouth of the bridge, he saw a patch of shadows in the corner detach itself from the surrounding darkness, shifting and swaying in the breeze. Only there was no breeze.

He ran, his heavy work boots making a sucking sound each time they pulled free from the sticky, thick red Georgia mud.

May 1922

"Yeehaa!" The boy leaped high in the air and came down like a bullet, clutching one knee with both arms to maximize his impact. The water flew up and around him in a wide circle, splashing the two other swimmers and provoking screams of protest.

"This is a great swimming hole," the boy said after swimming back to the shallows to join his friends. "How come we never been here before?"

A second boy, taller and stockier than the first, shrugged his shoulders. After a moment, he pointed wordlessly at the dark shape squatting across the creek a hundred yards upstream.

"Folks say all kindsa things 'bout that bridge," he said barely above a whisper.

"Just another bridge, ain't it?" Steve's mother had only come back to Alvaton last month to live with her parents on their farm. Steve's dad had died of pneumonia last winter.

"Aaarrrgghh!" Will's head disappeared beneath the water as his hands flailed uselessly on the surface.

Steve watched, horrified, until Will's head reappeared on the surface a few feet away. Wade popped up shortly after, screaming with amusement.

"Gotcha!" he yelled. "Betcha thought some big snake'd snatched ya, dincha?" He howled with laughter until Will forced his head under.

Wade came up sputtering, and the three boys splashed and played for another hour until a long, low rumble caused them to look up.

"Was that thunder?" Wade asked uneasily.

"Naah, just a big truck goin' across th' bridge."

"It mighta been thunder," Steve argued. "Lookit them clouds." The sky above them had turned a deep purplish-black, the clouds hanging low and pendulous.

"We better head home."

A long, crooked finger of lightning darted from the clouds and reached to the ground, as if to punctuate Wade's nervous statement. The wind blew up with a startling suddenness. The tall oaks, sweetgum trees, and pines that bordered the creek swayed and danced in the unexpected onslaught of wind.

"Let's make a run for it," Steve shouted and dashed for the barnlike structure spanning the water.

Hesitating for a long moment, Will and Wade followed him.

Steve darted into the bridge and flattened himself against the inside wall just before his friends approached. Fat drops of rain were slamming down, their impact creating tiny puffs of smoke to rise from the red dirt, miniature explosions. The day had turned almost completely dark, and the interior of the bridge was crowded with shadows. The frequent flashes of lightning were more blinding than illuminating, creating illusions of motion within and without.

"Boo!" Steve jumped out at Wade and Will. Their terror was so pronounced that they froze in their tracks, their faces almost comical caricatures of of fear. Wade's face instantly drained of color, and from Will's mouth tumbled a piercing shriek.

"Omigod," gasped Wade. "That's not funny."

Steve wasn't laughing. He was taken aback by the intensity of the reaction he had provoked. Both his friends stood outside, pounded by the rain.

"Git outta the rain, you idiots," he finally said.

Their teeth chattering, Wade and Will exchanged a long look before moving into the shelter of the bridge. The thunder sounded like God himself just across the field, and the rapid flashes of lightning gave each boy's face a ghastly glow.

"Really blew up a big one, didn't it?" Steve tried to resume a normal conversation. The other two boys stared over his shoulder, to the deep gloom of the inner bridge.

"Whatsa matter, y'all? You act like you seen a ghost." Steve turned to look behind him. He saw nothing.

Just as suddenly as it had come up, the storm was gone again.

"Let's go."

All three boys took off across the field as fast as their legs could take them. They got to Steve's grandma's farm in record time, and scrounged some apples before ascending to the hayloft. The sun, strong again, streaked through all the chinks and cracks in the old siding, making a crisscrossed pattern of golden-silver, with dust motes floating lazily, turning and sparkling like fairy fireworks.

"What's wrong with that old bridge?" Steve lay flat on his back, watching the sunlight.

"Should we tell, Wade?"

The other boy slowly chewed a chunk of apple. "Gotta swear never to tell, Steve," he said at last. He swallowed. "Somethin' bad's bound to happen if you do."

Steve sat up.

"Aaron Johnson tol' his mama, an' the very next day he fell out of a tree and busted his arm up."

Steve nodded and leaned forward. "Tell me," he insisted in a hoarse whisper.

"A man hung himself to death on that bridge," Wade hissed. "He'd been betrayed by his best friend."

"Or maybe it was his girlfriend," Will put in darkly. "Nobody knows for sure."

"He thought about it and thought about it, till he got so caught up in it he wrapped that rope 'round his neck and threw it over a rafter.

"It started stranglin' him but it was real slow."

"His eyes bugged out 'n' he couldn't hardly see anymore . . ." Will interrupted eagerly.

"He stuck his tongue out . . ." Wade clutched his throat and made strangling noises.

"It got all swole up an' turned purple . . . "

"Then he died, swingin' back an' forth on the middle of the bridge!" Wade finished with a flourish.

"Oooh." Steve was properly appreciative. They sat silent for a moment, chewing their apples reflectively.

"You ever seen that ghost?"

"My mama won't ride through that bridge after dark," Wade said flatly. "My gran'pa, neither."

"My uncle saw it once, an' said he's never been so scared in all his life. He thought it was the devil come after him."

"Today when we was waitin' out that storm, I swear I saw that body swingin' in the shadows."

"It don't feel right on that bridge."

"Mebbe we should go back after dark, make sure it wasn't our imagination." Steve tucked the apple core absently into his pocket.

"Naaah. Can't." Wade was fidgeting with his apple core, picking each seed out and flicking it down to the floor below.

"Me, neither." Will's tone was decisive.

Steve said nothing, just looked from one friend to the other. Soon the other boys found excuses to leave and went on their way, leaving an unusually quiet Steve to eat supper with his grandparents and his mother.

"Kin I be excused, please?" he mumbled after wolfing down a second helping of everything. Released, he raced up to his room to wait until dark.

Slipping out of the house after bedtime was easy. His grandparents went to sleep right after sunset, and his mother closeted herself in her room. Steve crept slowly and carefully down the stairs, skipping the third step down because of its loud and telltale creak, and cautiously pulled open the kitchen door.

He was nearly across the yard and to the road when a shapeless form materialized beside him. His heart nearly stopped and then he recognized the furry creature.

"Hey, Prince," he said softly. "Good boy. Attaboy." He patted the collie roughly on its side, and the dog followed slavishly at his heels.

Afraid of holes and other pitfalls in the field after dark, Steve took the long route on the road to the bridge. As he approached the dark, forbidding structure skulking low over the banks of the creek, his footsteps slowed unconsciously. Prince whined and stuck his cold nose into the palm of Steve's hand.

Steve fumbled in his pocket for the candle stub and the matches he'd snitched from the kitchen before supper. As he entered the mouth of the bridge, he paused to scratch a match on the rough wood of the portal. It flared briefly, then sputtered out.

He tried again, and this time the flame caught and held long enough for him to touch it to the candle's wick. Armed with this meager light, Steve stepped resolutely forward into the bridge. By the candlelight—flickering wildly in the draft created by his movement—he could faintly see the great crossed beams that had kept the structure standing firm through decades of high winds and roaring floods. Above, the rafters were black with age. He shuddered, thinking about a rough sisal rope tossed over the rafter with deadly intent.

He moved forward, examining every square foot of the bridge as his circle of light revealed it. At last he was at the far end of the bridge and his light had uncovered nothing more threatening than a big beetle ambling along through the shadows.

Just then, at the far end of the bridge, he heard a faint rustling noise. Steve froze, the candle held high to illuminate as much as possible.

The rustling sound turned into a shuffling noise that seemed to reverberate though the passageway, and Steve's bones turned to water. The shambling footsteps steadily approached the terrified boy, closer and closer to his wavering circle of light. Though Steve strained his eyes until they felt as if they'd pop out with the effort, he could make out nothing beyond a shifting, obscure mass of shadows, only slightly more black than the gloom surrounding it.

At last, unable to withstand the suspense, Steve flung down his candle stub with a shriek of utter terror and fled out into the safety of the open road with Prince at his heels.

September 1938

"Ella, you can't do this," the young man moaned in misery. "I can't stand this anymore!"

The young woman on the wagon seat beside him crossed her arms resolutely.

"I ain't changin' my mind this time," she said. "I cain't marry you 'n' that's final."

"But I love you," he protested. "Don't you care about that?"

"It ain't right. Preacher tol' me so 'n' he's a man of God. He oughta know."

Just then, lightning cracked close enough to make the hairs on the back of her arm stand up. "See there?" she said matter-of-factly. "God sez so."

"Yer mama was only cousin to my daddy," he protested again. "It ain't like we was cousins."

"Too close to marry, an' that's that."

The clouds opened up, and the rains descended. Great sheets flew across the road, battering the wagon, the mule, and the occupants with its fury.

"Let's git outta this rain," the man said wretchedly. "Git up, Bess." The mule headed for the covered bridge down the road, eager to see shelter ahead.

"Don't take me in there, Jonathan O'Kelly," she warned. "I ain't sittin' in that bridge."

He shrugged. "You don't believe in ghosts 'n' things, now, do you? I thought the Bible said that was a sin."

"I've been in that bridge in daylight, but it's too dark in there now." She shrank against him.

It was true. The storm had leached most of the daylight out of the sky and the mouth of the bridge yawned black and empty. "I don't care," he said. "Bess is goin' anyway, whether we want to or not."

The mule trotted into the shelter of the bridge and stopped as soon as it was under cover. "Here, you dumb mule." Jonathan flicked the reins. "Pull the wagon in, too." The mule moved forward a few paces, and the woman moved closer to the man.

He slipped an arm around her. "I wouldn't worry if I were you."

She moaned, a strangely feral sound.

"I've never seen nothin' strange on this bridge, 'n' I've been crossin' it all my life," he said, trying to comfort her.

She crouched even lower on the seat next to him and he flicked the reins softly to urge the mule farther into the shadows.

"Don't, please, Jonathan," she pleaded.

The man's strong arm circled her protectively.

"Nothin's here, Ella," he repeated.

Her eyes swept from side to side and stopped, riveted by a movement from the far left corner of the bridge.

Intent on the mule and the wagon's progress, Jonathan never saw a thing. Never saw the mass of shadows detaching itself from the darkness. Never saw the swaying, swinging form. But Ella did. She began to babble incoherently, her voice rising to a shriek as she lifted both her arms to ward off the clotted drift of darkness that dangled, suspended from the rafter dead ahead.

The mule and the wagon were expelled from the mouth of the bridge with unnatural force. Jonathan anxiously patted the woman's face and arms.

"Ella?" He queried. "Ella, wake up. Stop this foolishness. Ella?"

His voice trailed off, drowned by the fierce growl of thunder from the west.

January 1946

"Helen, do you suppose it needs more gas?"

The car sputtered and coughed and then jerked along for another hundred feet.

"We're only half a mile from the farm. Jack can get it fixed if we can just . . . "

The engine sputtered again and Helen stomped hard on the gas pedal. The sudden motion made her hat slide down over her eyes, and she shoved it back, crushing the expensive trim that had seemed so important just two hours ago.

"Oh, come on, you old thing!" She spoke from between clenched teeth and pressed again on the gas pedal, as if by force of will she could make the engine turn over and carry them the half-mile to her cousin's farm.

The car resisted and stubbornly rolled to a stop just inside an old covered bridge. "Well, isn't it just like a picture postcard?" Betty got out and ran her hand along the massive old beams that supported the structure.

Helen stayed behind the wheel, twisting the key and pressing the gas pedal in a vain attempt to keep moving forward. "This is exactly why Howard says ladies shouldn't travel alone," she muttered. "He'll say 'I told you so.'" She struck the wheel with one gloved hand in frustration.

The passenger door opened with a click. "What a lovely old bridge," Betty said brightly, slipping into the seat. "I'll bet it's been here forever."

"My cousins always said it was haunted," Helen retorted tartly. "I'd just as soon be up at Jack's farm by sunset."

"It is getting dark, isn't it?" Betty looked around at the shadows spreading like pools of oil from the corners of the bridge.

"It's downright spooky. Jack told me somebody hanged himself out here a long time ago."

Betty looked around again.

"Where?" she asked in a tiny voice.

"In a corner somewhere. See, over there, where the shadows are deepest?" Helen was still wrapped up in the frustration of this, her first visit to the home place in five long years. As she gestured, she noticed a smudge on the tip of her glove and exclaimed in annoyance.

The gold and red splendor of the Georgia sunset was perfectly framed by the mouth of the bridge. To the right, the shadows shifted and stirred. Betty shivered.

"I wish this car would start," Helen repeated, twisting the key again.

"Maybe we should just walk up to your cousin's house."

Helen's only reply was a small, unladylike grunt as she pressed hard on the gas pedal. She didn't want to traipse up the dirt road, arriving at Jack's door like a bedraggled stray kitten.

As soon as the sun slipped away, the shadows crept across the floor, tendrils splaying longer and wider from each side of the bridge until finally they met in the center, leaving the occupants of the car in a dusky half-light.

Betty twined and untwined her fingers, looking from side to side anxiously as Helen, grim faced, thumbed through the owner's manual.

"Maybe it's the choke," she muttered as she opened the door to stand near the hood of the car. Betty hurried to stand beside her.

"It's getting so dark," Beth insisted. "Please, let's just go on and your cousin can come back and fix it later."

"Sshhh," hissed Helen. "What was that?"

"I didn't hear anything." Betty fixed her hand tightly on Helen's forearm. "Let's go."

Something stirred and rustled in the far corner of the bridge. Helen fixed her eyes on the spot, straining to make out the details, but no definite shape resolved itself.

"Get your purse." Helen opened the car door long enough to snatch up her new pocketbook and then took long, striding steps away from the source of the noise, through the darkest part of the bridge.

"Wait," Betty squealed, slamming the passenger door shut and tottering forward on the spiky little heels of her best shoes. The two women trotted as quickly as they could out of the barnlike structure, only slowing when they were a good hundred yards out of the mouth.

"Who," Betty gasped, "Who was it that died in there?"

Helen threw a glance over her shoulder and kept up a brisk pace, heedless of the red dust stirred up by her fashionable shoes.

"It's been a long time," she finally said. "No one knows. But they say he'd been jilted by his lover and that she found his body, twisting and turning, dangling from the rafters just minutes after he died."

Betty's mouth opened into a little red "o."

"She went crazy after that. But anybody'd go crazy stuck out here for long," she concluded. "It was probably just some old raccoon we heard. Look at my shoes." The brightly lit farmhouse lay just ahead.

October 1958

Two teenagers danced around the wagon that had stopped right outside the Alvaton Bridge. The sun was nearly gone, obscured by a bank of clouds on the horizon.

"Hurry, Billy, hurry," urged one. "Someone'll be along in a minute, and we gotta hide the wagon."

In the bed of the wagon lay a supine form, one motionless arm protruding from the rough weave of an old horse blanket. A third teenager stooped over the figure, working feverishly.

"I'm hurryin' as fast as I can, Cecil," he complained, brandishing a hand unattached to the body. "If you'da been more careful throwin' this thing in the wagon, it might not have broke into a million pieces."

The third boy was busy fashioning a noose from a long strand of rough hemp rope.

"Ready when you are, Billy," he sang out.

Cecil and Billy carefully lifted the mannequin out of the wagon bed and carried it to the mouth of the bridge.

"Where should we hang it?"

"Over there, in those shadows," Cecil commanded. "Easy, now." The mannequin's eyes stared straight ahead as they slipped the noose around the cool, slender neck.

"Maybe we oughta dress it? It kinda gleams there in the shadows."

"I think it looks perfect. First person to drive through here's gonna pee in his pants."

They stepped back. The light flesh tones of the mannequin caught and reflected the remaining illumination on the bridge. The head was hidden by the shadows up on the rafters, and the legs were suspended, motionless, just to the left of the mouth of the bridge.

Billy grasped the foot and slowly set the body spinning. They raced out of the bridge and Cecil drove the wagon a half-mile down the road, hiding it in a little grove of trees before sprinting back to crouch in the cover of some bushes with his friends. As they waited for their first victim, they passed a pocket flask back and forth.

"Sshhh, somebody's comin'!" They could hear the slow clop-clop of a single mule coming to the bridge. No gleam of moonlight or glitter of stars broke the velvet blackness of the country night.

They could hear the old black man mutter to himself or his mule as he entered the bridge.

"Dontcha worry 'bout spirits or haints, now. Jest git along home now and git to supper."

The shriek of terror was so bloodcurdling it made the hairs rise on the necks of the boys hiding in the brush. After a moment, they looked at each other and grinned. The mule and wagon came clattering out of the mouth of the bridge at a nearly impossible speed. The old man rocked back and forth on the bench seat, moaning, before he disappeared from view down the road.

Suddenly, Cecil clutched his midsection and groaned.

"What's in that flask, Billy?"

Cramps bent him over double, and he hobbled into the woods, wracked by great waves of nausea.

He lay curled up on the ground beneath the trees, his head gradually clearing. Whatever had made him sick was now on the ground a foot away. He felt better.

Cecil staggered to his feet and made his way down to the stream to rinse his mouth and duck his head underwater. Refreshed, he returned to the mouth of the bridge.

"Billy?" he called.

He cautiously advanced into the bridge, looking for his friends. The shadows were so thick that even the bright gleam of the mannequin was masked, its location only given away by a faint shifting and stirring of the shadows in the far left corner of the bridge.

"Billy?" He whispered now, vaguely uneasy by the impenetrable gloom enveloping him. He could hear some movement over by the mannequin, and he suspected some trick. He crept slowly toward the corner, straining his eyes to see through the shadows.

The mannequin didn't look quite right, but that didn't register in his mind until hours later. For when he touched its foot to make it spin a bit on the old, frayed rope, his hand met not with cold, lifeless plastic, but with flesh still warm from the blood that had coursed through its veins only minutes before.

Alvaton Bridge, in Meriwether County, Georgia, burned down about 1985, according to local sources.

There is a beautiful bridge, built around the same time, outside Gay, which is also in Meriwether County in the west central part of the state. To find it, take Georgia 85 north out of town. Go a few miles and turn left onto an unmarked road. Follow that road until you come to the "T" intersection of Covered Bridge Road; turn left. The bridge is about a half-mile down the road. Covered Bridge Road is not paved, but it is in good condition; use caution if the road is muddy.

EMILY'S BRIDGE

Would you please turn off that noise?" Without waiting for a reply, the woman driving reached over and twisted the knob, cutting off the radio with a click. The teenaged girl beside her slumped lower in the seat, scowling.

"I can't hardly hear myself think," the woman complained. "And if we're going to meet your grandmother before midnight, we don't have any time to waste."

The narrow road through the center of Vermont twisted and turned, headlights only revealing a few hundred feet at a time. A pounding rain obscured the driver's vision even more than the darkness, and the wipers squeaked and whined as they struggled to keep up with the deluge.

"I wish they'd mark these country roads better," the woman complained again. "Who knows if we're still on Route 100?"

The sullen teenager still did not speak, only examined her fingernails in the dim light of the dashboard instruments.

"Honestly, I don't know why I bother." The woman slapped the steering wheel in frustration. "You used to enjoy traveling with me. What happened?" Before the girl could reply, a blurred shape bounded into the center of the road. A scream tore from the driver's throat. Brakes shrieked. The car spun wildly in a full circle.

Only an instant later, it was all over. The car stood slightly askew in the center of the road, and the two occupants were inside, breathing hard. "Are you okay, Beverly?" The woman reached for her daughter.

"What was that, Mama?" The girl's voice quavered.

"A deer, I guess. I don't know. Thank God we didn't go off the road."

She restarted the engine, and they continued down the road, a little more cautiously now. The road twisted again, and the woman braked, slowing down for the blind curve just in case.

A few minutes later she spoke again. "I haven't seen any road signs for miles. Have you?"

The girl shook her head, mute again.

"Damn." The rain poured down. Ahead, a structure loomed, its mouth wide and black in the tenuous gleam of the headlights. The driver braked, puzzled by the presence of a barn straddling a major highway.

As she approached, she saw her headlights illuminating more rain on the other side, and she laughed. "Now I know we're lost, Beverly. There aren't any covered bridges on Route 100." She pulled slowly into the structure, her tires making a deep rumbling noise on the old wooden planking.

"But we can get out for a minute and stretch our legs without getting wet, and I want to take a look at that map."

She threw the car into park and opened her door. The rain clattered loudly on the tin roof of the bridge. As she exited the car, stretching, she heard Beverly opening the passenger door. The driver stared with curiosity at the massive wooden beams, black with age and hewn from trees that must have towered a hundred feet off the forest floor. The gleam of the headlights did more to illuminate the road ahead than the interior of the bridge, so shadows hovered close.

Running footsteps interrupted the woman's study of the bridge. She heard the car door slam, and then the car horn blared urgently, the sound bouncing all around until it filled the structure. She ran back to the car and jerked open the door, furious.

"What in God's name has come over you, Beverly?" She pushed the girl's hand off the car horn and slid into the car.

Her daughter's ashen face startled her. The girl was trembling, her teeth chattering so loudly she could barely force out her words. "Let's go, Mama," she sobbed. "Get me out of here, okay?"

Stunned, the woman complied, starting the car and pulling out of the bridge into the rainy night. A few miles down the road, she began to query her daughter. "What happened, Bev? I've never seen you so scared in your whole life."

"Didn't you hear it?"

The woman was genuinely puzzled. "Hear what?"

"There was a woman screaming for help. Her voice echoed all through the bridge."

The driver shook her head and said nothing. They drove on, lost in the turbulent darkness of the night.

****

"Old maid, old maid, yada-yada-yada." The three little children hooted and called after Emily, but she just picked her skirts up out of the dust and continued, her market basket lightly swinging on her arm.

"Some people should learn to teach their children manners," she muttered, watching the road carefully for sharp stones. Last week she had tripped on a stone while she was walking away from this very group of nasty children, and they had shrieked with laughter. She had begged her father not to make her go to market today, but he had insisted.

"I'll not have you becoming a recluse, girl," he boomed. "God knows why you haven't found a husband yet, but you'll not find one hiding away in your room—that's for certain!"

Emily had peered around his bulk in a mute appeal to her mother, but she had not raised her eyes from her sewing. Emily's shyness was interpreted by most of the ladies of Stowe as arrogance, and she had been additionally cursed with three vivacious, pretty sisters, all younger than herself. She knew what all the matrons of the town whispered about her. "Poor Emily," they tittered behind their hands, "So tall and awkward, it's no wonder she hasn't got a beau! But her sisters are sure to be married in no time."

And of course, they were, one to a dairy farmer who lived north of Stowe and another to a poor but eminently respectable preacher who served a congregation in Morristown. Her third sister, the youngest of all, had snared a lawyer who had whisked her away to live in splendor, Emily supposed, in Burlington.

So Emily suffered in silence for the most part, not even really hoping that someone might come galloping into Stowe to carry her away. It would have to be a stranger, because there were very few unattached men in Stowe, and those invariably cast their eyes toward younger, more pliable women.

Emily had thought that perhaps her father's repeated comments about her matrimonial state might end when she turned thirty—but they did not. In fact, if anything, their frequency had increased over the past six years. Her mother had become more withdrawn, so Emily bore the brunt of her father's disappointment.

"I'll not always have the means to support you, girl," he would grumble as she served his supper. "I'm getting old, and it's time you found someone to take on your care."

She didn't eat much, Emily pondered as she walked down the road toward home. She got one new dress a year, and it had been three years since she'd asked for a new pair of shoes. In fact, the soles of these were so thin, the rocks cut her feet, but she didn't dare ask for new ones. Surely she wasn't that expensive to maintain. She was so caught up by her thoughts that she did not hear the jingle of a horse's bridle approaching or the soft plopping sound of hooves in the dust.

"Oh, Emily," trilled a familiar voice.

Emily looked up to see Jenny Mueller, her eyes alight with mischief, riding in a handsome buggy beside one of the most attractive men in Stowe, Donald Manning.

"Good afternoon, Jenny, Donald," Emily said stiffly, moving to the side of the road. "Pleasant day for a drive."

They rode on after exchanging a few words. Emily tucked a stray strand of hair behind her ear and squinted her eyes against the dust as she walked the remaining quarter-mile to her father's house.

"Jenny's hat was crooked," she thought scornfully. "And her hair was all mussed. I don't doubt that she and Donald have been driving through the kissing bridge."

After she had unloaded the market basket and kissed her mother hello, Emily went to the old upright piano and began to work out a new piece. Her sister in Burlington had sent her the sheet music, and Emily poured her whole heart into the plaintive notes as she played.

****

"Isn't this a perfect campsite?" The man stretched out his legs and rubbed his hands in anticipation of the potatoes baking in the hot coals of the fire.

"I still think we should've asked permission," his companion said doubtfully. "Surely somebody owns this land." Above them, to the left, loomed the gentle folds of Mt. Mansfield. The leaves were brushed with the faintest tinge of yellow or red, and the evening breeze held a promise of winter's chill. A few hundred feet in front of them was a line of trees marking the banks of Gold Brook.

"It wasn't fenced," his friend pointed out. "And I sure wasn't gonna pay $15 for some dumb patch of dirt at that KOA. Didja see all those kids running around, screamin' and yellin'?"

The other man just shook his head and poked at the fire with a long stick. "Dinner'll be ready about dark," he said. "I hope you're hungry."

They ate in silence and then rose to take their plates to the stream to rinse them off. A few late fireflies flickered in the trees ahead, but the road and the woods were otherwise devoid of light.

"I'm always surprised at how dark it is in the country," one camper remarked. "It's like walking around in a black velvet curtain."

"I wish I'd brought a flashlight."

A sudden noise, like thunder, startled both of them. "Damn," one swore. "There wasn't any rain in the forecast, was there?"

A light broke through the trees and the two men realized what the noise had been. "It's that old bridge," the first man said in relief. "A car was going across it and made that noise."

"I didn't know we were that close to the road."

"Let's go up to the bridge and check it out."

Inside the old structure, their voices reverberated strangely. They could hear the murmuring, babbling sound of the stream below as it coursed over rocks and pebbles. Suddenly, through the mouth of the bridge, a dazzling stream of light poured in, blinding them.

"What the hell?"

The light flashed again and again. Then, just as abruptly, it was gone. The sound of the crickets resumed.

"It wasn't a car, was it?"

"I didn't hear one, did you?"

"No, but maybe it was car lights reflecting off of something."

"I dunno. It sure didn't look like a car light to me."

"Whaddya think, it was a ghost or somethin'?" His friend punched him playfully on the shoulder.

He shivered. "Let's get back to the campsite. You bring any brandy?"

****

Emily was walking home from the market again, humming a little from the new piano sonata her sister had sent last week. She heard a buggy approaching and she moved to the side of the road.

"Emily." The buggy stopped a few feet in front of her. It was Donald, alone this time, his face shadowed by the overhanging canopy.

"Donald," Emily nodded. "Out for a drive?" Her eyes, shaded by the brim of her hat, ran across his shoulders and down his arms. Even at rest, loosely holding the reins, their strength was apparent. A sudden, unbidden thought of those arms around her in an embrace made the color rise to her cheeks.

"A bit warm, isn't it?" His eyes, too, had been scanning her face and form.

"I imagine it's cooler out by the creek," Emily ventured, and then bit her tongue in confusion. She didn't want him to think that she was hinting for a romantic ride down shady, cool Gold Brook Road.

Donald leaned forward, and Emily noticed what a nice smile he had. Then she noticed his eye and covered her mouth in dismay. "Oh, my," she gasped. "What happened to your eye?"

His grin grew wider. "Aww," he said, "I walked right into a tree branch the other night after I put Amelia here in the barn. Smacked me right in the eye. I felt pretty silly about it."

"Did you try a cold compress?" As soon as the words came out, Emily scolded herself silently for being such a busybody.

"Yeah, nothing seemed to help, really." He fidgeted with the reins and Emily realized he was trying to figure out how to say something. He's shy like me, she thought, and the thought warmed her.

"I've heard that you really like to play the piano," he said. "I'd like to hear you sometime. I wish I had a musical talent like you do."

"But what about Jenny Mueller?"

His face changed. "Her father said my prospects weren't good enough to suit him."

"Oh, I'm so sorry," Emily stammered. "That is, I . . . "

"I'm not sorry," he said bluntly. "Truth is, Jenny was a little . . . " He groped for the right word. "A little flighty for me," he finished. "I guess she's pretty young, really."

Emily did not know what to say. She turned a deeper shade of red.

"I guess I should talk to your father about calling on you?"

She nodded, relieved that Donald had at last found the words.

He reached out and lightly touched the top of her hat. "You have such pretty eyes," he commented. "But I can't see them when you hide your face like that."

"Thank you," Emily stammered.

"See you later," Donald called, and the horse and buggy ambled down the road toward town.

Emily stood on the side of the road, her heart pounding. She would not fly into a tizzy, she admonished herself firmly. This probably meant nothing at all.

But still, her footsteps were unusually light as she walked the rest of the way home. Almost like walking on air. And that night as she brushed out her hair before bed, she felt uncommonly pretty.

****

"Stand right here."

The girl obliged, shifting a bit to the left.

"No, no, that's not right. Too much shadow on your face. Turn to the right."

Patiently the girl moved again. She shivered a little in spite of the heavy parka enveloping her.

"Let me try this." The photographer knelt down, angling the camera up.

"For heaven's sake, Bob, it's just a snapshot. Hurry up, would you? The poor kid's freezing." The woman lounging against the side of the car held a steaming cup of coffee. The bright December sun warmed her, although there was more than a foot of snow on the ground.

"This is such a beautiful bridge, I want to show it off in the picture." The man fiddled some more with the lens and then decided to change it.

"Don't move, honey," he warned his subject. "With the blue sky from the opposite end of the bridge and the sparkling snow on the roof, it looks great."

"But I'm cold, Daddy," the girl complained. "Just take a picture of the bridge, okay?" Without waiting for a reply, she wandered farther back into the shadows.

"Hey, Mom?" The girl's voice echoed oddly coming out of the bridge.

The woman leaning against the car straightened up and drained the last of her coffee. "What, baby?"

"C'mere. This is really strange."

As the woman peered into the structure, she gasped. "Catherine, get your parka back on! It's 30 degrees out here!"

"It's not cold right here, Mom." The girl stretched out her arms and whirled around. "Come see. It's warm right here!"

Dubious, the woman advanced to near the center of the bridge. As soon as she got within two feet of the girl, she, too, felt the inexplicable warmth. Her face broke out into a light sweat. Her skin prickled.

"This is weird, Catherine," she protested. "Something's not right. Let's get out of here."

"Aww, Mom, you're no fun." The girl skipped toward the mouth of the bridge, stopping short a few feet away to put her parka back on.

"Brrr. You're right, Mom, it's too cold to be out here without a coat. Beat you to the car!" In an instant, she was away, her long legs flashing in the uncertain light of the bridge.

****

Emily's face beaded with sweat, and the stays of her corset were digging painfully into her skin. The market basket was heavy because she had bought the sugar and coffee they needed. She trudged down the road, thankful for having successfully bypassed the Kendalls' house with its horde of rude children.

Donald had not called on her during the past week or communicated with her father, apparently. The only news was from her sister in Burlington. She informed them that she was expecting a baby early next spring. This news had, of course, prompted a barrage of sarcasm directed at Emily from her father. "Some women in this family, at least, are fulfilling their God-given potential. I suppose now we'll have grandchildren to care for us in our old age, and I thank God for that. Eh, Margaret?" He poked his wife, but she just took another stitch and pretended not to hear.

Emily snorted and shifted the market basket to her other arm. She was tempted to leave the basket by the gate when she passed it on her way to Gold's Brook to cool off. A few steps farther down the road, she decided to do just that. She hurried a little, eager to reach the shaded, quiet stream, its drowsy murmuring a perfect counterpoint to her melancholy thoughts.

She heard a buggy coming up behind her, so she moved to the side of the road, almost automatically. She had jumped so often this past week at the sound of a buggy and been disappointed so often, that she forced herself not to look around again.

"Emily?"

The buggy had stopped right in front of her, and Donald's familiar face peered around at her. "I'm so glad to see you!" He jumped down and hurried toward her, taking the basket off her arm. "I've had to go out of town, that's why I hadn't called, but I was on my way now to speak to your father."

Against Emily's will, a little bit of relief blossomed at his words. Her conscious mind rejected his facile words, but some part of her responded.

"You're not mad at me, are you?" He took her chin in his hand and tipped her face up toward his.

Caught unaware and defenseless, she could only smile and shake her head.

"Will you please honor me with your company?" With a little bow he indicated to his horse, Amelia, standing patiently in the traces. "I could give you a ride home and then speak to your father."

"I was actually going to leave my basket at the gate and go down to the brook and cool off," Emily replied, amazed at her own boldness.

"I would be most glad to accompany you, then," Donald said, his smile growing larger. "I couldn't think of anyone I'd rather go driving with."

Knowing she was crossing the bounds of propriety, Emily gathered her skirts in one hand to step up to the buggy's seat. The thought of Donald wanting her company brought such a delicious chill running across her skin that the hot July sun was almost forgotten. She didn't care, she thought defiantly, if she was endangering her reputation. What did an old maid like her have to lose anyway?

Donald climbed up to the seat next to her and rested his free arm casually across the back of the bench. With a small smile, Emily leaned into the curve of his arm, reveling in the feeling of being desired.

****

"You can't catch me!" The long, lanky form of the thirteen-year-old was scantily clad in a two-piece swimsuit. Her wet, bare feet slapping noisily against the planking of the bridge, she ran through the mouth and down the bank to the water again.

"I'll get you!" Her little sister screamed ineffectively—the older girl's head was under-water and she couldn't hear the threat. From the top of the bank, the younger girl could see the remains of their picnic lunch on the other side of the brook and her parents dozing in the shade.

"Mary Ellen threw mud at me, Mama." She hollered mightily, but neither of her parents stirred. "They don't care," she thought unhappily. "Nobody cares." It was hot up here, out of the water and the shade, so the little girl turned and walked back to the bridge.

"I guess they'd care if I was gone," she grumbled, and that gave her an idea. She ran to the center of the bridge and began to scramble up the big beams, preparing to hide while the rest of the family searched frantically. She'd done it before, with pretty fair results.

Halfway up the beam, she stopped. It was cold here. Not just cool, like a shady spot, but downright cold. Like a refrigerator.

"Patty?" Her sister appeared, silhouetted at the opening of the bridge like a picture. "I'm sorry I threw that mud at you."

"Come here." The little girl beckoned to her sister.

Mary Ellen advanced cautiously. "What?"

"Do you feel that?"

Goosebumps popped up all over the girl.

"How'd you do that?"

Patty shrugged. "I didn't. It was just here."

"Let's go, girls." Their dad stood at the far end of the bridge with a newspaper in his hands. "Your mom's ready to get back to civilization."

"Daddy, come here."

He walked toward them. "Did you find a bird's nest?" When he reached the area where they stood, he recoiled.

"Whoa! That's really cold."

"What makes it do that, Daddy?"

He shrugged. "I don't know. Maybe something with the water in the stream. Let's scoot before your mama starts hollerin' for us."

With their arms wrapped around themselves for warmth, the two girls scurried out of the dim structure and into the bright summer heat beyond.

****

Emily wadded up another piece of paper and threw it angrily in the stove, watching it shrivel and turn gray and take flight in one of the currents of heat that whirled inside the cast-iron structure.

She couldn't come up with the right words, no matter how she tried. It had been two months since she had climbed in the buggy and gone to Gold Brook in search of a stray breeze, and now she was chilled inside and out. Donald had never called on her father. Never, in fact, ridden down the road in front of her house again. And she had gone far, far beyond the limits of proper conduct with him. The implications of her impulsive actions that hot July day made her shiver all over.

Even if she did manage to compose a letter to Donald, she had no idea how to get it to him. She could hardly appear on the doorstep of his parents' house, note in hand. Perhaps, she thought with a grim little smile, one of the Kendall ruffians would deliver it for her.

More likely, she thought, they'd tear it open and read it aloud for all the world to hear. And she couldn't bear the shame of that, she thought. Bad enough to be an old maid. But to be revealed as the most foolish of women, one taken in by the most timeworn stories of all, tricked blind by her own vanity. Her thoughts chased round and round, like little mice in an empty room scrambling to find even a crumb of hope.

"Writing to your sister, Emily?" Her father entered the kitchen, shattering the silence. "I expect you'll be starting dinner soon, won't you? Your mother's too tired to cook today."

"Yes, Father," Emily mumbled obediently, rising to her feet and sweeping the paper into her apron pocket.

"You are getting stout, my girl," he commented as he left the room. "Watch your figure or you'll be an old maid forever!"

****

It was a picture-perfect autumn day. The trees had put on their most brilliant foliage, the sky was an impossibly deep, rich shade of blue, and not a breath of wind threatened to dislodge a single leaf or move a cloud in to blemish the sky.

"Days like this only happen once or twice in a lifetime," declared the woman, pulling the brim of her hat down to shade her eyes. "I've never seen colors this bright before."

Her friend just grunted softly, preoccupied with trying to thread the film into her camera.

"Look up, Marilyn, look around you," she commanded with a laugh. "You'll be so busy trying to put film in that damn thing you'll miss it all."

"There." Marilyn snapped the camera closed with a satisfying click. "Let me take your picture so we'll remember this perfect day forever."

"Oh, no, you don't," her friend replied. "Take a picture of the bridge, but leave me out of it. My behind is as broad as that mountain, and I want no record of it."

"Suit yourself." Marilyn busily shot pictures of the trees in their splendor, the brown wood of the bridge in pleasant contrast to the brilliant red foliage, the blue sky, the mountain, and the water in the brook.

"You'll shoot anything that stands still, won't you?" Her friend stood in the mouth of the bridge. "Put your camera down and come see this marvelous old bridge."

They stood admiring the massive old beams, and Marilyn sighed. "It reminds me of that old bridge east of town, you remember?"

"How could I forget?" Her friend hooted. "I got into so much trouble in that bridge, I had to get married!"

Marilyn look startled. "You did not."

"Well, almost," her friend conceded. "My, how Kenny loved to spoon in that old bridge."

"That's what I was thinking. Ed asked me to marry him in that bridge."

"You still miss him, don't you?" The woman slipped her arm through Marilyn's.

"Don't you still miss Kenny?"

"Of course I do. Every day." Just then, a gust of wind snatched of her hat, sending it sailing into the shadows deep in the bridge. Her silver-gray hair, carefully combed that morning, stood up nearly straight, blown by the wind. She retrieved her hat.

"That's odd," Marilyn said. "I was watching those trees outside the bridge, and I didn't see them move."

"The wind certainly isn't blowing now," agreed her friend. "Maybe it was Kenny, saying hello. He always did love to play tricks."

"Oh, I wish you wouldn't say that," Marilyn looked up nervously. "You know I don't believe in that stuff." She shivered, and the two women returned to their car, the perfection of the day somehow marred.

****

Emily's mother was bent over, her needle flashing in and out of the fabric she held. Emily noted vaguely that she had never seen her mother sew so fast. Her father's voice thundered somewhere above her, but Emily had stopped trying to make sense of his words several minutes before. "Disgrace," "shame," "sin," "humiliation," "tarnish." Words like these figured prominently in her father's tirade.

Emily laced her fingers over her swollen belly and sat as still as she could, next to the warmth of the fire. It was cold all the time now, and the trees were stripped bare. Emily imagined that they, too, might feel a little humiliated, with their clothing all fallen away, and their bare bones exposed for all to see.

"If you'll not tell me who is responsible for this outrage, then I'll send you to your room until you come to your senses!" He pulled her up roughly by her arm, causing her to gasp with the sharp, unexpected pain. Her mother did not look up from her stitching. Half-dragging her, Emily's father stormed up the stairs to her room, thrust her inside, and slammed the door. Minutes later, Emily heard the rattle of the key in the lock and the tumblers sliding into place.

Emily did not talk for five days. Once a day, her mother brought in a pitcher of water and carried out the chamber pot, with her father glowering in the doorway, his arms crossed. Neither parent spoke to her.

On the fifth day, she gave in. "I don't want to hurt the baby," she said. "If I tell you who the father is, will you let me eat?"

Her father nodded grudgingly, and Emily saw a faint glistening trail its way down the pinched and furrowed face of her mother. A single tear.

"It was Donald Manning. But I don't think he'll have me."

"Oh, he'll have you all right," her father said grimly. "Margaret, fix the girl something to eat."

Emily sat at the kitchen table and did not comment as her father left with his old musket in hand. A few minutes later, she called her mother.

"Mama," she said softly. Margaret turned to her with questioning in her eyes.

"Come here," Emily said. She took her mother's hand and laid it gently across her stomach.

"You can feel it," she explained. "It moves around a lot, especially when I'm trying to sleep. Feel that?"

Margaret snatched her hand away and turned back to the stove. The room was filled with the quiet sound of her weeping and the occasional log settling in the stove.

After a meager meal of bread and cheese and a wizened old apple, Emily climbed heavily back up the stairs to her room. It was dark before she heard the door slam downstairs, and she could hear the rumble of her father's voice through the floorboards.

He spoke for a good five minutes, barely hesitating in his tirade. Emily's mother spoke so seldom now anyway that the pauses were more for him to catch his breath rather than for his wife to respond. Soon Emily heard his footsteps ascending the stairs. She sat in her chair, unbraiding her hair to prepare for sleep. He threw open the door and spoke without preamble.

"Donald and the preacher will be here at nine tomorrow morning," he said shortly. "I'll expect you to redeem yourself by behaving properly."

She nodded.

"I hope you appreciate all I've done for you," her father said bitterly, skewering her with his eyes. "I've told Donald he can have my best saddle-horse as a dowry."

She nodded again, her eyes in her lap, her fingers frozen in the soft tangle of the single, thick braid. As soon as he left, Emily picked up her hairbrush and began to run it through her hair in long, rhythmic strokes. The baby within turned and rolled lazily, and she savored the sensation. Her hair fell in thick clouds all around her face, and she dreamily brushed it until her eyes felt heavy with sleep.

****

"Mama, I had a dream last night," the little girl announced as she carefully poured milk over the garishly colored cereal. "It was about a sad lady."

"Mmmm. Pass the milk, would you, dear?" Her mother held a guidebook open on the table next to her. The waitress had refilled her coffee cup and she stirred milk into it while reading aloud.

"Historic Stowe Hollow Bridge. Two miles north of town on Gold Brook Road." She looked up at her daughter. "You want to go see a neat old bridge today, honey?"

The girl pouted. "I wanna tell you about my dream," she insisted. "You weren't listening to me."

"You're right, I wasn't. I'm sorry." She closed the guidebook, but held her finger inside it as a place marker. "Tell me your dream."

"Oh, it wasn't much," the girl said happily. "Just a sad lady in a white dress with flowers. She had pretty long hair."

"Did she look like me?"

The girl studied her mother carefully, then shook her head.

"Not at all," she said decisively. "This lady had brown hair, and she was fatter and older."

"Thanks, honey." The woman laughed and opened the guidebook, while the little girl cheerfully spooned multicolored mush into her mouth.

It was midmorning before the woman pulled the rental car off onto the shoulder of the road. "Here we are, honey," she said. "We drove straight to it. I'll have to tell your daddy what a good map reader you are."

The girl climbed out of the car, her braids swinging with her movements.

"This is it, Mama," she said excitedly.

"I know, it's the bridge I read about at breakfast."

"No, Mama, I mean this is where the lady in my dream was."

The woman looked closely at her daughter, then knelt down to her face-to-face.

"You dreamed about this bridge last night?"

The girl nodded confidently.

A shiver passed over the woman, but she quickly shook it off. "Let's go over there." She pointed to a field not far from the stream. "I bet we can see the mountain real good from over there."

"I wanna look at the bridge, Mama."

The woman shrugged, and moved closer to the structure, clutching her daughter's hand tightly.

****

When her mother gathered up Emily's hair to braid it as always, Emily protested. "It's my wedding day, Mama." She pushed Margaret's hands away.

Margaret inclined her head and moved to get Emily's dress. She helped her daughter pull it over her head and smooth down the white folds delicately embroidered with flowers. The bodice was snug, and the unfashionably high waistline helped to mask Emily's ungainly belly.

"I don't know if Father will want me to wear this," Emily warned.

"It was my wedding dress, and I saved it for you. You'll wear it." Emily caught a fleeting glimpse of the woman who had once ruled this household. She wondered if time had worn her down, or if her father's force of will had changed her mother into this meek, silent specter.

Emily wondered what marriage held in store for her, but time did not allow for long speculation. She had just long enough to run a brush through her hair before her father called her down to the parlor.

Emily smiled wanly at the preacher, who was politely sipping a cup of tea as they waited for the bridegroom. She felt vaguely shamed and wondered if the preacher knew that this whole exercise was a farce, a sham with a foundation in deceit and threats.

"Donald will be here soon," her father assured the preacher. Emily lifted the corner of the curtains to peer out the window. On the frozen, rutted road, the sound of horse's hooves rang with an incongruously joyous air. Donald was bringing the buggy.

Emily's father went outside to the porch to greet his prospective son-in-law. "Donald."

"Morning, Mr. Smith." Donald jumped down from the buggy. "I'd like to see that mare again, if I may."

Emily stood in the doorway of the house. Donald's peremptory demand made her feel even more ashamed. He wanted to examine his payment more closely, she thought bitterly, before he makes the final commitment.

Donald came out, leading the mare with her saddle on. Emily had wandered out to the buggy and touched the fringe on the top with wondering fingers. The buggy that had looked so elegant just six months ago now looked a bit shabby. Amelia, the horse, stood a little swaybacked.

With an effort, Emily hoisted herself up to the buggy seat, trying to recapture the feeling she'd had when Donald had first told her how much he loved her. It had been in the dim recesses of the covered bridge over Gold Brook, and the water rushing beneath the bridge had seemed to echo his words.

Donald swung himself up on the mare's back. With a wild cry, he dug his heels into her side and wheeled out of the yard and onto the road.

Emily's father roared in protest, and Donald laughed mockingly as he rode, "You'll never catch me!"

Emily sat in the buggy, stunned, as her father ran into the house for the old musket. He flew back out to the buggy and mercilessly urged Amelia to follow Donald down to Gold Brook Road. In his anger, he barely noticed Emily's presence. They galloped down the road, the buggy bouncing and flying from rut to rut. Ahead lay the bridge, filled with shadows. One of them was Donald, bent over the straps that secured the horse's saddle. It had loosened abruptly, and he was forced to dismount to cinch it tight.

"You bastard," roared Emily's father. "I'll kill you for this!" He ran, pell-mell, into the bridge while Emily struggled to dismount from the buggy. Her hair blew in clouds around her face, and her white dress caught and reflected the brittle January light.

Donald threw a glance over his shoulder and abandoned his efforts to fix the saddle. He stood and ran to the portal of the bridge.

"I'll never marry her!" His defiant cry cut right to Emily's heart. He swung up to the giant beams of the roof, out of range of her father's musket. Her father roared again in impotent rage, and backed off to get a clear shot. Donald stood on the roof of the bridge. Suddenly, his arms flew up in the air and cartwheeled violently. He'd lost his balance. As Emily watched, horrified, he slipped and tumbled to the rocks below.

She ran, heedless of the sharp stones and steep bank, down to his crumpled body. Blood pooled around his head, and his eyes stared sightless up at the gray, cold sky.

Emily's keening cries rose through the branches and up to the sky beyond. She would mourn this loss forever.

Emily's Bridge, also known as Stowe Hollow Bridge, is in Lamoille County in north central Vermont. To find it, take Vermont 100 north out of Stowe, and drive for a couple of miles until you reach Gold Brook Road. The bridge is straight ahead.

CROSSINGS

The girl banged the spoon against the side of the metal bucket. "Soo-ey! Soo-ey!" Her eyes scanned the underbrush, searching for a sign of life. Next to her, two little ones danced and yelped in imitation. "Soo-ey! Soo-ey!"

With relief, the older girl heard the pig crashing through the underbrush. It foraged most days, but Becca said it was better to bring it in before dark. The pig, Patsy knew, was of paramount importance to their family life, and Becca had put her in charge of its care.

The little children squealed and scattered as the big old sow lumbered toward their sister and the feed bucket. The pig and the children turned and headed back for home in the clearing above Sandy Creek.

Edward and Ella were fighting when Patsy and the two youngest came back into the house.

"That's my cat-eye! You traded it to me last Sunday!"

"Did not! You stole it, and I'm gonna tell Mama!"

"Stop it, you two." Becca scooped up baby Frank and plopped him on her hip. "You'll be fast asleep when Mama gets back. If you go fetch me some blackberries, I think I could scrape together a cobbler for dessert. Git on."

Distracted by the prospect of a sweet dessert, the two scampered out the door.

"Don't . . ." The screen door fell back into place with a loud slam and tottered a bit where the hinge was missing a couple of screws. ". . . slam it," finished Becca.

"Honestly, when will those two grow up and quit squabblin'?" Patsy picked up a bowl of peas and started shelling them into a cast-iron pot.

"They're too close in age, Mama says. When they get to the ripe old age of twelve, I'll bet they'll turn into little angels."

Patsy shot her sister an exasperated look. "You're not that grow-up yourself, smarty-pants."

"Pretty soon I'll be old enough to get married and get out of here," Becca retorted. "Take Frank, I'm gonna light the stove." She handed the toddler to her sister. "Rosa, stand back, now."

The five-year-old watched the ritual lighting of the stove with wide eyes. First Becca pumped the handle to get the kerosene into the burner chamber. Then she quickly struck a match and tossed it at the burner, stepping back to avoid the low whoomp of gas igniting. It took two tries tonight.

"I hate that thing," she said, tucking a few straggling strands of hair behind her ears. "I'll get me a modern gas stove, just you wait and see." She and Patsy shelled peas in silence for a few moments, letting Rosa play with the baby.

Edward and Ella burst though the door with a cupful of berries in their bucket.

"Looks like more found their way into your bellies than in the bucket," commented Patsy as Becca took the bucket and rinsed the berries.

"Wash up, now," commanded Becca. "Supper's almost ready." She mixed a little flour, a little sugar, and some water and spooned it over the berries before sliding the pan into the oven.

"Why are you so bossy, Becca?" Ella grumbled. "Do this, do that, morning till night."

"She's bossy Becca, that's why," chortled Edward. "Bossy Becca, bossy Becca!" Soon all the children but Patsy and baby Frank were circling in a ring, chanting noisily. Baby Frank cooed and clapped his hands with delight.

"Hush, now," Becca said. "Let's eat."

"Beans again," Patsy said sadly. "I hate beans."

"Cobbler for dessert," reminded Becca. "It's in the oven."

"Did you light it?"

"Oh, drat!" Becca went back to the oven and bent over to light it. After three tries, she had to concede defeat. "It must be nearly out of kerosene," she said as she sat down again. "The peas barely got cooked."

"Yuck!" Edward spat out a mouthful. "They're hard!"

"They're good for you, Edward. Don't waste food."

"We could eat the cobbler the way it is," suggested Rosa.

"Yuck!"

But after trying it, the children scraped the pan clean and declared the unbaked cobbler a success.

"Can we go swimming, Becca?" Edward was the first to clear his plate.

"Please, please!" begged Rosa and Ella.

"Pwease?" said baby Frank, tugging at Becca's skirt.

"You silly goose, you don't know how to swim!" The oldest girl patted her baby brother's soft, downy head and turned to her other brother. "Have you fed the chickens?"

"Yes, I mean, I'll go do it now!" he darted out the door, slamming it again as Becca winced.

"Ella, Rosa, Patsy, let's do the dishes right quick so Mama won't have to."

Their chores completed, the six children traipsed down the hill to the old ferry road. To the right was the covered bridge that provided the main thoroughfare to and from Goldman. There were usually one or two travelers every hour or so, and Becca liked to sit on a little rise overlooking the bridge, keeping an eye on the passersby as well as her brothers and sisters playing on the sandy beach that lay beneath the red-painted bridge.

She heard a distinctive sputtering noise just east of the bridge and her heart rose. It sounded like the old DeSoto her father drove, and she stood and shielded her eyes from the sun to watch the car approach.

She waved, disappointed, as the LeMays crossed the bridge and headed downhill toward Goldman and their hardware store. Behind her, just as she began to sit down again, she heard a piercing whistle.

"Rebecca Johnston, what are you doing playing around at the kissin' bridge?"

"Johnny Oates, you scalawag, I'm not playin', I'm watching my brothers and sisters."

The lanky boy, dressed in overalls but no shirt, hunkered down in the grass next to her. "Were the blackberries good?" he inquired solemnly.

Becca's hand flew to her mouth, to wipe away any telltale stain that might have lingered after supper. "How'd you know?" she gasped.

"I ran across those little devils fighting over blackberries on my way to the store," he laughed. "I was hopin' some made it back home."

Becca laughed in response. "They're always fightin'. It comes as natural to them as breathin', I guess."

"How d'you like your summer vacation so far?" The boy picked a long blade of grass and began to fiddle with it, watching the five youngsters splashing around in the creek below them.

"Well, I wouldn't call it vacation, exactly. You look like you've been puttin' in some time in the fields yourself."

"It don't hardly make sense to grow anything anymore, with the prices we been gettin'. My pa says he'd as soon set back and collect a government check, but that makes my ma fly into a fury."

"My father quit tryin' to make a livin' on these hills years ago. He says all he ever harvested was rocks and grief anyway."

The two teenagers sat in silence for a moment before Johnny jumped up. "I better get back to the house," he apologized. "My pa wanted this pack of Camels after supper, and ma was cookin' when I left."

"Bye." Becca watched his long legs stride across the grass and scramble over the rocks to reach the road. Johnny made her feel happy sometimes, with all his jokes and cutting up, but the thought of becoming a farmer's wife dismayed her.

On the other hand, it seemed coldhearted and calculating to ignore Johnny's attentions just because he had the misfortune to be born and raised on a farm. That was about the extent of her choices around here, she had to admit, unless she wanted to make friends with Hank Webber, the minister's son. Heaven only knows, though, where he'll end up, she thought as she stood and brushed off her skirt. Smiling a little at the inadvertent pun, she walked down to the creekbed to collect her family.

They were splashing and shouting so loudly they hardly heard her. Baby Frank was in the middle of it all, on Patsy's shoulders, crowing and clapping his hands every time his brother or sisters shouted.

"Let's go home, now," Becca repeated. "It'll be dark soon, and the skeeters are out. They'll eat you up."

The children protested, but Becca was firm. "Out. Now. Or we can't come back tomorrow."

When they finally straggled out of the water, Becca poked Edward. "Race you up the hill!" With a whoop, she gathered her skirts high above her knees and ran furiously, her long legs pumping, up the path to the house on the hill. She only just beat Edward, who complained that she'd had a head start.

Minutes later Patsy came trudging up the hill holding Rosa's hand and carrying the baby on her hip.

"No fair, Becca, I've been watching Frank all day. He's gettin' too heavy for me." A whining note crept into her voice, and Becca threw her a look of disgust.

"Don't carry him then, Patsy. He can walk."

Tired and cross, all six children cleaned their teeth before kneeling down by the side of the big double bed where Edward, Ella, Rosa, and the baby slept.

"Now I lay me down to sleep," they chanted in unison. "I pray the Lord my soul to keep. If I die before I wake, I pray the Lord my soul to take. Amen." Patsy tucked them in while Becca straightened out the quilts that made a pallet for the older girls.

"Patsy, what's 'die' mean?" asked Rosa sleepily.

"Never mind, Rose Red," Patsy said, stroking her hair.

"It's what that fat ol' pig's gonna do this fall," giggled Edward.

"Hush, now."

"He kicked me," whined Ella. "I want Mama."

"Mama will be back soon. Go to sleep."

The warm glow of the kerosene lamp woke Becca hours later.

"Mama?" she whispered.

"Yes, honey?" Even by the soft, forgiving light of the lamp, she looked worn. Almost old, Becca thought.

"What was it?"

"A girl. A big one, and it went hard on Sally."

"She's all right?"

"Yeah, just wore out. Like me. That baby fought for 13 hours. I guess it didn't see much out here worth bein' born for."

"Aw, Mama." Becca crept out from the covers and wrapped her arms around her mother. After a moment, the older woman reciprocated.

"I'm sorry, Becca. I'm just tired, I guess." Sarah smiled at her oldest child and suddenly looked more familiar. As she stroked the girl's hair, Becca snuggled up closer, warmed by the luxury of undivided attention.

"Let's go to sleep, honey."

Wordlessly, the girl clambered down to the pallet on the floor and nestled spoon-style next to her sister. As her eyes closed, she heard the familiar murmuring sound of her mother's heavy braid of coal-black hair being loosened and brushed, stroke after stroke, until the girl fell asleep.

The next morning her mother had a skillet full of scrambled eggs nearly ready when Becca wandered into the kitchen.

"I think the tank needs filling up, Mama," she mumbled. "I couldn't get the oven to light last night."

"We had blackberry cobbler for dessert and it wasn't even cooked, Mama!" Edward, although not exactly clinging, was hovering close enough to wrap his arms around his mother's legs if he felt the urge. Ella and Rosa, too, were right underfoot and baby Frank rested effortlessly on his mama's hip. The woman moved around through this small cluster of humanity with an easy grace, seeming to know without looking where to place her feet in order to avoid her children's bodies.

A car rattled to a stop outside, the sound of its labored ascent to the house masked by the noise of breakfast being prepared. "It's Daddy!" shrieked Patsy, and the children tumbled like an avalanche into the yard, even Becca forgetting in her haste the precarious state of the screen door hinge.

Sarah turned off the skillet and walked to the door, wiping her hands on her apron. The sight of her husband, overgrown with joyous children like an old barn covered with honeysuckle, brought a small smile to her lips.

"Yes, yes, of course, I brought you all something, I always do, don't I?" He looked to-ward the house. When he picked out the shadowy figure of Sarah, he waved gaily. "Even got something for your mother this time, couldn't forget my own true love now could I?"

He disentangled himself from the children, and his lurching gait as he walked toward the house again filled Sarah with a hurtful surprise. He'd come back from France with the injury more than 16 years ago, but the sight still had the capacity to make her heart ache with a dull echo of the pain she'd felt when she first saw his mangled leg.

"How'd it go?" She closed her eyes for an instant. She had meant to greet him first, ask how he felt, instead of demanding an accounting. She saw the welcome fade from his eyes.

"Great, just great. Cotton's down lower than it's ever been, 15 million men are out of work, the banks are foreclosing on every other farm in the county, and men are lining up by the dozens to buy cigars."

"I'm sorry, Ed. I shouldn't have asked that way. I didn't mean it, I've just had a hard week and . . . "

"You want to talk about a hard week? I've driven no less than a hundred miles every day, stopped at every two-bit crummy little store and practically begged men who don't give a damn to please, please buy my cigars!" By the time he finished, he was nearly yelling. But the effort seemed to exhaust him, and he dropped into the chair nearest the stove.

"Mama always says a cup of coffee perks you right up." Rosa's solemn little voice as she tugged on her father's sleeve sent the tension in the room underground for the moment. Ed laughed and pulled the little girl up on his lap. Ella scrambled up to his other knee, and Edward leaned against his father's shoulder. The two older girls sat down at the table, eager to hear about their father's adventures while he was away.

"Sally had her baby last night, Ed. Another girl."

"She pay you this time?"

"Her mother gave us three dozen eggs."

"Our hens stop laying?"

Sarah briefly closed her eyes again, but her back was to her husband. "That's all she had, Ed."

"I'm hungry, Mama," Ella whined.

"And I could use that cuppa coffee, Sarah," Ed said, tugging gently on one of Ella's braids.

"Here, Becca." Sarah handed Frank to his sister and reached for the matches. She pumped the stove vigorously, and with a practiced flip of her wrist, tossed a lighted match toward the burner pan. It failed to catch, and she tried twice more with no success.

"The tank's empty, Mama," Becca reminded her.

"I'll fill it," Ed volunteered. He spilled the girls off his lap and went to the shed outside for the five-gallon can.

"Nearly empty," he said cheerfully, swinging the can so they could hear a little liquid slosh. "I'll send you down to town this afternoon to get a refill."

After he poured the last few drops into the small cylindrical tank attached to the stove, he set the empty can by the back door. Becca sliced bread and Sarah turned the burner on beneath the eggs and the blue speckled coffee percolator.

"Put the can in the shed, please, Edward," she said without turning around.

"It's empty, Sarah. It can sit there during breakfast."

She didn't answer, just shrugged her shoulders.

After breakfast, Ed brought out the gifts he'd collected during the two weeks he'd been away. "Hair ribbons for my beautiful girls." He presented them with a flourish to Becca and Patsy. "New shooters for my marble players." Ella and Edward held up the oversized marbles and turned them round and round, catching and fracturing the light streaming into the kitchen from the window over the sink. "And for Rosa, my pretty little flower," he reached into his worn leather valise and carefully lifted out a tiny, mewling ball of fluff. "Her very own mouser!"

"Ooooh, Daddy!" the children chorused. Edward had long refused to get a cat, saying that another mouth to feed was a wasteful expense.

"Kitty?" said Frank, toddling forward to touch the curious bundle.

"Edward?" queried Sarah.

His first reply was an eloquent shrug. "It was free," he explained lamely. "I took to it."

Edward and Ella played marbles in the kitchen, while Becca, Patsy, and Rosa amused themselves with the kitten. Before lunch, Sarah announced that she had plans for the children.

"I'll fix you a picnic lunch," she declared, "to take to the creek, and then you can all go to the hardware store and get the kerosene can refilled."

"Oh goody!" shouted Edward.

"What's for the picnic?" asked Ella.

Sarah thought fast. "Deviled eggs," she said. Ed, still sitting at the table, grinned.

"Here's a quarter for the kerosene, Becca." Ed bent close to his oldest child and whispered as he pressed an extra coin in her hand. "Take them to the store and give them each a nickel to spend on candy, too. Tell them to share with baby Frank."

With a flurry of activity and a few false starts, the caravan of six children set out down the hill to the creek for lunch and a swim, and then across to town.

"Be careful!" Ed and Sarah stood watching in the doorway. Patsy carried baby Frank, Edward toiled under the burden of the kerosene can, Becca hauled the picnic basket, and Ella carried a blanket. Only Rosa was not pressed into service, and she flitted forward and backward between the group and the house at first, reluctantly leaving her precious kitty after many attempts to persuade her.

"Let's swim first!" yelled Ella, dropping the blanket halfway as she scrambled down to the creekbed.

"I'll beat you into the water!" shrieked Edward. "Last one in's a monkey's uncle!" With a loud hoot, he tossed the kerosene can aside. Rosa raced past him, her little legs pumping wildly to keep up.

Patsy set baby Frank down and held his hand as they scrambled to the shallows, where Frank liked to watch the shadowy little fish dart back and forth.

Becca was hot, but she felt like she should maintain her dignity and not splash and play in the water like the children—just in case someone special came across the bridge. Or even, she thought, if Johnny Oates happened by. So she lay on her back above the creek, cushioning her head on her crossed arms, staring upward at the billowing, shape-shifting clouds sailing slowly and majestically across the blue.

"Help, help, I'm drownin'! Help!"

Her brother's cry galvanized Becca, and she half rolled, half ran down the bank to the water's edge. Heedless of her dress, she splashed into the creek up to her knees, her eyes frantically scanning the water's surface for a sign of her brother.

There, under the bridge, in the shadows, she thought she saw a hand rise up out of the water. Just as she took a deep breath, preparing to dive into the deepest area of the creek, a giggle behind her brought her up short.

She whirled around to see Patsy, with baby Frank on her shoulders, and little Rosa, covering their mouths to unsuccessfully stifle their snickers. Becca turned around again in time to see Edward swing down from the cross-bracing on the underside of the bridge, and hang there, hooting like a monkey and grinning at Becca's panic.

"Fooled ya, didn' I?" he taunted. Ella also appeared from behind the stone piers, grinning sheepishly.

Becca sloshed furiously out of the water. As she walked past Patsy, she threw a slap across her cheek so hard the girl rocked with its force.

"Don't you ever, ever play a trick like that on me again, you hear, Patsy Ann Johnston?"

Patsy's eyes filled with tears and Frank began to whimper. "I didn't do anything, Becca, I didn't even know where he was till you jumped in the water, I swear."

Becca didn't reply, only stalked back up the bank to sit and sulk. When the shadow of the bridge was directly beneath the structure, she called to her brothers and sisters.

"Let's eat, you rotten little beggars. Or maybe I should let you all go hungry."

They were all subdued as they ate. Little Rosa slipped her hand into Becca's and squeezed it softly, a mute apology for the trick.

Becca felt bad, seeing the imprint of her hand still on Patsy's cheek. Edward and Ella were wary of Becca's anger and ate at a distance, only speaking to request more food.

"Look, Edward, she's right. That was a really nasty trick. She's the one who's supposed to be lookin' out for us, and she'd catch it if anything happened." Patsy broke the tension as the last deviled egg was divided between Edward and Ella.

"She wasn't watching us, anyway," the boy pointed out. "She was bein' her usual stuck-up self, off moonin' at the clouds."

Ella poked her brother. "Say you're sorry, Edward."

"Sorry, Becca," he mumbled, unable to withstand pressure from all sides. "But you did look funny, all soppin' wet an' mad!" With another holler, he took off across the bridge down toward town.

"Oh, forget him," Becca said, standing up to brush crumbs off her skirt. "Ella, you take the kerosene can. I'll stick the basket and the blanket under the bridge, and we'll collect 'em on the way home."

She held out her arms for baby Frank and touched Patsy's cheek gently by way of apology as she passed her younger sister.

"Becca, it's got a dent in it," Ella cried, picking up the can from where Edward had flung it down in his haste to go swimming.

Becca sighed and ran her hand along the side. "It doesn't feel like it's got a hole in it, anyway," she said. "Let's go."

They trooped across the bridge, still cool inside despite the heat of the summer day. It was dark, with only small pools of light filtering in from the narrow windows below the eaves.

"Spooky old bridge," Patsy commented.

"They call it a kissin' bridge," Becca said. "I guess 'cause it's so dark."

Ella and Rosa ran ahead. It was only a little over a mile to Goldman, and they knew Edward was somewhere close by.

"Have you ever been kissed, Becca?"

The older girl thought for a moment before replying. "Who have I ever met that I wanted to kiss?" she asked.

"I dunno."

Their feet scuffed up a cloud of dirt as they walked. Baby Frank's head nodded as he succumbed to the lethargic pleasures of a full stomach and the rocking gait of his sister.

"He's gettin' heavy, isn't he?" Patsy gave a nod toward the baby.

"Yeah. He'll start walking all the time soon, I 'spect."

"You think Mama'll have another one?"

"I dunno, Patsy." The two walked in a companionable silence the rest of the way to town. Ahead they heard the little girls squeal as Edward jumped out of the bushes at them.

"Gotcha!" he hollered. "I'm the Lone Ranger!"

"The Lone Ranger's a good guy, Edward," Patsy called out. "And if you're not good, you can bet Papa'll want to know!"

Mr. LeMay at the hardware store gave the children a hard stare as they came in the door with the kerosene can.

"No credit," he barked. "And I don't need any more eggs," he added nastily.

"No sir, we've got cash today," Becca said stiffly, holding up the quarter for him to see. Grudgingly he took the can from her and led them out back to the kerosene pump. He pocketed the quarter without a word when the can was filled.

"May we leave it out back here while we go to the store?" Becca asked politely, but inside she was seething with anger.

"I can't watch over it, but if you want to, it's fine by me," he said gruffly. "I've got a business to run."

Becca turned and led the little troupe of children through the alley and out onto the main street.

"Daddy gave me a quarter to share with you," she said as they approached the grocery store. "We each have to buy a little piece of candy for baby Frank, though, since he's too little to get his own nickel."

Ground rules established, they swarmed into the store. Mrs. Byers gave them a warm welcome. "It's Mrs. Johnston's children," she cried, slipping off her stool to come meet them. "How is your mama? You'll have to tell her my girl Eva and the baby are doing so well, we never could've managed without her."

"Thank you, ma'am," Becca mumbled.

Mrs. Byers' stream of words continued as she helped the children choose some candy. "It was a hard birth, you know, but oh, he's been such an easy baby. I think it goes like that, don't you? I know women whose babies came out smooth as silk, just like that," she snapped her fingers, nearly dropping a jar of peppermint sticks.

"But then, my, weren't them babies colicky? I never did see a fussier baby than that LeMay boy. He's fourteen now and still a handful." She toted up the assorted peppermint sticks, licorice strings, and brightly colored jawbreakers on a scrap of brown paper. "Let's see, that's twenty-six cents. Don't give that precious baby those jawbreakers, he's liable to choke on those, why I saw a little girl, she was two years old I think, and she just turned blue."

Becca was having a fierce, wordless struggle with Edward and Patsy, trying to get each of them to surrender a licorice string in order to reduce the bill by a penny.

"Her daddy, though, turned her upside down quick as a wink and pounded her on the back and that jawbreaker popped out, pretty as you please," Mrs. Byers chuckled. "They didn't give that girl any jawbreakers for a while, you may be sure." She stared at the two bedraggled licorice strings the victorious Becca held out.

"Please, ma'am, we don't need these," Becca said. She neatly dodged the kick Edward directed at her shins and held out the quarter.

"Take them, take them," the storekeeper said cheerily. "You each want a little paper to wrap your candy in? Here, take this cracker for the baby, he'll like that much better anyway."

Frank, awake again, reached out his fat, grubby fingers for the saltine the lady held out. "Oh, he's a sweet one, he is," she cooed. "Let me wrap that candy up so it doesn't spoil your supper. Your daddy's home today, isn't he? I thought I heard him come through town this morning,"

"Goodbye!" yelled Ella, and the three younger ones dashed out the door.

"Well," said Mrs. Byers, caught up short. "Well, you be sure to tell your mama I said hello." She stopped to take a breath and Patsy swooped down to retrieve Frank. "Goodbye, Mrs. Byers," Patsy and Becca chorused, then "Thank you," as they made their escape.

Laughing, they ran all the way to the rear of the hardware store where the kerosene can waited. Edward and Ella were designated to hold baby Frank's hands as he toiled down the road, taking three steps on short, fat legs for every one his big brother took. Patsy and Becca took turns carrying the kerosene can.

"Oh, this stuff stinks to high heaven," Patsy cried as they reached the bridge. "I'm 'bout to choke on it."

"I'll carry it now," Becca offered. "Get the basket and the blanket—they're under the bridge in those bushes."

"I wanna swim some more," whined Edward. "I'm hot, an' I wanna get a drink."

"Go get a drink then, Edward, but don't you dare get back in the creek," Becca ordered. The boy tumbled down the bank, Ella and Rosa close behind. Becca and Patsy continued up the hill toward home, shepherding baby Frank ahead of them. He was tired, but struggled valiantly to climb the hill.

As they reached the side yard, angry voices spilled out through the tattered screen door. "Your children haven't had a new pair of shoes in two years! How dare you put a four dollar pair of shoes on your feet when we can't afford meat for the table?"

"I can't make a living going around looking like a bum!"

"You can't make a living! Go on, get out of here!"

Patsy and Becca looked at the ground, oddly ashamed to be overhearing this exchange. Frank sat down suddenly, hard on his bottom, and began to howl. Just then, the sharp sound of a hand striking flesh rang out across the yard.

Seconds later, Ed stumbled out the door, his bad leg dragging. He held his hand up to his face, where a red welt was rapidly rising across his cheek.

Without seeing the children in the yard, he cranked the car and drove down the hill, honking his horn in farewell to Edward, Ella, and Rosa, straggling up to the house.

When Becca timidly pushed open the screen door to enter the kitchen, her mother sat staring straight ahead. Fresh marks of tears tracked her cheeks, and her nose and eyes were red and swollen, but her voice was stony.

"Your daddy's gone back to work. I've got a sick headache, so keep the kids quiet, all right?" She pushed away from the table and rose to enter the bedroom. "Put the kerosene in the shed." The bedroom door closed with a little click.

Becca set the kerosene can down and rounded up the children.

"Let's go swimming," she suggested grimly. "Mama don't feel good."

"Is it a baby?" squealed Rosa.

"No, dummy, her tummy never got big." Ella shoved Rosa, but not too hard. Becca grabbed *Wood's Natural History*, a book her teacher gave her last year when she graduated, and followed her brothers and sisters back down to the creek. Halfway down, Frank sat down again and began to wail.

"He's tired," Becca complained. "I guess I'll have to carry him."

While the children splashed and played, and baby Frank napped on the blanket next to her, Becca lost herself in details of odd animals in far-off places. Time passed easily, and soon, it seemed, her stomach was growling and the others were clamoring for food.

Frank woke up howling. "His diaper's wet," announced Patsy. "Come on, let's go!"

All six children climbed the hill again, hearing the agitated squawks of the chickens before their yard came into sight.

"Everybody's hungry," said Becca. "You go feed the chickens and I'll start supper, okay?"

The bedroom door was still closed so Becca made as little noise as possible, setting out plates, bread, and butter and one of the last jars of applesauce from the cellar. Pumping the stove, she lit a burner under a pot of water and began to slice potatoes into the water.

A horse's hooves came pounding up the road, and Becca heard the chickens and the children scatter. She went to the door to see who rode up in such a hurry, and heard the bedroom door open behind her.

"Who is it, Becca?" her mother murmured.

The gangly young man trotted up to the door and practically wrenched it out of Becca's hand.

"My wife," he panted. "Mrs. Johnston, she's bleeding and you've got to help her."

"May, that's your wife's name, isn't it?" Sarah's voice became brisk, businesslike, and Becca felt a twinge of anger at this sudden recovery. "She's not due for another seven weeks. What happened?"

"I dunno," the man wailed, and Becca realized he was not too much older than Johnny. "She started feelin' poorly, and then she started bleedin'. Please, please come now, Mrs. Johnston!"

"I'll head that way. But you'll have to ride to Doc Sullivan's house. I can't do much if she's bleedin'."

"We can't afford the doctor!"

Sarah pulled sharply at his arm. "You love your wife, don't you?"

He nodded dumbly.

"Get the doctor. He gives credit, same as me." Sarah crossed her arms and watched sternly as the man mounted his horse and rode away to fetch the doctor. Then she disappeared into the bedroom for a moment for her bag.

She gave each child a quick kiss on the crown of the head, and a firm reminder to them all. "Mind Becca, now. I may be late."

Becca had just finished slicing potatoes into the water when she gasped. "Patsy, I left my book down at the creek!"

Patsy looked doubtful. "It's gettin' dark."

"I know, but I can't leave it out, it'll get ruined!"

"Run and get it, then. I'll watch them."

Becca flew out the door, only to return a moment later. "Don't touch the stove, now."

"We won't, worrywart." Rosa was playing patty cake with baby Frank, and Ella and Edward were huddled in the corner. Patsy fiddled with the wick on the lamp, then laid forks around the table.

"Frankie made a stinky one, Patsy," Rosa announced. "Pee-yew!"

"I got the last one, too," muttered Patsy. She held Frank at arm's length as she carried him into the bedroom where the clean diapers were kept.

"That one's mine, Edward. I got two red ones and one black string."

"No, you ate all your red strings. It's mine!"

The shadows were long, and the breeze nearly cool down by the bridge. Becca lingered a moment after she picked up the little gray book with cardboard covers.

"Rebecca, is that you?" Johnny's lean form materialized out of the darkness of the bridge opening.

"What're you doin', Johnny?" Becca felt a warm sort of pleasure steal over her at the sound of his voice.

Edward shoved Ella, hard. "Give me back my licorice," he shouted. A stray breeze, the first of the evening, stole through the screen door and made the flame under the burner dance. Rosa watched, popping her thumb in her mouth, fascinated by the movement of the bright blue flame.

"C'mere," Johnny urged, pulling Becca's hand. "The sun's just right to make these wonderful shadows on the bridge."

"Aw, Johnny," Becca protested, but she let herself be led along.

"See," he whispered, moving close and pointing over her shoulder. As she turned her head to look, his lips grazed her cheek and she turned back, startled.

The flame was out. But Rosa knew what to do because she'd seen her big sister do it countless times before. She climbed up on the kitchen chair and took down the box of big kitchen matches. She scratched one slowly along the side of the box.

"No, Johnny," Becca said softly, just as his lips met hers.

He dropped his hands and the two flew apart as a massive roar broke the silence, shaking the wooden floor of the bridge.

The sound seemed to tear an answering scream from Becca as she ran out of the bridge toward home. Johnny followed close behind, but the heat was too intense, the flames too bright. Both children crumpled in the grass on the crest of the hill as the house burned and then collapsed in a shower of sparks like a vision of hell itself.

****

"I'm sure there's a bathroom, it's a state park, isn't it?" The man was a little testy, four hours in the little blue Toyota beginning to wear on his nerves. "Here we are. Look, bathrooms."

He pointed to a small building in the center of a grove of trees. His wife and daughter piled out of the car and sprinted to the structure.

"Looks more like an outhouse to me, Dad," his son commented. "When did you say the bridge was built?"

"Oh, 1860 or something like that. Let's take a look." They wandered slowly over to the weathered old structure, the boy reading with curiosity the graffiti scrawled on the concrete piers.

"Let's see what's on the other side," the man suggested when his wife and daughter joined them. Across the bridge, to the left, was a faintly marked path.

"I'll bet there's a clearing up there, where we can get a good view of the bridge." The woman had her camera. "Let's take a look."

The boy and the girl raced ahead. Their parents, hand in hand, climbed the hill more slowly.

"This is really cool, Dad," the boy announced. "There's these foundations, all over-grown with honeysuckle, and they're all charred and black."

"Must've been a big fire," the man mused.

"How sad," said the woman. "We can't see the bridge from up here. I was wrong. Let's head back down, and maybe I can get a good shot from the creekbed."

"Where'd the kids go?"

"I hear somebody splashing in the creek."

"Sounds like a good idea to me."

"I don't want them to get their clothes wet. We've got another three hours before we'll stop for the night."

Just then, the children appeared before them, flushed and panting. "We hear some kids playing in the creek," said the boy. "Can we go, please?"

"You can wade in, but don't get your clothes wet," their mother said.

"And watch out for glass," warned their dad, as they raced down the hill.

When the couple arrived at the bridge, the two children were standing in the middle of the road, their shoes in their hands, puzzled.

"Not getting in?" called their mother.

"We can't find those other kids," said her daughter. "They were here—we heard them. But when we got down here, they had disappeared."

The woman shivered and wrapped herself in her arms. "It's a little chilly here in the shadow of that old bridge," she commented.

"It sounded like a lot of kids," her husband said doubtfully. "Where could they have gone?"

The boy looked up as if to reassure himself that the sun was in its rightful place. "I'm cold, too," he said uneasily. "Can we go home now?"

The family resumed their road trip in a troubled silence that only began to lift when they returned to the sleek new expressway. Behind them, they left a creek whose quiet, sandy shores sometimes echoes with the joyous laughter of unseen children.

Sandy Creek Covered Bridge is near Hillsboro in Jefferson County, Missouri, which is in the east central part of the state. To find it, take Missouri 21 north out of town and continue until you see Goldman Road on the right. Turn right onto Goldman Road, which twists sharply back to the right and makes a "T" intersection with LeMays Ferry Road. Turn right again, and go past the Goldman Volunteer Fire Department and a row of houses; the road ends at a state park. The bridge is closed to vehicles, but foot traffic is welcome.

THE NOISIEST MILL

As the dark clouds flitted anxiously across the the blank face of the moon, the shadowy bulk of the mill towered over the little girl, all four floors devoid of light and unnaturally quiet. She reached for the comforting warmth of her father's fingers, and he squeezed her hand in response.

"Quiet, isn't it?" He threw open the door to the main floor of the grist mill. "I'll get a lamp lit in just a wink."

A matched flared and flickered and then caught on the wide wick of the kerosene lantern that hung on a nail by the door. The meager light made the hulking machinery of the mill seem oversized and threatening, and Ruth stayed close to her father. Even though she had spent most of her waking hours at the mill since she was born, this big echoing room lost all familiarity by lamplight.

The miller took the lantern and crossed the room, stepping up onto the broad staging platform for the giant millstone, which had been shipped all the way from France. As he carefully began to sharpen it, she watched his fingers fly.

His hands were big, with long stocky fingers, a palm almost as big as his daughter's face, and knuckles that were knotted and gnarled as if in protest at the endless round of lifting, loading, tinkering, adjusting, scraping, and hammering. He maintained all the equipment in the mill, from the giant turbines downstairs that turned the great millstone to the grain-cleaning apparatus that stretched up to the third floor and back down again.

Every time something broke down, he would fix it again, sometimes making small modifications to make the mill run more smoothly. The top joint of his third finger on his left hand was missing entirely, a sacrifice to the mill's machinery and, as he often said, a constant reminder to be alert around the great forces at work in the Kymulga Grist Mill.

He had the utmost respect for the raw power of the creek rushing by right outside their windows. The dam allowed him to control its turbulence somewhat, but that was a tenuous control at best. Coupled with the mighty turbines, the water had the power to make almost anything happen, and he held a reverence for that capacity that approached a sense of awe at times. Other forces that lay beyond his sight but were nevertheless undeniable also commanded his respect. He was a big man, but arrogance was not one of his failings.

"Tell me a story, Papa," Ruth begged. This was the great privilege of coming back to the mill with him at night, once the millstone had cooled from its labors, to watch him sharpen the stone. During the day the noise from the equipment and customers' demands on the miller's attention made storytelling impossible. Ruth and her brothers and sisters cherished whatever time they had alone with their father. Ruth had been granted the honor of accompanying him by herself this evening.

"Well," he began, watching his hands very carefully while he sorted through the stories tumbling around his mind. "A scary one?" He glanced up at his youngest child.

She nodded eagerly and then crossed her arms across her chest, hugging herself and rocking gently in anticipation.

"Not too long ago, there was a fine lady who lived across the creek. She had to have the best of everything, no matter what the cost. But some things are just too dear.

"She went visiting some friends one day, and their son had just brought home a splendid black stallion. His coat gleamed, and his mane was long and silky, his gait was proud, and his neck arched so gracefully that she made up her mind she had to have that horse.

"Her horse and buggy were in the stable. Her horse was a perfectly good bay gelding, nice and gentle and well-accustomed to the lady's ways. But the lady had decided that she couldn't live without that stallion. The young man didn't want to sell and argued that she couldn't handle the horse, but the lady was so stubborn, he finally gave in.

"He warned her that the horse wasn't tolerant of loud noises, and he could easily take fright and run away with her and the buggy, but the lady didn't pay him a bit of attention. She just had the stable boy hitch up that lively black stallion, and she went on her way.

"Well that horse gave her no end of trouble. It kind of got to be a joke around here about the lady and the horse she couldn't control. But she was proud as the Devil and twice as stubborn.

"One night she took it in her head to go visit some friends and show off a fancy new dress. Her husband told her not to go, but she ordered that black stallion hitched up to her buggy anyway."

The miller's hands, which had been flying on the millstone sharpening it in preparation for the workday tomorrow, now stilled. He leaned closer to his daughter.

"It was a clear night, and the stars were all out, shining down on the earth like a million angel eyes, watching out for little girls and boys. But they weren't watching out for stubborn proud ladies. No, sir.

"That horse pranced and danced down the road, and clip-clopped through that very bridge out there." He gestured to the left with his free hand.

"He was just at the mouth of the bridge when a sound as big as thunder came roaring by, and he screamed and jerked and reared up. Just as the lady was thrown from the buggy, the engineer of the nine o'clock train to Montgomery gave a friendly little toot on his whistle, and the horse, more scared than ever, turned and trampled that lady to death."

Ruth had crept into his arms as he narrated this part of the story. He held her tight.

"Now sometimes when the stars are watching bright-eyed from heaven and the nine o'clock train is due any minute, you can hear the clip-clop of hooves dancing through the bridge. Sometimes when the train is rushing by, you can hear the scream of a horse or maybe it's the cry of a stubborn lady who wanted her way at any price."

Ruth shivered and then reached up with both little hands to pat her father's cheeks. "Papa, are all your stories true?"

He thought for a moment. "I don't know, Ruth. Sometimes they sound true, don't they?"

"Tell me another," she pleaded.

"Not tonight, Ruth. It's time to go home."

When they reached the door he blew out the lantern and hung it back on the nail. As he closed the door behind them, he held Ruth's hand tightly. "Don't be afraid if we see her," he whispered.

"See who, Papa?"

"The lady. She wanders around some at night in that fancy new dress of hers. But she won't hurt you."

"Carry me, Papa." Ruth held up her arms and her father complied, holding her close as they walked through the night.

****

"Marcia, this is crazy." The young man carried a blanket and followed the woman as she led the way down the railroad tracks.

"They quit running trains along here in 1967 or something. Believe me—we lived right next to the tracks, so I oughta know, right?" said Marcia.

"What makes you think they didn't tear down the old covered bridge right after you left?" He grumbled but still followed her.

"I read about it in the paper. It's really cool. You'll like it."

"It's dark, and the skeeters are eating me alive."

"It's because you're so sweet."

They walked along the tracks in silence for a few more minutes, the faint beam of her flashlight feebly illuminating a few feet in front of her.

"Aha! I told you so!"

A few hundred yards to the right was a dark shape that looked like a barn, with stairs leading up to it. Only the rushing sound of water indicated that the barnlike structure was a covered bridge.

"Here's a road. Look, we could've driven right up."

"I forgot," she said sheepishly. "Besides, it's blocked. The park's closed at night."

"Great. So we're not supposed to be here at all, right?"

"Get romantic," she commanded him. "This is supposed to be romantic. Look at all those stars."

They stood hand in hand and stared up at the brilliant night sky, punctuated with millions of gleaming points. When she tugged the blanket out of his arms to lay it out on the grass, he did not protest.

They had just settled down when a hollow knocking sound resounded from the bridge. "What in God's name is that?"

"It's a horse. It sounds just like a horse on the bridge."

"That's ridiculous. There's no way for a horse to get on that bridge. It'd have to climb up all those stairs."

The steady clip-clop of the hooves continued, drawing closer and closer. All at once, a thundering roar filled the air.

"Holy cow, it's a freakin' train!" Marcia jumped up, yelling to be heard over the noise. The hoofbeats accelerated, and over the high, mournful whistle of the train they heard a scream—horse or human, they couldn't tell.

Suddenly it was quiet again. The cicadas resumed their noisy song, and the bass harrumph of the bullfrogs started up again.

Marcia touched her boyfriend's arm. Her hand trembled. "Randy," she whispered. "That wasn't a real train."

He looked at her with questioning in his eyes.

"We'd have seen or smelled it," she explained. "Touch the tracks."

They did. The unused steel was cold enough to send chills through their fingertips.

****

Ruth and her two middle brothers walked with their father back to the mill just before bedtime. The weather had turned cold, almost overnight, so all four walked quickly to get out of the chilly night air. The mill was dark and cold, but at least the wind wasn't blowing inside. Outside the closed wooden shutters, the creek babbled and moaned like a living creature.

"Ralph, help me swing the stone over," commanded the miller. "Ruth, stay clear, now." With very little effort the great stone was levered up and swung over to a spot where the miller could easily bend over it and prepare it for another workday. The system of balances and counterbalances was perfectly designed so that a single man could manipulate it with ease. The miller was teaching his sons the trade.

Once they had all settled in a semicircle around the miller as he worked, Andy asked for a story. "Papa, tell us that story about the fight on the bridge," he asked eagerly.

"That's a great story, Papa. Please?" Ralph chimed in.

The miller looked doubtfully at his youngest daughter. "I don't know," he said slowly. "I don't want to scare Ruth, and that's a mighty bloody story."

"I won't get scared, Papa." Ruth sat up straighter so she'd look older. "Do tell it," she urged.

Again the miller kept his eyes on the task in front of him as he organized the story in his head. "Well," he began, "this old bridge used to be the only way across Talladega Creek for miles and miles, so anybody with business in town or who had to get to the county courthouse had to come right down here. And if you waited long enough, you'd see most everybody in the area either here at the mill or crossing the bridge.

"Not too far from here lived a farmer, Simon was his name, I think. He had two strapping boys, big and strong and both of 'em just as smart as a whip. They grew up, and like all brothers, they had fights every now and then. Sometimes they'd even slug it out, but it never was anything serious because deep down they really loved each other.

"The older they got, the more they started to look alike. They were both six feet tall in their stocking feet and could lift up the back end of a loaded wagon with one single hand without turning a hair.

"Trouble came in the shape of a young woman—Louisa. She was beautiful, but you know what your mama says about beauty."

He paused in his work for just a moment to touch Ruth gently on the cheek. "Beauty is as beauty does," Ruth quoted dutifully. "Go on, Papa."

"Louisa may have had fair skin and golden hair, but her heart must've been black as night. She set out to win both men's love, and when she did, she set them against each other.

" 'Oh, Peter is so strong,' she'd say to Paul. 'I believe he could break that big old tree over there in half like a toothpick.' Then Peter would call on her, and she'd say something like, 'Your brother is so smart. He told me the other day that he's figured out a way to get twice as much cotton from your farm as you did just last year.'

"Well, the jealousy between the two brothers grew and grew until it was a monstrous thing. Their father tried to reason with them, to tell them what Louisa was doing, because to anyone else, it was as plain as the nose on your face. But the brothers were blind.

"At last, when she had worked them up to a fevered pitch, she told them that she couldn't decide who to marry. She laughed and said she would never be able to choose unless one of them was gone.

"Maybe she didn't know what she was doing. But Paul was so overwrought that he decided to kill his brother. So he lay in wait, right inside that bridge over there." He pointed to the window on his left, tightly shuttered against the rising autumn wind.

"So Peter was on his way home that night, walking easy with hands in his pockets, whistling a little tune. He figured that this thing with Louisa would end up all right because most things in his life did. He wasn't two steps inside the dark, shadowy bridge before a figure flew at him in a fury.

"Peter fought back as hard as he could, but being surprised put him at a disadvantage. First his attacker had him by the throat, but Peter managed to get his hands round the other man's neck and choked him just long enough to get him to let go. Then the other fellow started kicking and kicked so hard that one of the side slats of the bridge was kicked out, and it floated down the stream.

"Peter let loose with a roundhouse punch that would have flattened any other man, and the two of them rolled and tumbled and fought up one side of the bridge and down the other. Peter still had no idea who his assailant was.

"They bloodied each other's noses, and they could feel their fists were wet with blood, but neither one of them would admit defeat. It's hard to believe, but they kept up this fight all night long, till dawn was peeping in the eastern end of the bridge. Sometimes they'd get tired and crawl off to separate corners for just a minute or two, but then they'd catch their breath and one or the other would fly back into the fray. It was a monumental fight.

"When the first little bit of light started creeping into the bridge, both of Peter's eyes were blackened and one had swollen completely shut. His ribs hurt so badly he could barely breathe, and his throat was sore from being throttled. The other man was just as bad off, but neither one was going to give up.

"Peter's assailant cried out for the first time, and Peter saw the glint of steel as his opponent pulled out a knife.

"The knife was coming straight at Peter's heart, and he twisted it back and plunged it into the chest of his brother just as Paul cried out 'Louisa!' Too late, Peter realized it was his brother, deranged by jealousy.

"Paul died in Peter's arms. Peter left the state that same day. Louisa died a bitter old maid years later. They say the boys' father died of a broken heart. Some nights you can hear whistling coming toward the bridge. If you dare stay, you'll hear the noise of a fight like none you've ever heard before, and the anguished scream of a brother killing the one person who loved him best."

The millstone was turning and turning and Ruth cried out in horror. "Papa, look! Your hands!"

As the stone turned and the miller's hands flashed, drops of blood were flying off, spinning into the air to land on the floor in a gory pattern. The miller laughed and stopped the stone. "It's all right, Ruth. It's just my knuckles got so dry the skin cracked." He held out his hands for her inspection, but she flew into his arms, sobbing.

"There, there, girl," he soothed. "It's all right. It's just a story, that's all. Just a story."

****

"What on earth does this old thing do?" The machine was rectangular, on four legs, with a spout on one side and evil-looking teeth on the inside of the main housing.

"It shucks corn. How many people have we had today?" The woman's knitting needles made a muffled clicking noise as she set her knitting bag on a stool in the old corn room. A Coca-Cola cooler hummed in the corner, and an idle late summer breeze made the wind chimes on display next to the window sigh.

"Five, I think." The other woman straightened out the little stack of maps next to the cash register and then moved on to organize the wooden toys for sale on a card table next to the door.

"Maybe we'll get a school group or two when school starts up again. Or has it started back already?"

"I don't know. I no longer keep track. I'll be going now, if you'll be all right?"

"Sure. Thanks for taking my morning shift. Did you enjoy it?"

The other woman shrugged. "I wasn't much help to the people coming through, but the diagram explains the mill pretty well. I'm glad I could help you out. I'll do it again, if you want me to sometime."

Edna stood in the doorway to watch her friend walk out to her car and wave goodbye before turning back to her knitting. If she spent an hour a day for the next three months on it, she could have a sweater done for each of her grandchildren by Christmas. Afternoons as a volunteer for the Historical Society here at the old Kymulga Grist Mill were dependably boring. Perfect for knitting.

She was just turning to the critical part at the top of the sleeve when she heard whistling. Glad for the distraction, she lay down her knitting and stretched, heading for the door to greet the visitors. She hadn't heard their car, but not everyone followed the sign and parked outside the corn room that the Historical Society had turned into a store. She was at the door when she heard a terrific pounding on the bridge a few hundred yards away. Without thinking, Edna went toward the bridge at a jog.

"Is it a dog fight?" she asked herself as she trotted toward the structure. But she didn't hear any whining or barking sounds that dogs usually make. As she watched, something inside struck the side of the bridge with such force that the siding quivered under the blow. She slowed her steps, not sure if she should approach. She wished she'd grabbed her knitting needles as at least some form of self-defense, but she had left them stabbing the ball of yarn in the old corn room.

Edna stood there, undecided, until she heard the sickening, mushy sound of a closed fist making solid contact with flesh. She shuddered and turned toward the corn room and the telephone. This was a police matter.

More thuds and soft grunts of pain or surprise followed her as she hurried back to the store. Then a car horn and a friendly voice dispelled the noise.

"What's up, Edna?" It was Barclay Smith, another Historical Society member.

"Oh, I'm so glad you're here," she stammered. "We've got to stop them before someone gets killed."

He jerked the car to a stop, raising a cloud of dust in the gravel parking lot. "What are you talking about?"

"On the bridge," she gasped. "It's a terrible fight."

To her surprise Barclay smiled. He climbed out of the car and took her elbow firmly. "Steady now, Edna," he advised. "Let's go see."

The bridge was empty. Although she paced over every inch of the floorboards, there was no sign of any kind of struggle. Barclay leaned against the portal of the bridge and watched her search.

"You act like you expected this," she accused him, as she settled down on a bench in the sunshine.

"I've heard it too," he admitted. "It always happens when I'm here by myself. And it always starts with the sound of a man whistling, walking up the road."

"Let's go back to the mill." Edna stood up, dusting off her slacks. "I feel safer there."

****

One night, the miller's house was packed full with strangers and anxiety. Granny Holcomb was there, but Ruth knew she never came unless someone was sick. Ruth's mother wasn't exactly ill, but something was awry. The bulge of her belly had just begun to reach noticeable proportions beneath her full skirts and apron. Under the cover of the unfamiliar activity, Ruth and her two middle brothers crept out of the house to join their father at the mill.

When they opened the door expecting to see the miller at his customary spot on the platform, darkness was all that greeted them. Andy tumbled back out of the shadowy space so quickly that he stepped on Ruth and Ralph. "It's dark in there," he said by way of apology.

"You're not scared of ghosts, are you?" Big brothers are good at goading.

Andy bristled. "Course not."

Ruth stepped back to look at the windows.

"Must be fixing the cleaning system," she whispered, seeing a flickering light in the upper story. "He's got his lantern up there."

Ralph looked up and squinted.

"Maybe if we go up there he'll tell us a story while he's working." He poked at his brother. "If you're not too scared to go up in the dark."

In answer, Andy led the way into the echoing, shadow-filled main room, with its hulking machinery and long, spiderlike extensions that groped blindly up to the ceiling and beyond. Ralph and Ruth followed, the little girl reaching for the warmth of her brother's hand, as much for reassurance as for guidance.

Single file, they crossed the room in darkness, shuffling a bit to avoid tripping over any unexpected obstacles. Although the moon was bright outside, the shutters on the ground floor were all tightly closed and latched. The blackness inside was absolute.

At the back of the big room where the noise of the creek was loudest, they reached the stairs. They climbed up, placing one hand on the wall to guide their progress and staying as far as possible from the open side of the stairs. Andy expected to see the welcome gleam of the miller's lantern as his head emerged at floor level of the second story, but only the cold light of the moon showed. The shutters here were left open, except in the coldest weather, to vent the heat and noise and dust that rose like smoke when the massive machinery was running.

"He must be on the third floor," Andy whispered as Ruth and Ralph joined him at the top of the stairs. "Let's go."

Some instinct made the children move as quietly as they could. No one had told them to go to bed; indeed, in the general flurry of anxious women and preparations, they seemed to have been forgotten. Someone sent the older boys, Robert and Charles, to chop wood for the stove. The two oldest girls were in the middle of all the fuss with such a distracted and grown-up air that Ruth was reluctant to approach them.

The stairs to the third floor were narrower and steeper. Andy led the way, creeping quietly, pausing after every step to listen for a sound that would indicate his father's presence. His heart fell as he peered over the edge of the stairs—the third floor was also empty. The tubelike contraptions reaching up from the floor below, the long boxes that agitated the grain to make the chaff fly up and away, all lay still and noiseless before his disappointed eyes.

But above him, accessible only by stairs so sharply inclined and narrow that they were more of a ladder than stairs, he could see a glimmer of light. Andy gestured to the other two to wait while he tiptoed to the foot of the stairs that led to the fourth and highest floor. No equipment was housed up there. It held mostly odds and ends, bits of obsolete equipment, unused lumber, and so many huge rat traps that the children had always been forbidden to climb these final stairs.

Above him, Andy could hear an unearthly, tuneless sound, a cross between humming and moaning, and the scratching, scrabbling noises of hands at work. Goosebumps prickled along his spine until he recognized the sound as his father's peculiar brand of singing. Tone-deaf and acutely aware of it, the miller was in the habit of muttering or moaning his hymns under his breath, barely above the threshold for hearing.

Andy crossed back to his big brother and Ruth. "I don't know what he's doing, but we're not supposed to go up there," he whispered uneasily. "Let's go home."

"They'll just tell us we're in the way," Ralph pointed out, truthfully enough.

"I want my daddy." Even at a whisper, Ruth's voice threatened to break, and the scant light from the opened shutters showed her lower lip protruding stubbornly. The two boys looked at each other, knowing from prior experience what that lower lip signified.

Shrugging a little, disclaiming any responsibility, Andy started for the steep little stairs. Ruth pushed ahead and began climbing, Andy was so close behind, she was almost supported in his arms as she rose.

Their two heads appeared at floor level at almost the same time. Their father sat in a chair near the window, the red lantern at his feet. A shower of wood shavings had made a little mountain by his side, and he carefully, methodically, ran his plane across the two-foot-long rectangular box he gripped between his knees.

The smell of new wood cut cleanly through the familiar odors of the mill, and Ruth watched her father, fascinated as always by the sureness of his motions and the grace of his hands. His back was half-turned to the stairs, and his plaintive humming had masked the sound of the children's footsteps.

At last Ruth became aware of a frantic tugging on her skirts. Andy was below, gesturing wildly for her to descend. Reluctantly she complied. Something told her that her father was not to be disturbed. Just as her view of him disappeared, she realized what had made the picture of her father so incongruous: the tears sparkling on his cheeks were something she had never witnessed before.

****

The rain pounded down so fiercely that its sound cloaked even the rushing noise of the swollen creek outside the corn house. Edna yawned and set down her magazine. Early spring was always slow here at the mill, and the rain made it even less likely that visitors would take the detour from the main road to see the old mill, no matter how historic. They might get five people through here in a week.

"Maybe I should just bring a cot," she mused aloud. Her voice was oddly loud, even competing with the steady sound of the rain. She cleared the frogs from her throat.

"Is talking to yourself a sign of senility?" She laughed and stood to stretch her legs. She picked up a feather duster and idly ran it over the shelves of little knickknacks Historical

Society members made to sell here at the mill. Her own handiwork was among them: little needlepoint magnets to hang on your dishwasher to tell if the dishes were clean or dirty.

"As if you couldn't see it with your own two eyes," she chuckled to herself. "The things people buy."

A noise from the main room of the mill made her set the duster down with a little click on top of the glass display case.

"Hello?" Edna moved to the Dutch door that separated the corn room from the main mill. She peeked around the door frame just in time to hear the stairs at the back of the mill creak and groan in protest at the weight they bore.

"That's strange," she thought, crossing the mill floor. "I didn't hear a car." The crunching of wheels on the gravel parking lot usually made enough racket to bring her out of the most exciting of daydreams. She stood at the bottom of the stairs and looked up.

"Hello, there?" she called. "You'll need to come pay the admission price at the store, all right?"

When she received no reply, she got irritated. "Some people," she huffed as she climbed the stairs. "No manners at all, I declare."

Once on the second floor, she looked all around. No one was there. But the stairs behind her creaked distinctly, and she turned sharply.

"Look here," she began, but no one was on the stairs. She walked to the foot of the stairs that rose to the next floor. Above her, unseen in the shadows, she heard footsteps again. She shuddered involuntarily.

"Who's there," she croaked and then cleared her throat to call more forcefully. Just then an unearthly sound came floating down from the highest floor in the mill. The fourth floor, which housed only meaningless scrap and bits of rusted machinery. The noise was a cross between humming and moaning—its very tunelessness made it all the more plaintive. Accompanying the sound, in bizarre counterpoint, was the the scraping, scratching sound of a plane moving patiently back and forth against wood.

* * * * * * * *

The miller had five children arrayed in front of his chair this night as his hands flashed and blurred white at their work. "Tell us a story, Papa," they chorused, and he was silent for a few moments, chewing the inside of his cheek thoughtfully.

"Well," he began. "This one is absolutely true. It happened a few years ago, when I first came here. And there's really no proper ending, so don't go complaining about that now."

"We won't, Papa," Ruth assured him, her hand touching his knee. He favored her with a sweet smile before continuing.

"I was looking out the window at the creek one day, you know, like I always do." The dam that stretched across Talladega Creek was of critical importance to the mill. It alone gave the power that enabled the giant turbines below the mill floor to turn. Maintaining the dam required constant vigilance—a stray log could puncture the structure and cause the whole dam to crumble and fall away downstream.

The children nodded, eager to hear the rest of the story.

"I saw something out there, just kind of bobbing up and down. It looked to be nearly six feet long, so I decided I needed to get a closer look.

"I went outside and scrambled down the bank of the creek, right next to the dam. I looked, and saw it was a body. I didn't know what to do. We hadn't lived here that long, and I didn't want to make trouble.

"I stood and watched it for a minute. It was all bloated up and awful looking. Then I got to thinking about whether the man had had a family, you know, and I decided I needed to fetch it out and at least give it a decent burial.

"I went to get a pole so I could get it out of the water, and when I came back, it had floated up over the dam and was riding the current. It was gone out of sight in just a few minutes."

"Who was it, Papa?"

"I don't know."

"Was it a colored man?"

"I couldn't tell, Andy."

"What happened next?"

"I don't know. I suppose it fetched up in the Coosa River somewhere. Or maybe it floated all the way to the sea."

The children were silent for a while, contemplating the rigors of such a journey. "Who was it, Papa?" Ruth asked.

"I told you, I don't know. This story doesn't really have an ending." The miller shuddered. "Poor devil. I hope when I'm gone someone'll lay me in a nice peaceful grave."

"Don't say that, Papa." Ruth put her arms around his neck and hugged him tightly, careful not to get near the grindstone. "You'll live forever. Promise me."

The older ones smiled at the child's naive demand.

****

The tires on the car crunched and ground to a stop on the gravel surface outside the corn room. Edna had just slipped the padlock over the hasp and turned in annoyance. The sign at the gate clearly stated that park hours ended at six. When she saw the Iowa tags on the car she relented somewhat. A tall young man unfolded himself from the driver's seat and called over to her. "I know it's almost six, but could we look around a minute? I don't know when we'll be back in Alabama."

Edna shrugged and turned to unlock the door. "Just for a moment," she warned. "There's no time for the full tour."

"Thank you so much," the man said warmly. "Come on, Ellen!" He gestured to the woman still in the car.

"Where are you from?" Edna switched on the light and headed for the cash register.

"Des Moines, Iowa. We came to Childersburg just to see the mill."

"It's $2 each, please." She made change for a five and handed him a map and a diagram of the mill. "The money helps the Historical Society keep up the maintenance, you know." She led them into the main room of the mill.

"We still grind corn here every Wednesday. You can buy a bag if you like. I'll rest outside while you look around, if you don't mind. We've had a lot of visitors today. Mind the stairs and don't go past the third floor."

"Thanks again for letting me in. My great-grandfather was the miller here a long time ago."

"Is that so?" Edna pinned him with a sharp gaze. "You'll have to sign our guest book. What did you say your name was?"

"Watkins. Robert Watkins. This is my wife, Ellen." The woman by his side nodded and smiled.

"Well, I'll be. There was a miller here by that name once. A long time ago." Edna was intrigued. "Let me tell you a little about how the mill works." Forgetting her fatigue, Edna gave the visitors from Iowa a full tour, only skipping the climb up to the third floor. She explained the function of each piece of equipment in complete detail while Robert listened attentively.

Dusk was falling when Edna climbed into her car and drove away, raising a cloud of dust as she pulled out of the gravel parking lot. The cloud hung still and lifeless next to the old mill; not a breath of wind stirred the sullen August air.

"Let's go look at the old covered bridge, Robert." Ellen tugged at her husband's arm and he good-naturedly followed her.

"Isn't this just beautiful?" The last light of the day streamed into the mouth of the bridge, filtered by the leaves of the redbuds that crowded close to the creek and the lattice structure.

As they stood there listening to the hush and murmur of the creek below, a new noise broke into their consciousness. A strange groaning, like giant gears shifting and turning.

"It's the mill," Robert whispered, hurrying outside to look at the massive old building.

The moaning of the turbines steadily grew, and turned into a whining sound as they approached full speed. Then a deep-throated rumbling began, rhythmic and insistent. A clanging, clamoring sound of equipment, rattling and banging, rolled out from the mill and across to the bridge where they stood.

"There's no one there," whispered Ellen. "This can't be happening."

They stood in silence, clutching each other's hand tightly, as the noised swelled and crested over them. In a few minutes the sounds died away, leaving an August night that was lacking even the prosaic cicada's song.

"When did your great-grandfather die, Robert?" They were walking slowly back to their car, ready to head for the lights and noise of Birmingham.

"I'm not sure he did, Ellen. I'm not sure he ever did."

The old Kymulga Grist Mill and Covered Bridge are located near Childersburg, in Talladega County, Alabama. Tours of the mill are available from late March through September, and there are many special events throughout the season. For details, contact the Childersburg Heritage Society at (205)378-5482 or (205)378-7436.

To reach the mill, take U.S. 280 west out of Childersburg and turn left onto Kymulga Mill Road (Alabama 180). The mill is a few miles on the left.